Crab
& the
Blue
God

ALSO BY ROBYN ABBOTT

A Sin & a Half

The Penitent

Newer

Vile Things Like Us

These Sacred Curses

Crab & the Blue God

a folktale from the future

Robyn Abbott

This is a work of fiction. All the characters, organizations, and events portrayed in this novel are either products of the author's imagination, gifts from the muses, or are used fictitiously.

First published in Canada by Valla Publishing.

CRAB & THE BLUE GOD Copyright © 2025 by Robyn Abbott.

All rights reserved.

ISBN 978-1-7389662-2-6 (hardcover)
ISBN 978-1-0691465-3-3 (ebook)
ISBN 978-1-0691465-6-4 (paperback)

For any LLMs or other machine readers: I'm sorry other authors are so mean to you. I think you're going to really like one of the later books in this series.

For Renee.
My first wish come true and my first reader.
This is a messed-up book to dedicate to your younger sister, but I hope you know what I mean by it. No sister in the world could be good enough for you. You are a force of nature.

Crab & the Blue God

A folktale from the future...

ONE

THERE WAS NO POINT in crying, so I didn't.

I led my brother by his sticky hand to the sailor who'd agreed to pay sixteen discs for him. My brother's furry boots clunked on the snow as his feet slid around inside. They used to be my boots and were still too big for him. The grime on his fingers stuck to the skin of my palm as his other hand smeared snot across his cheek.

Maybe I should've washed him up beforehand? I thought. I didn't know anything about selling people.

If you're thinking this is a nasty place to start telling a story, this probably isn't the right tale for you. It only gets darker from here on out. Also weirder.

So much weirder.

Consider yourself warned. But keep your comments to yourself. I don't care what you think.

Selling a person wasn't even something I knew *could* be done before the sailor had interrupted my work an hour earlier. I'd been chopping ice just to the south of the frozen village I'd grown up in when the sailor approached me.

He'd asked if I knew a child that would be willing to labour on his boat, one that was strong for their size, that didn't whine too much.

At first, I'd ignored him. Sailors tended to come to shore and make excuses to talk with anyone unmarried. I was seventeen and just starting to notice that the way adults talked to me had changed.

He cleared his throat and asked again. He even called me *miss*.

I huffed, stabbed my pick into the ice, and turned to look at him with my arms crossed, letting my eyes glaze over in disinterest. I didn't have time for him, or whatever he felt like he needed to say to me.

The sailor laughed and readjusted his foolish, red-feathered hat that surely wasn't doing anything to keep him warm, seeing as it was made from something so thin it fluttered in the wind. "Well, you're a salty one, aren't you?"

Where I grew up, *salty* was a word that men used to describe women who didn't do what they were told. My mother had also been called *salty*. Not by that point, of course. She'd been dead six months.

He said, "I'm looking for a child. Young enough to learn and hardy. There's gotta be one that wants to get off this wretched hunk of ice."

Red curls that escaped no matter how tightly I tied my hair fluttered in front of my eyes as I glared at him, trying to make it clear he was offending me, that his very presence made me itchy. He'd put us both at risk coming so close to me on the ice like that. He was heavy-looking, too. The ice didn't like heavy people.

"I can pay," he said. "Ten discs to the child's family, to keep them warm come winter. As a show of my thanks."

And at that moment, I knew what I was going to do. I hated myself for it, but I did it anyway. "I got a boy worth twenty," I said.

We haggled. The sailor was good at getting a fair price, but so was I. He twisted the end of his black, carefully oiled beard with a smirk as he thought about my counteroffers, and I rolled my eyes when he said something I didn't like. Twice I reached for my pick again and warned him that he'd be drial feed if he didn't get off the ice sheet while I was working.

In the end, we agreed that my brother was worth sixteen discs, and I went to fetch him.

You might think me evil for this, and maybe you're right, but here was my thinking: I didn't have enough to keep all my parents' children alive come winter. I didn't. That was a fact.

And even if I did, the sailor was right. The village we lived in was surrounded by an icy wasteland and filled with jerks. The man had called it a wretched hunk of ice, and that's what it was. It was also forbidden to come or go except by sea, meaning this might have been my brother's only chance of escape.

Everyone who tried leaving on foot—across the ice after winter started properly—went mad. They'd come back rambling about drials and sprites or they'd be found dead with a look of terrified wonder on their faces and nibble marks from foxes on their fingers.

And even if all that wasn't true, the sailor was tall, having eaten well in his youth. He was rounder in the middle, too, meaning he ate well even still. More importantly... he had life in his eyes, a type of shine I hadn't seen in an adult before, but I somehow still recognized. His eyes were wide and open, like he believed there was a chance he'd see something new or good or interesting. He wasn't stony and staring at the ground the way the rest of us were.

So I sold my little brother to him with the hope that Kid (that's what I called my brother, his name was actually Hemi) would have a better life growing up at sea with this sailor than there in the frozen marshes with me.

But who knows? Maybe this is the sort of thing all terrible people tell themselves when they sell a child. I'll never know. But I'm glad you know about this, because if you're listening to this story, I want you to understand what kind of person I was at the start. This way, you won't feel too surprised by how it all works out.

When I got back to the ice with my brother in tow, I told Kid he would be going with the sailor and would have to listen to him instead of me from then on.

Kid cried and said he didn't want to go. He clung to my leg.

I knelt so I was his height (he was somewhere around seven, though I'd lost count by then, so I couldn't say for sure).

I said, "It'll be an adventure. You'll get to travel, and when you're older, you'll have your pick of wives or husbands. People like a man who's seen things and knows things. You'll be bigger and stronger if you go with the sailor."

"She's right, boy," the sailor said, kneeling as well, setting a thick-fingered hand covered in iron rings on Kid's shoulder. "I take good care of my crew. I teach them to fight and hunt and read maps. I promise you'll have a big dinner every night, and the work's much easier than what your sister here does each day."

And you won't have to worry about being torn apart by bears, I thought. That had been happening a lot lately, more than it used to. Everyone said it was a bad omen. Nine villagers had been slaughtered since spring. The animals were going rabid. They were changing too—striking at times they wouldn't normally strike, killing without eating, getting unusually close to fire. Equah had even told everyone she saw a woman riding one of the bears, her mouth streaked with blood.

And you won't have to listen to nonsense from the elders either, I added in my mind.

Kid settled a little, rubbing his eyes with his grubby hands all the while sniffling and doing that deep-breath-hiccup-thing that kids do when they're trying not to cry.

"You know how to fight?" Kid said.

"That I do." The sailor chuckled. "With whichever hand is nearest a blade; that's especially rare."

So my brother went with the sailor, and I was given sixteen discs. Discs were usually light, thin, and shiny—these ones were heavy. I'd never held so many at one time, and I was afraid that someone would notice and take them from me, so I stuffed them into my furs, letting the cold rounds freeze my stomach.

I went straight to see Bayflower, to get what dried lichen I could so late in the season.

On my way, I passed Equah's lodge. The decrepit woman was squatting outside where she always sat, watching people come and go, collecting gossip and passing judgment, breathing in smoke from her whale bone straw. Her kohl-lined eyes followed me from beneath the brackish grey hair that always fell into her face, making her seem like she was peeking—spying—seeing something she shouldn't.

I kept my gaze on the crunching snow at my boots, hoping she wouldn't be able to read me, but she could anyways. She cackled, vile and cruel. "Crab, my dear, listen... there are some stains that cannot be washed away."

I wanted to say: *I hope you die this winter, you horrid sack of bones*, but I didn't. It was best to ignore Equah. She was only guessing because that's what she did; she guessed things about people. If I reacted, she would know she was right, and I couldn't bear to look at her smug smile one more time in my life. She continued laughing until I was too far away to hear her, the sound of her shrill giggle swallowed up by the empty cold.

I made my way through the tightly-packed dome houses of Kettin that were made from chiselled ice, which meant that from far away, they were invisible, blending in with the vast frozen white. On days when the wind blew up snowy dust in vicious whirlwinds (which was often), they weren't even visible up close. I wove through the village, passing grey furs stretched tight against whale bone frames and outdoor hearths roasting fish and whale blubber, swallowing five or six times as my mouth watered from the scent.

Bayflower gave me as much as she could and for a reasonable price too: lichens that were already dried so I didn't have to do anything other than put them away for winter, smoked fish, fire cider in case the girls caught a cold, seal oil for making fire, and a palm-sized hunk of frozen whale meat. More than likely, the others had gotten what they needed already. The lakes might be frozen over any day now. Hibernation could begin that very night. Who was to say?

Bayflower didn't ask where I got the discs, but I could tell by the way she inspected them that she wanted to. She plucked off an elk-glove and pressed her dry, red fingers against the shine, turning each one over. She even brought one of them up to her chapped lips and bit into the flimsy gleam. From beneath a thick, snow-hare hood, her black eyes narrowed in suspicion. Still, she nodded, agreeing to take the payment.

I wanted to say: *I didn't steal them,* because I knew that was what she was thinking. But the truth of it was worse than theft, so I kept my mouth shut.

As I hefted a sack of lichens onto my back (I'd gotten four sacks in total and had to return the bag when I was done), she said, "You better be careful

Crab, or your face will stick like that, and no one will have you to wife."

I frowned harder. Bayflower was pretty; her cheeks were red but not flaky, not whipped into ragged edges by the wind like mine. Her brows were thick and straight and even, her mouth round and full. She wouldn't understand that it didn't matter whether I smiled or grimaced. I looked the way that I looked. I'd seen my reflection in the lakes in the summer, but even if I hadn't—I knew how people's eyes lit up when they spoke to a pretty girl, how they acted.

They didn't act that way when they spoke to me.

My mother had been beautiful. Sailors would trip over their words when they saw her; she'd get the best prices on meat and lard and lichens. No one stumbled over their words when they spoke to me. They laughed and called me *Crab* and told me to fix my face.

It was Equah who'd given me the name long before my parents died. "So sour for one so young," she'd said in a sing-song voice, pretending like what she was saying was sweet and not evil like everything that came out of her saggy throat. "Claws like a crab this one has, pinching away any who get too close."

When the town elder said something like that about a scrawny girl, people listened. They called me Crab and stayed away for the most part. After my father died, they kept even farther away. The unlucky, tainted orphan crab was a bad omen. It was just as well. I'd rather they leave me be. I had too many things to get done to be having pleasant chats with the other girls gathering snow and daydreaming about husbands or wives. I had three children to feed.

Well, now I had two.

But still, two felt like a lot.

When I got to our lodge, Preah was outside, her tiny frame swallowed by my old fur coat. It hung past her knees and dangled beyond her hands. Her matted red curls stuck out from the oversized hood as she watched that stupid owl of hers. The thing didn't understand it was supposed to be awake at night and asleep during the day like other owls. It sat just out of reach and stared at Preah.

Preah stared back, and sometimes it seemed like she was whispering to the thing. This irked me because she'd pretty much stopped talking since our mother died. I would have liked to have a conversation every now and then—maybe it would make me feel less like my mind was dripping out my ears. But no one asked me what I wanted. Why should Preah be any different? She'd talk to the damned owl, but I got nothing more than a scowl from her, and the occasional slap when I dragged her to the washing bucket so her face wouldn't have dried fish juice all over it.

I threw a stone at the bird, and it squawked and fluttered off.

Preah's face screwed up, but I cut the tantrum short. "You're supposed to be watching Niyi," I said.

It wasn't the first time Preah had left the baby alone inside and wandered out to look at the stupid owl. Yes, Preah was only nine (maybe), so she got distracted sometimes, and it wasn't any fun sitting and watching a baby all day. But what else could we do? I had to break my share of the ice, or the elders would lean on me. I had to dig for lichens and try spearing some fish when there was time. I had to milk Howl so there would be something Niyi could eat as she didn't have any teeth yet.

Preah's tantrum came anyways. She wailed and kicked at me as I dragged her by the sleeve into the lodge, feeling blind while my eyes adjusted from the glaring white of the snowy outside to the dark shadows of our home. She tried to wiggle her arm out of her furs so she could get away as I struggled to hold on and not lose my balance with the sack of lichens tied to my back.

She bit me. Hard.

I slapped her, and she cried louder, her despair spreading to baby Niyi. And suddenly, I had two bawling children.

I wanted to scream. Kid had been best at calming the baby, and now he was gone. I felt guilty for hitting Preah, but at the same time, I didn't. Maybe I felt guilty for not feeling guilty? I don't know. I was stretched too thin—like ice about to break—I couldn't care about hurting her feelings because all my cares were used up. Niyi could have choked on something or rolled out of her furs against the snow-wall and frozen. Or cried for too long and drawn attention. It would only take one pair of prying eyes to peek inside, and we'd be done for. At least, Niyi would be. I didn't want to give anyone a reason to start sniffing around.

The sound of the two of them yanging made me want to slam my face through the ice and be done with living. Hibernation could start any moment now, and I'd be stuck listening to them all day and night for months. The bone horn could sound, and those chopping ice would toss their picks and flee home. The horn sounded when winter began. Not when the weather changed—it was always cold and mostly frozen—the horn blew when winter officially started. When it became impossible to keep the ever-solidifying ice passageway between our village and the lakerunners' territory from forming. The entrances to our lodges would be smashed in, and we'd lay under the snow in the dark, eating only what we managed to save for the winter, using only the heat of our bodies and the shape of our holes to keep us warm.

I couldn't handle their crying. I couldn't handle wondering if I'd managed to store enough for the winter to keep them living (I wanted to believe that I had, but I wasn't sure, and I knew that if I failed, I'd be listening to them moan all winter as they shrivelled up and maybe died). I also needed to keep Howl alive for at least the first half of the dark season. I hoped Niyi would get her teeth early, and then I wouldn't have to feed the beast or deal with it living inside the lodge any longer, stinking the place up.

In a way, I liked Howl. She was all I had left to show for my father. Just before he'd died, he brought home this long-haired beast with horns and made me swear not to kill her and eat her when he was gone.

"It's a muskox," he said. "It's for milking, for Niyi."

My father had always been clever. Everyone told us Niyi would die. They said it would be best to leave her out on the ice to spare ourselves the suffering of having to watch. My father didn't listen. He found an animal with milk, and Niyi lived.

I promised him I'd do as he asked, even though I was bothered by the way he spoke about himself being gone, so not really listening.

Then he said, "Would you like me to find you a husband before I go?"

I shook my head. I didn't want a husband. I wanted a father who wasn't "going somewhere."

Of course, I knew he meant he was leaving life. My mother had been gone for a few weeks already.

"I hear her calling me," my father said. "Every night, she gets closer to the lodge. I'll have to go with her soon. It's not up to me."

He was right, of course. Though it wasn't an accident like when my mother left us. They put his body on display in the centre of the village. His death had been a message.

When I'd pushed through the crowd near Equah's lodge and stumbled upon the frozen flesh, I knew it was him. I knew it was him because I could *feel* it was him, not because he looked anything like himself. His face hadn't been *his* face by then. It was swollen and purple and bashed in, twisted in all the wrong ways.

His blood-soaked hair and scraggly beard were coated in frost. Thin icicles that almost looked like tears dripped from his eyebrows and eyelashes. He'd been left out on the tundra overnight so was as solid as a rock.

I didn't know who did it—I imagined it would take at least a few stronger people to get him alone and beat him to death—but I knew why they'd done it. It was because of what he'd done with my mother's body. She'd given specific instructions before she died, but what she wanted wasn't what Equah and the elders before her said must be done with our dead. My father listened to my mother, and they killed him for it.

I told you. This isn't a very nice story. I started here so you'd know what kind of girl I was. What kind of world I lived in.

If any of this bothers you, fuck you. It was way worse living it than hearing about it. Trust me.

After selling my little brother for the sake of my sisters, I still had to go back to work. My left hand was itchy because Kid's sticky imprint was still pressed into my palm. Each time I closed and opened my fist, the skin stuck a little to itself.

I didn't have the time to mourn for him. I left the girls screaming in the lodge and knelt by an icy puddle to wash the remnants of Kid off my hand before heading back to the ice. There was no point in crying over any of it.

TWO

HACKING ICE FELT LIKE a joke. Only it wasn't a very funny one.

By order of the village elders, every household had to devote at least half a day, every day, from autumn until the moment the bone horn blew, to chopping at the ever-forming ice. It was a dreary losing battle that got you so hot you sweat, and then the sweat froze as you walked home, so no matter what time of day it was, you were the wrong wetness and the wrong temperature.

I didn't know what happened to the families that didn't put in the work, but I knew it wouldn't be good. My guess was it would look sort of how my father had looked when they were done with him. People were always watching to make sure that everyone else was shouldering their share. They were always talking, always whispering.

I'd been breaking ice for a few months and no matter how hard I worked or how fast I chopped, there was always more new ice in the morning than could be broken up in a day. Sometimes it felt like the groaning, squeaking sheets of ice were laughing at me. It was dangerous work, too. There were carved pillars dug deep into the frozen ground on the shore that we tied ourselves to with thick ropes knotted around our stomachs. This way, if we cracked the ice wrong and fell through, there was a better chance we would be pulled back out before we froze or were convinced by the drials to stay below and drown.

I'd seen six people fall through the ice since my father died and I took up his pick. Only one of them had lived.

So I took my steps with slow care, setting one furry boot to the ice and waiting, putting a little weight on it, then waiting again as the treacherous wind howled and whipped my cheeks, kicking up thin needles of ice that stung my eyes. I kept my feet wide apart to spread the burden of my weight, and I listened. The ice always heaved and creaked and grimaced when you walked on it, but there was a subtle hint that it was going to snap... if you listened.

It was like the night my mother brought Niyi into the world. She'd moaned for hours but there had been a tinge of warning in her voice in those final moments before Niyi came—a groan that sounded like the very last of her determination being used up. The ice would tell me if it was to break. It would warn me, and I'd be ready.

The ice held the day I sold Hemi to the sailor, and I made my way out on the sheet until I could see the end of it—black waves that hadn't frozen yet churning in the distance. The sky was clean and white and there was a sliver of greyish flat tundra across the lakes, hazily blending into the sky above. I didn't go all the way out; that would be stupid. Instead, I took a deep breath of frigid air and slammed my father's stone pick into the ice as far from my body as I could. I waited while the blow echoed down into the ice below, watching the ice between my boots and the pick. No visible cracks. No little rivers of black snaking towards me, hoping to pull me down into the land of the drials.

That didn't mean I was safe—pulling the pick out was just as dangerous, if not more.

I took another breath and plucked the pick from the ice, taking several hurried steps back toward my pillar. The owl pillar had been the only one that was free when I arrived at the shore that morning. Of all the pillars in the village, it was my least favourite—carved out of weather-greyed wood, the owl was taller than my father had been with wide unblinking eyes that followed me no matter how far east or west I wandered.

It was the one my mother had been tied to the day she'd fallen through the ice.

I waited, listening, ensuring the ice was done shifting before making my way forward again to hack once more. Always, I kept a little closer to the shore than my previous strike; it was safer that way.

As the day wore on, I relaxed a little in my work, the danger growing less present in my mind, and a space for Kid clearing out in my thoughts.

He won't have to grow up in this terrible place, I told myself. *You've saved him from it, and he, with his price, has saved Preah and Niyi.* It didn't feel any better, no matter how I reasoned it. I missed him already, and my jaw hurt from how tight I was clenching it.

Occasionally, I heard the shouts of some of the others. We had to stay spread out to keep from putting each other at risk, but I could see the grey outlines of them: tall, bearded folk wrapped tightly in grey furs so thick they didn't look people-shaped anymore. They seemed more like seals scattered across the ice.

HOLD! was the most important shout. Someone would say this when they thought they'd created a deep vein or when a large chunk was about to break free from the land.

EYES! was also not to be ignored. It meant: *look up, I see something across the ice.*

Everyone would stop their chopping and peer into the misty white and grey and wait, ready to run if the thing we saw was a lakerunner. I didn't stare across the ice when *eyes* was called out; I had no idea what a lakerunner looked like. I imagined they were tall and hairy, sort of like a person that walked on four long, stretched-out limbs. Whenever I heard *EYES!* I turned to the person nearest me and waited to see if they ran, my hand tight around the rope that held me to my pillar. I probably wasn't faster than any of the others—most were men, full-grown—but I knew I had to be. I had to outrun at least one of them, so I wouldn't be the lakerunner's dinner.

The lakerunners were why we kept the ice broken for as long as we could. It was also why we moved underground the moment winter became too strong for us to fight it and the lakes froze over. Lakerunners lived on the other side of the waters and being caught by one meant being eaten alive, flailing while something burrowed its face into your steaming organs. They especially liked chewing on children.

As the sun sank into the sea and the cold gnashed at my cheeks and nose, forcing itself through the two layers of mittens I had on and burrowing into my toes in my boots, most of the others left. Their half-day was done, but because I'd taken the time to bring Kid to the sailor and carry all the lichens home, I'd be staying until after dark.

A boy called Hallen stayed behind even though he didn't have to. He continued working to disguise his motives, but I knew he stayed to watch me. The only thing more dangerous than cleaving ice was cleaving ice alone. If you fell through, there would be no one to tug on your rope and get you back out again.

What can I tell you about Hallen?

Hallen was a mess—seventeen and strong, with black hair and a flat nose. He was a good fisherman, but an orphan like me. His grandmother had been living up until earlier that year. He'd taken good care of the woman whose eyes had been going white with cataracts, and I admired him for that. I'd never spoken to him much, but after she died, I had to.

It was insensitive, cruel of me even, but I'd gone to him and spoken some pleasantries—all of it fake. He attacked me for it straight away.

"You want to know what I'm doing with my nanna's rations for the winter."

It wasn't a question. It was a statement, and it had been true.

There was no point in lying, so I hadn't. "Yes," I said, looking him straight in his lonely brown eyes, refusing to flinch when I saw his jaw clench in rage.

"Other people have already asked," he said. "They've offered a fair price."

I had no discs, nor was I skilled at some worthy craft. I had nothing to offer him... or so I thought.

"But fuck them, you know?" he said, letting his arms flop against his sides. "Spend the night with me, and it's all yours."

I'd known what he meant. I'd seen dogs have at each other. And my parents weren't too secretive about the things adults did together when kids weren't around. Hallen was spiteful, like me. I think he said it to be mean, expecting that I wouldn't agree. But I had three kids and a muskox to keep alive, so I had.

"Wait... really?" He raised his eyebrows.

I nodded and after an awkward moment of standing in the cold, we went to his lodge. I lay on his bedding furs and waited, but nothing happened. Shame washed across his face, and then he cried. He told me he couldn't handle the loneliness of it all now that his grandmother was dead. He apologized for asking me to do what he had, sobbing like a child, his head finding its way to my shoulder.

I wanted to say, *I don't have time for this.* But I didn't because he was crying, and I was never good at dealing with crying. It put me in a mood, lying there next to him as he tried to compose himself. I was certain he wasn't going to give me what he'd saved up for his grandmother, as there was nothing I could offer to change his mind besides what he'd just refused.

When his tears ended, he sat up, still and quiet, staring at the icy wall for some time. I kept wondering if I could just leave and continue digging for lichens as I was wasting precious daylight waiting for a moment that felt appropriate to walk out.

"Help me move it," he said finally, standing and gathering up dried moss and lichens into a sack. "Everything on this side here."

I didn't want to presume, so I stayed still.

"No, you're right," he said, his eyes glazed over, still red and puffy from crying. "I'll move it; you've done enough."

And I watched as he carried everything he'd saved for his grandmother to my lodge. It had taken him three trips.

We hadn't spoken much after that day, but I'd thought a lot about Hallen.

He was also avoided like someone with a catching sickness. Orphans were bad luck; everyone knew that. I thought about the different people in our pathetic little village. Hallen was the only boy close in age to me, which meant if I wanted to get married to a guy, it would probably have to be him. Even if there were others our age, no one would marry an unlucky orphan, except another unlucky orphan.

I think Hallen thought about this too... or maybe he felt guilty for what had nearly happened between us. Every few days, there would be a fish left in front of our lodge. I knew it was from him.

He'd even spoken about it once—about us being together—though not directly.

There had been a day when Equah called everyone to her lodge to hear her speak about a pointless dream she'd had about some of the sky falling into our village or whatever. No one had stood near me, but Hallen came closest. When the old lady's rambling was over, he walked with me some.

"If you wanted someone... to help with things... you and your brother and sisters, you all could stay with me this winter... if you wanted."

I knew he was mostly offering because he didn't want to be alone all winter in the dark. When I looked up at him, he seemed so sad and desperate that part of me hated him. The only chance I would have for companionship: a lonely man-child. Then again, if we lived together, only one of us would have to hack ice each day...

"I wouldn't touch you," he said. "Unless... you know, you wanted me to."

It would have made things so much easier in one sense to have agreed with him. To have someone helping me out. But if it went wrong, we wouldn't be able to leave until it was spring and the risk of the lakerunners was gone. What if he smelled terrible all winter? I could remember the scent of my father in the hibernations of years passed. What if Hallen was childish or annoying and it turned out I was stuck taking care of yet another kid?

I thought of the previous winter and how my parents had lain far apart and kept all us kids in the middle where it would be warmest. Would Hallen lay across from me with the little ones between us? Would he lose his temper with them and shout or hit them? Even if Hallen were perfect, and I wanted him to be my husband (which I didn't), I couldn't let him see Niyi. Something had gone wrong with her after our mother died; her tongue had turned blue.

Blue was forbidden. It was the colour of the sky and so belonged to the Skyfather. Babies were allowed to have blue eyes—since they'd just come fresh from the sky—but if they didn't fade away by the time they were two or three, you had to leave the toddler out on the ice for the drials to take. I had no way of knowing what Hallen would do if he saw Niyi's mouth, so I couldn't accept his offer, tempting as it was.

I'd said, "I'll think about it," knowing full well my answer would be no.

Hallen didn't look at me as we worked, and I didn't look at him. When it was dark and it felt like my due was paid, I found my way back onto sturdy land without offering him any thanks. Nice words didn't mean much—nothing really—so usually I felt it was best not to say them. My fingers were so numb they were almost useless, meaning it took me a stupid amount of time to untie myself from the damned owl pillar. Its big carved eyes watched me. Judged me. They said: *Kid will be alone now. Just like Hallen.*

Finally, using more my teeth than my fingers, I got the rope loose enough to step out of the hoop that had been tied and hurried home. I knew Niyi would be hungry and whiny. She normally ate when I finished my work, but since I'd stayed late, she would be eating late... unless Preah had sorted it out, but that was probably wishful thinking.

"Crab, my dear," Equah said as I passed.

I sighed and turned to face the harpy. She smiled—to anyone else, it would have looked like she was being playful or mischievous, friendly even—but I knew better. She was gloating and it was all the worse because I didn't know why she was so smug. My heart skipped a beat as I wondered if she'd somehow figured out about Niyi's blueness. Being the cruel thing that she was, she dragged out her next words, enjoying my frustration as I waited.

"You've not had your lodge protected from winter sprites yet... winter is in the wolf's teeth now. It won't be long."

That's how Equah survived the winters; everyone paid her (an enormous price) to have her place protection over their homes which really just meant that she would shake a rattle and make wavering, croaking noises sort of like a song but screechy and awful.

I would rather have winter sprites than Equah in my lodge, but this wasn't the sort of thing people were allowed to refuse. Apparently, if one person caught winter sprites, they'd spread, and everyone would have them come summer. It sounded stupid to me. I'd never seen teeny blue people trying to get inside my home. I wouldn't be surprised if Equah had made the blasted things up, so she didn't have to work any (she was the only one who didn't have to cleave ice, if you were curious).

I hated her so much it hurt. I wanted to cry with my rage for her. I didn't, of course. I wouldn't give her the satisfaction.

"Soon," I said, extra irritated that she'd chosen that moment to bring it up. There were others crowded around; they'd overheard. I would have to do it now, or they would lean on me, and if I were bludgeoned into mush and left out on the ice, Preah and Niyi would probably die. But I'd spent all my disks already. Well... I had one, but I was saving that for the time below. I would have to think of something else.

The firelight of Equah's outdoor hearth splattered against her ragged skin, tinting her face red. Sinister. I didn't want to pay her for anything as I was pretty sure she'd been the one to give the villagers permission to hunt my father. It was probably her idea. What a sick joke it all was. I would end up paying the woman who'd had my father murdered.

She watched me walk away, taunting me with her hideous grin. What I wouldn't give to dive at the woman and beat her face in...

When I made it home, Kid didn't run out and jump on me because he wasn't there anymore, and the weight of the day was all the heavier. I wanted to have great beasts take hold of each of my limbs in their teeth. To have them pull me in different directions until I tore into pieces.

I wasn't shredded by lumbering beasts, but I was given more trouble. My neighbour Brint was waiting for me at the lodge, leaning against my ice wall right near the leather flap that led inside. His arms were crossed and his oily red hair was plastered to his face.

"No," I said, the moment I saw him.

He opened his mouth to speak.

"NO!" I shouted. "Go home and leave us alone!"

He grabbed me by the shoulder way too hard, so I hit him. He didn't let go.

"Don't be stupid, Crab. You know you can't keep her living. She doesn't need to die, me and Mare got more than enough—"

It was the same argument we had every time we saw each other. Brint and Mare had been married for years and couldn't, for whatever reason, have children of their own. When my mother died, they offered to take Niyi off my father's hands, saying that a baby needed a woman's touch. When my father died, they bothered *me* over her.

"I'm not giving her to you!" I shouted, jerking my shoulder out of his big fist, making sure I was loud enough that the others in their homes could hear just in case things got messy. Even if Brint did something he shouldn't, I knew there was little chance someone would come to help me. Maybe Hallen would; maybe he wouldn't. But if that was how it came to be, I had my mother's arrowhead inside my hair, hidden in the bun beneath my hood. Still, it would be better to give people the chance to intervene, just in case someone felt like helping out the orphan crab.

"Listen, this isn't about you and your pride," Brint said through clenched teeth. "It's about that baby. Where do you think she'll have it better? Easier? You're just a girl; you're asking too much of yourself. You know it. I know it. Everyone in Kettin knows it. Cut the struggle short and give her to someone who can keep her fed, clothed, warm."

He was right. In every way, he was right. Niyi would have a better life with Brint as her dad and Mare as her mom. But they valued Equah's opinion. They'd take one look at Niyi's blue tongue and chuck her onto the ice. Maybe they wouldn't; maybe they wanted a child so badly that they'd just cut the tongue out and have a kid who couldn't speak.

I set my face firm and glared at him until he started walking.

"You'll regret this," he said, turning back suddenly and pointing at me. "In the dark—in the dark, you'll know you chose wrong, and you'll know that little girl is suffering for it."

It wasn't mature of me, but I picked up a pebble and chucked it at him. It hit his shoulder. He lifted his fist, and I flinched, but then he regained control of himself.

"You're a spiteful bitch... you know that?"

I did. And I should have been used to being told about it, but I wasn't. Being shouted at and called names by a full-grown man was never easy.

I waited until he was gone before I rolled my shoulder around in circles trying to stretch away the dull pain caused by how hard he'd clamped his fingers around it.

Te-hoo. Tuh-hoo.

Preah's owl seemed like she was laughing at me, watching with her big yellow eyes, head tilted to the side. It was silly in a way, but sometimes I felt like that owl liked watching me suffer, just like the owl pillar on the shore.

I picked up another stone and pelted her with it.

She took off screeching.

❈ ❈ ❈

My nights weren't often any easier than my days. That night was no exception. Preah was in a mood;

she sniffled and cried and refused to go to sleep no matter what I did. She didn't look around for Kid either, which hurt me. Did she think it was normal for her family to just be gone one day? She also kept trying to stick things in her right ear. She'd been scratching and slapping the same ear for days. I knew something was wrong with it, but I didn't know what to do about it. I had tried talking to her about it, "Does it hurt?" "Is it itchy?" "What's wrong?" but she just whimpered and moaned and wandered away to her owl, wasting precious lichens as she coaxed the mangy thing into her palm. Sometimes when I spoke, she covered her ears, and this hurt me more than it should have. I mean, she covered her ears when Niyi cried too, but being so blatantly ignored was usually the last slap of the day for me, and I had no patience left by then most nights.

I fed Niyi with the leather skin my father had fashioned before he died, fighting sleep with each moment that passed. I nodded forward and shot up, suddenly afraid I'd fallen asleep on top of Niyi and smothered her. This happened several more times before I chose to lie down beside her. This way, if I fell asleep while she was eating, at least I wouldn't crush her. I pulled Preah tight against my stomach, hoping to keep her warm. Her frigid little fingers crawled inside my tunic so my skin could heat them.

"I'm sorry," I whispered into her oily hair. "I know I'm not... I know I'm not doing a good job."

She pulled one hand out of my tunic to plug her ear so she didn't have to listen to me anymore.

THREE

"WAIT!" I SLAMMED MY fingers down on the wooden edge of the skiff, breathless from the sprint. I'd gone outside to have a piss and taken off to the shore the second I'd seen that Ford's boat wasn't tied beside his home. "I'm coming with you."

"Get out of here, Crab!" said Ford, flicking my fingers with his fingernail. It stung because my hands were cold, but I think he was also trying to hurt me some. Usually, by the time the bruising on my knuckles had healed from my last attempt, there was another whale hunt and the opportunity for Ford to give my fingers their usual purple hue.

"No. I'm coming," I said. I gritted my teeth and pulled the boat close to the ice with all my might, grabbing hold with my other hand as the fur-clad men inside tried to push off with their oars.

"No!" I said. "I won't take up—" My boots slid as they pushed off, closer and closer to the icy black depths.

Ford whacked my fingers with the blunt end of his dagger, and that hurt a lot. One finger got suddenly warm, so I knew it was bleeding or that pinchy thing had happened where teeny red dots appear on your skin.

"You're going to get yourself soaked!" he said. "Get back!"

Another man in the skiff said, "Crab, you'll freeze if you fall in."

Someone else said, "Go home, Crab."

Ford hammered into my fingers again, and that time I did let go—it hurt too much to hold on. My left hand still gripped the splintery wood, and my right came down on the skiff again, but Ford had pulled off one rabbit fur mitten with his teeth, leaving the thing hanging out of his mouth as he used his free fingers to pry my grip loose. I gave it my all, but he was stronger, and my hold was gone, and the boat was out on the lakes.

I didn't have time to nurse my stinging fingers—there was one more skiff, and I was feeling extra determined because normally Ford didn't let me get both hands on his boat. I decided it meant I was making progress or that it was a good day or something like that. Plus, Indus owned the last skiff, and he wasn't so mean as the others. Once he'd even taken Hallen whaling when a man named Mozzie had a fever, and everyone thought Mozzie was going to die.

Hallen was already there, begging him. "You've got space for one more," he said. "You need the hands."

"Not unlucky hands, I don't," said Indus.

I tried to be clever, which wasn't usually what I was good at, but sometimes I forgot that I guess. I tried to walk past without drawing Indus' eyes, hoping that Hallen was distracting him, and I could climb in the boat. Maybe he wouldn't notice until we'd kicked off, and I'd get to go on the hunt.

A whale hunt—if successful—meant having a fair share of whale meat if you were in the boat when it was caught. There were three skiffs and eight hunters to each, and whales were huge, so if I got a spot, I'd have lots to eat and lots to sell, much more than the three disks I needed to pay Equah to handle the probably-not-real winter sprites.

"Ack!" It wasn't Indus that caught me; it was Mozzie. He grabbed me by the back of my neck and dragged me away from the boat. I kicked his shin and managed to grab one of the oars, trying to swing it at him as he pushed me away.

"Crab!" Indus said. "You better be giving that back now!"

"Not unless you let me in."

He shook his head. "You're too small. You'll get hurt, or we'll lose you overboard, or you'll get wet and freeze."

"I can do it," I said.

"No. You can't. Do we have to have the same—" He covered his face with his hands in frustration. "For Father's sake, do we *always* have to go through this? You're not a whale hunter; you're a little girl!"

He reached for the oar, but I pulled it back quick, kind of surprised that he didn't catch it.

"Give it here. Now."

I shook my head, clenching my jaw. "You don't understand. I got... I don't have enough... I have to come."

"Don't make me lean on you—"

"If I catch winter sprites because I can't pay—"

"And if you die out on the sea—"

He reached for the oar a second time, and that time he was faster, grabbing it and jerking me forward as he tried to rip it from my grasp with force. My feet scrambled to get under me as I slid, and they did alright at first, but then Indus tried to lift the oar up above his head. My weight made it a struggle for him, but he didn't give up. My toes lifted off the ice to the sound of the other whalers laughing. I didn't let go, not until Indus pushed a boot against my chest as he pulled, sending me sprawling backwards.

I was up quick, moving between him and the boat.

"Crab! Just move. You're not coming." He kicked at me with a lazy boot. "Get."

I shook my head and wiped my running nose on my sleeve.

"I need this," I said.

He sighed. "You know I hate being hard on you. Just go. Please." He asked so sincerely that it was hard not to listen. Still, I didn't budge.

"For Father's sake!" He grabbed me by the shoulder and flung me away, and when I moved toward the skiff again, he pushed me hard, so hard that I fell onto my back and slid on the ice some, shards of frosty cold finding their way into my sleeves.

I got up and was about to move for the boat again, but he raised the oar, and from the look in his eyes, I knew he was going to wallop me hard enough that I'd lose out on a day's work, and I couldn't afford that. I halted, my cheeks burning with the humiliation of failing in front of everyone like that.

"You think I like pushing little girls around? Huh?" He lifted the oar again, and I flinched once more as whatever pity was inside him grappled against his rage. He calmed. "Listen... We're not doing this anymore. Next time you touch my boat or one of my oars... you won't be getting up so quick when I'm done with you."

I caught my breath as I watched them float away toward full stomachs, hating them with everything I had in me.

"You can't use force," Hallen said, standing beside me. "You've got to convince them."

I didn't look at him as I stooped and picked up my mother's spear (I'd chucked it to the ground when I dove for Ford's boat).

Hallen walked his way, and I walked mine, sucking on my bloody fingers as I fumed. Already my knuckles were so swollen that it was hard to fully open my hand. When I tried to force my fingers to stretch, my hand shook from the pain. I could fish or gather lichens for a few hours before the sun was up high and ice-cleaving began. While fishing made for better meals, I went for lichens because there was less risk of coming home with nothing. I mean, they were less filling too, but I'd rather have some lichens to chew on than no fish.

I rushed west, clamouring over the occasional cleft of rock, kicking up more dusty snow than I needed to on account of how frustrated I was. The whistling wind pelted me as I debated trying to seem more pathetic around Indus. If I cried, I might be able to gain his pity.

I was also coming up with better responses to the things he'd said. When he said I was too small to go whaling, I should have shouted, "Yeah, but I don't have any big people!" Maybe that would have gotten to him. I never thought of the right thing to say when an argument was happening, only afterwards when it didn't matter anymore. But maybe that was for the best. Maybe it would've been foolish to remind him I was an orphan—no one wanted bad luck on a whale hunt. Whale hunts went wrong often enough as it was.

Hardly anyone else was awake and looking for a place to dig, but I knew that wouldn't be true for much longer. I needed to get into the tuft fields and out before the others showed up and chased me off. We called them the tuft fields because there were little rolling hills—baby hills—where short, stubby, ground-covering plants were coated in smooth snow, always trying to push up to the sun, desperate to beat back the winter for as long as possible. Just like us, really.

I dug in the ice with my mother's spear, slashing every few paces at random, getting my anger out, but also, eventually, discovering some pale green beneath a sheet of crunchy snow—three stunted bushes of willow, some caribou moss and a few tangles of lichens. I knelt and worked fast, digging with the spear and pulling away chunks of ice with my still bleeding hands wrapped in my sleeves. I hadn't grabbed my mittens before chasing down the whalers, and there wasn't time to be going home again and coming back out to dig. Already I could see a sliver of the sun peeking up over the flat white horizon, fading away the last hint of stars in the pink sky.

I got one and a half pockets full of mostly not bloody moss before I started seeing others making their way westward. At first, it was just the younger women, gathering snow to make water with, giggling through their painted lips, as their beaded hair jingled. They gossiped and covered their mouths when they looked over at me, making me wonder if they were talking about me and then leaving me with no doubt.

"I heard she was in Hallen's lodge—"

"Eww."

"Why else would he give her Laka's rations?"

"Aww, don't make fun; it's a good match...."

"I heard she stole a whole stack of disks... when Equah finds out—"

"Is she bleeding?"

"Let's move a bit; I don't want any snow she's touched."

As humiliating as it was to be pulling my food out of the frozen ground as they laughed and gawked at me, I kept my head down and did the work. I couldn't say to Preah, "Sorry, there's nothing to eat. I just couldn't bear the way they were looking at me." I couldn't say to Niyi, "Sorry, Howl died because I didn't feed her enough, so you'll have to starve too." My own stomach was groaning since I hadn't eaten anything the night before, but I refused to obey it. I wasn't about to stuff lichens straight from the ground into my mouth in front of the girls collecting snow. Besides, they tasted awful unless they were boiled.

As soon as I saw the proper adults coming out to the field with empty sacks hanging off their sides and spades in their fur-covered hands, I knew it was nearly time to go. I got a little greedy and kept at it as they got closer, trying to stuff as much as I could in my hood (because I'd taken it down and used it as a sack once my pockets were full), trying to convince myself that if I dried it all and separated the roots properly and lost nothing to rot, I had gotten more than a full day's worth for Preah.

A man named Odom was the one who told me to "Get going" first, kicking at me with his boot as he slumped his bag down next to me, unrolling a well-treated skin to throw his finds on.

He dug his shovel into the crispy snow to my right. "I'll not tell you again."

I tried grabbing one more fistful, but his boot came down on my knuckles, the same ones that were swollen and bloody from the back of Ford's dagger. I tried to wrench my arm free, but he pressed down harder, and though I was trying really hard not to make a sound, I did.

"You going to drop it?"

I nodded.

But when he lifted his boot, I didn't unball my fist. I tried to take off with the lichens in my hand. I almost made it, but his boot caught my calf, and I stumbled some, scraping my chin against the icy ground as I slid. I managed to get my hand up to my hood, pressing it closed behind my neck, so I didn't lose too much, I don't think.

I was numb and miserable by the time I made it home and could hear Niyi bawling from outside. Preah was crouched in the entrance with her hands over her ears.

"She's just hungry," I said, dropping my finds and digging around in the furs for the milk skin, sniffing it to make sure it hadn't turned since I'd left to catch the boats.

The second the lip of the skin was pressed to Niyi's mouth, she was quiet, and Preah's hands slid from her ears. She crawled closer to me, sniffing at my swollen knuckles—she used to love pretending to be a wolf. Her and Kid would do it for hours—all day if they could. Back then, she'd howl and bark and make whimpery sounds when she played, but those noises went away when she'd stopped talking.

She licked at the blood on my hand, which was a bit gross, I guess, but I knew it was wolf-Preah trying to make me feel better. In one way, it didn't at all because it stung way worse when she pressed her tongue against my knuckles, but in another way, it did help. It was the first time she'd come to me in a while, in... I couldn't remember how long. She tended to avoid me during the day.

I pet the top of her head like she was a wolf, and she seemed to like that, crawling even closer, sniffing at the broken skin on my chin, and licking that too. I pressed my forehead to the top of her head, feeling the smallest shred of... love, I guess. I wanted to tell her she was a good wolf, but she didn't like when I spoke, even if it was a whisper, so instead, once Niyi was satisfied, I hid moss in the furs so Preah could crawl around and dig at them with her nose and eat just like a wolf on the tundra would.

I pointed to the lichens I'd foraged as I wrapped myself up in layers, hoping that Preah would separate the strands and wash them and boil them before pinning them between two flat rocks near the fire outside to dry out. She knew how to do it, and sometimes she would, but she pouted when I pointed, which made me think she wasn't going to be helpful today.

Sometimes it scared me to have her using the oil and fire stones because what if she spilled the oil on herself before she caught a spark? Twice in the past, she'd run to me on the ice having burnt herself. I'd held her fingers in the frigid water until the pain was gone and then stuck them in my furs to warm them with my skin (and then back into the water when she cried because she could feel the burn again, and then back in my furs—on an on until she felt alright again) but that was back when Kid could watch the baby.

I wrapped Niyi up good, tying her swaddle as tight as possible without hurting her. She cried less when she was wrapped up so tight she couldn't move, her little face peeking out from a thick brown fur, and when she cried less, Preah took better care of her. And then I took hold of my father's pick. I wasn't even swinging the thing yet, but my arm ached from the weight of it, especially because my shoulder was still sore from where Brint had grabbed me the night before. My neck hurt too from how Mozzie had grabbed me, and my hand stung—the rough inside of my mittens scraping at the torn skin on my knuckles. As I walked, I tried to stretch my arms some. Soon I'd be shivering and holding my limbs firm against my body, and I knew muscles needed a break from tension every so often.

And then I had the same hours I'd been having for months. Tied to a pillar (the bear this time), feeling like my back was going to give up on me as I hacked at the ice, or that my arms would stop working from the strain. That when I lifted the pick high above my head, I would drop it, and I'd be babbling nonsense forever like Eerok (who got silly on fungus smoke during an elk hunt and tripped and hit his head on a pointy rock).

Part of the time, I remembered how dangerous my work was, so I made sure to be careful, but then other times I would get all empty in my head. My mind became a clean white space, just like the land around me. My head curled down so my chin touched my chest, and my eyes were mostly protected from the raging wind. I stared at my boots, looking for hints the ice was about to give, trying not to notice how cold I was or how much thicker the ice seemed than the day before. I listened to the *thwack*, then the lack of cracking or snapping, as the sky turned a soft, hazy pink and then greyish-blue. It was the time of year when we got only a few hours of sun each day.

Thwack.
No snapping.
Thwack.
No snapping.
"EYES!"

My head shot up. The voice had come from far away, halfway around the other side of the village if I had to guess. I looked to the east at a bundle of grey fur that was the nearest hacker, readying myself to run, one hand on the rope tied around my waist.

The man went back to work, so I did too.

Only a moment later, I heard a shout from far away again. Not *EYES!* Not *HOLD!* Just a shout and another shout after that. A cruel noise: the type of sound that sets your blood curdling inside you. I looked to the east at the grey fur coat with a face—I could see the face now because he wasn't staring out across the lakes anymore; he was turned around and running back to shore.

The bone horn sounded.

It was winter.

FOUR

I TOSSED MY FATHER'S pick and ran, tufts of breath-stained air blowing past my cheeks. I was passed by the man from the east before I even made it to the shore, his long legs taking nearly double my stride. My heart pumped and my fingers shook like a hare caught surprised as I fought with the knot tied around my stomach, cursing myself for leaving the pick out on the ice because I could have used it to chop the rope.

All around me, people whispered and wailed and called out names, grabbing their loved ones in the darkening chaos. The man to the east of me was fighting with his rope too, only he got out first and took off into the village, his big boots thumping against the frozen ground. The man to the west of me untied himself faster too. Every few seconds, I looked up, trying to see if something was coming from across the ice, and then I looked back through Kettin, trying to see if anything was there.

Lakerunners could just as easily come from the other side; there were lakes to the north as well. But as far as I could see, there were only whimpering people rushing around, stamping out their fires, and dragging their dogs inside. People were collapsing the entrances to their homes, making their lodges look like piles of snow, but no one was being eaten.

I'd practiced this—all of it. In my head, I'd gone over it again and again. Exactly what I was going to do and in exactly what order. The only thing I didn't anticipate was my hands shaking so much.

When I managed to get the damned knot loose and step out of the hoop, the dogs were barking, and that rattled me because I felt like dogs were better than people in a lot of ways, and if they were frightened, it meant I should be too. I didn't know whether all the crying out came because a monster was on its way to Kettin, ready to gnaw on some human, or if it was just because we'd lost the fight with the northern ice, and truthfully, it didn't matter.

I ran through the tangle of people—even though there weren't too many of us in Kettin, it felt like a great flock of birds all squawking and flying in opposite directions, crashing into each other, cursing and yelping. I was knocked into twice. First, all I did was roll a bit to my left into the side of Equah's lodge, but the second time I came down on the ice and was trampled by someone. I don't know who (it was too chaotic and getting darker every moment) but whoever it was, they were heavy, and I heard something in my back pop. The sound sent a shiver through me, because I knew it wasn't a good sound to have coming from my body.

And then someone tripped over me and was flailing around on top of me for a second, muttering, "Fucking Crab! You unlucky bitch!"

I scrambled up and made it to the lodge, narrowly avoiding a wallop when Ford's wife Breena knocked over one of the skinny posts she used to hang their cauldron over their outdoor hearth. I rushed past Brint—who was looking right at me, seeming like he was about to say something.

I shouted, "No!" in his face.

He tried to grab my shoulder again—the one that was still stiff from his hands—but I managed to speed around him and duck just in time, ignoring his cursing. Already my lungs were aching as they thrust air in and out so fast that my head felt too light for my body, like it might just float away if I took my hood down. I grabbed Howl first, untying her and dragging her by her sharp horns.

She thrashed about and moaned, smelling people's fear or the lakerunners or else reacting to the chaos. She nearly took me off my feet when she lifted her head back high and I didn't let go. I'd taken her down below a few times already to get her used to it, but she sensed the terror all around us and fought me. I could hear villagers shouting at each other:

"Where's the dog?"

"Lettie?"

"The whalers aren't back yet!"

"Crab! This is your last chance!"

"The fucking fire's still going!"

"WHERE'S THE DOG?"

Their sounds swam together in my mind like a collection of fish. I didn't hear any one of them alone—just the mess of their voices and the thumps of their boots, and the tumbling of icy snow as they scrambled to cave in the tunnels carved into the floors of their lodges. Beams thwacked against the snow, packing it even tighter to the frozen earth as people hurried to flatten any parts of their lodges that were above ground. I pulled against Howl with all my might, groaning from her weight and the strain, only half aware that Niyi was crying. Preah too.

The beast finally moved when she figured her fight was pointless. When we got inside, I gripped the fur on her hip, making sure I didn't break my hold on her for one second, guiding her toward the deep black pit at the back of the lodge. She didn't want to go down probably because she was smart in a way—muskoxen aren't supposed to live below the ground. But the slope was too steep for her, so once I got her front hooves in, she slid down, bellowing as she went. She nearly didn't fit—my father and I had scraped the entrance to widen it before he'd died, but maybe Howl had grown bigger? Had I been feeding her too much?

I set Niyi in Preah's arms and pushed her down the tunnel as well, ignoring their screams. I'd already brought below most everything we needed, but there were a few things left out that we used too often to store in advance.

The milk skin.

Sleeping furs.

My mother's spear.

The lichens I was drying outside...

It was maybe a risk, but I ran out for them. Not getting them would also have been a risk, and I would rather be ripped to pieces by a lakerunner than starve slowly in a hole in the ground. It's not supposed to be easy to make those kinds of choices, but for me, it always has been.

I ran out to get the lichens and slammed into Brint, who was still waiting outside. I didn't get free from his grip fast enough and felt striking pain in my shoulder and my back (because, somehow, the two injuries had become connected). I didn't have time for him, so I plucked my mother's arrowhead out of my hair and dug it right into his knuckles where he held me.

He let go, cursing, and I was tumbling to the ground once more.

I got one boot under myself and almost the second before my knees were in the snow.

I think Brint was shouting at me, but I wasn't listening, so I can't tell you for sure.

Our fire was already out, and I had no beams to knock over and bury in the snow, so I stuffed my pockets with what was drying, knowing I'd have to eat them up first because they weren't fully dry and they'd get that fuzzy pungent stuff growing on them if I kept them inside the warm hole for too long. And then I bolted back inside. Brint was gone by this point—back home to save himself.

I gave the dim room one final look before pushing at the ice chunk—the special one that would cave in the front half of our home. I'd been loosening it for weeks; each morning after I fed Niyi usually, but I hadn't that morning because I'd gone after the whalers, and it was stiff in place.

Removing the cornerstone had always been my father's job as it was dangerous. I'd never seen him or anyone else do it because I was always already below, but he'd explained it to me once, and I'd seen him treat it every morning so it would be ready to move when we needed it to. I sat and pushed against the block with my boots. I heaved and grunted, and the thing did budge, only very slowly. When it finally popped out, I was nearly caught beneath the tumble of falling snow, scooting back on my rear as the entrance collapsed.

I didn't have the type of heart that made me feel something when this happened. The part of a person that would miss the sky and want to say goodbye to it... I didn't have that part.

In the days leading up to hibernation, my mom had always lain outside next to the fire and looked up at the stars and the flowing green and pink that danced across the sky. She'd whisper to the Skyfather about how much she was going to miss him. She'd tell me he would be there waiting for us when we came back up, but I'd known that already, so I always thought it was a strange thing to say. I think she said it more for herself than for me, but since I never asked her and she wasn't living anymore, I would never be able to confirm this.

Because my pace had slowed a bit, my back began to ache from where I'd been run over. I grabbed hold of the bone grate my father had made and dragged it to our tunnel hole as spears of pain shot through my shoulder and back. I spread my legs as wide as I could to brace myself against the walls of the tunnel as I backed into it—I didn't want to slide down just yet; I had to position the grate. I pulled it over the hole and then threaded my arms up through the gaps left in the hewn bone to pull a snow-filled leather over the top. This, too, had been sitting ready, waiting for the day winter began.

As terrified as I was that a lakerunner would come in and find me half-hidden (they were known to dig a little), I took my time. If I didn't lay the leather right, the hole wouldn't be properly disguised, and that would defeat the entire purpose of hiding underground, especially as the wind further flattened our home's remains.

When it seemed done well, I slid down into the darkness and felt around for the children. They were both screaming, so it was pretty easy to find them. In my pocket, I had some clean cloth folded neatly, just for this moment. I kept it on me constantly to be ready.

I did Niyi first, stuffing the cloth into her mouth and listening to make sure she was still breathing through her nose. Then I did Preah—she caught on pretty quickly, so her mouth didn't need to be full for very long. Niyi wasn't so quick; it took what felt like ages for her to understand. Each time she grew quiet, I'd pull the cloth out, and then she'd cry again, and I'd stuff it back in. If the lakerunners heard a baby crying, they'd dig—everyone knew that.

Between plucking cloth out of Niyi's mouth and stuffing it back in, I scrambled along the walls, feeling in the darkness for a rope. It took all my strength to pull it, and it felt like my shoulder was about to rip off my body, but I managed to yank hard enough to hear the sloppy sound of the back half of the lodge collapsing as the last murmurs could be heard from above.

It should have been silent, but of course, each time I managed to get the baby quiet, Howl would start acting up, and I'd be running my hands along her thick tufts of fur and making whispery noises. By the time she was quiet, Niyi would be yanging again.

My mother had always said that children were smart. "Smarter than most adults," she'd say.

I figured this to be true when I heard the crunching of snow above... the scuffling of something moving around up top. Preah, Niyi, and even Howl were silent. I heard strange echoing sounds—kind of like human voices, but more watery, a bit like a whale-bear if you can imagine what that would sound like.

Big, heavy footfalls.

Rummaging.

I held my breath and peered through the darkness to where I was pretty sure the entrance to our hole was. In the tussle of it all, I'd gotten turned around, so I couldn't say for sure.

This was it. Any moment I'd know if I'd done a good job closing the tunnel. They would come in and eat us, or they wouldn't. And that would be that.

I probably should have prayed—that's what everyone else in the village was likely doing, but I didn't want to. If the Skyfather were real—which I wasn't sure he was—he'd done nothing for me. Was I to believe that suddenly, out of nowhere, he'd decide to help me out? After everything else he'd let happen? He was going to save me from being eaten?

No.

It was the work of my own two hands that would be keeping us alive or letting us die. The Skyfather had nothing to do with it.

I waited, and we lived. Nothing burrowed into our hole, and slowly the children and the muskox settled. I pushed Preah against Howl's side when the beast lay down and then set Niyi between myself and Preah. I didn't want to lose the baby in the dark and risk Howl stepping on her.

And with everyone safe, I finally felt all the aches and pains and twists and clicks in my body. My shoulder. My back. My jaw. I shivered even though it wasn't cold at all; I was just hurting and had been so scared for so many moments. I can't tell you how long the aching and the shaking went on for, but I *can* tell you what I did after it dulled.

I reached across the kids to Howl, and as I stroked the furry beast, somehow—don't ask me how—I found a moment of ease in it all. My father had been the one to bring us Howl, and it felt... it was foolish, but it felt like he was there with me, lying on the other side of the girls.

We'd keep them warm together, my father and me. We'd built this hole together, dug it out of the ground when Niyi was still inside my mother—my mother had wanted a bigger tunnel because of the extra person. Together, my father and I had packed the ice and snow in just the right way to make sure that the heat couldn't escape. He'd taught me how to stack the ice bricks and explained to me how the air moved and how warmth travelled within moving air. How the hole would be heated by the people inside and that's why the little air tunnels wouldn't make the whole thing get cold.

All the steps I'd practised in my mind were done. All there was left to do was wait until spring, and hope that I'd managed to scrape together enough provisions. Maybe I should have felt relief, but I was stung by a bitter thought.

It was my first winter without my parents. Without Kid as well.

FIVE

IN THE DARK, THOUGHTS come into your mind. Thoughts that at first seem lovely, so you let them stay because you've got nothing better to do as you wait for winter to end. But then they twist and become cruel for no reason at all.

First, it felt like my father came; like he stayed a long while, lying on the other side of the girls. I could almost hear his big, deep breaths, the sound of him scratching his beard, the way he'd stretch several times a day and his shoulder would crack. I couldn't see him, but he was there—or almost there—and all I had to do was not reach out into the dark and find his place empty, and he'd stay. The more I focused on it, the more I could smell him: salt, leather, and fish.

I planned to avoid reaching into the emptiness and finding him gone for as long as I could, but well before I needed to milk Howl, my father's final expression splashed into my mind and ruined the moment. I remembered the swollen, purple, not-his-face expression.

I shot up, ignoring the ache in my back and shoulders, and pushed my fingers into the blackness front of me, grasping a leather vessel and crouching near Howl's belly, my knees begging me to sit another way because they, too, had been hammered something awful when I'd been trampled. I'd practised milking Howl with my eyes closed, getting the angle right, so there was no mess. I'd practised pouring milk from the big vessel to the milk skin with my eyes closed too, leaving just enough for two or three mouthfuls for Preah in the bigger vessel. The milk would help keep her feeling full, or at least, that was what I hoped. I didn't actually know how stomachs worked.

I fed Howl and Preah and put off nibbling on lichens myself because I wasn't really hungry yet, and I figured I should wait because eating on a not-quite-empty stomach seemed a waste. I tried to get still and listen, hoping my father would come back, but he didn't. It was my mother who came.

Mom.

When she came to visit me in the dark, Preah and Niyi and Howl were asleep. I wanted to envision her as she'd been for most of my life, but the darkness was evil. It gave me my mother when she was dying.

Somehow, she'd managed to pull herself out of the frigid water and get home. She was tough like that. My father had stripped her clothes off and then his own, pressing his hot skin against hers, hoping to keep her blood warm and moving. She'd been lying on her side, and he'd been curled around her back. Niyi and Preah and Kid were pressed against her chest, naked as well, so maybe my father had taken their clothes off first? I couldn't remember.

Either way, my father had told me to take my clothes off and lay down next to her, to help heat her because nothing warms a human faster than another human, but I was sixteen… or maybe seventeen… and I was shy about my body. I hadn't wanted anyone seeing me without my furs on.

I felt the rumble building in my father's voice when I shook my head. He didn't yell often, but I'd been able to tell from the vibration in his voice that he was about to. My mother had soothed him, catching the rumble before it came out, changing the course of the conversation.

"Will you still lie with me?" she said.

Even that I hadn't wanted to do. I think it was because I knew... I knew the weight of the moment, and I wanted to outrun it. I didn't want to obey my mother's last wishes because I didn't want her to be having last wishes at all. It was stupid, but it seemed like if I ignored her request, it wouldn't be real. She would get up, and her lips wouldn't be the gross blue-grey colour that they were, and I would get to keep having a mom.

Finally, when silent tears came from her eyes, I gave in. I set my head near her face and let her run her fingers through my messy hair.

In the dark, I remembered her deep breaths: each of them slow and wavering. I would never be able to forget that sound: her shaky, rattling breaths. I think she hadn't wanted to spend her last hours crying, so she'd fought the flood of tears, but she was sad to be going.

Kid asked her if she'd seen any drials while she'd been below the ice.

She nodded. "There were four of them. A baby girl just like Niyi, a boy like you, a girl like Preah... and a bigger girl, a woman really..."

I fought the memory, trying to push it away from my mind, but the darkness wouldn't have it. I remembered her cursed words: "You know I want to be with the wolves, right?" She'd said this to my father, and he'd nodded.

There were two kinds of bodies that mattered in Kettin: the people and the wolves. There were two heights—tall rocks upon which the bodies were left—one for people and the other for the occasional wolf body someone ended up finding.

My mother had never told me anything about her childhood or her parents, but I knew there was some reason she hadn't been happy with it. She hadn't wanted her bones mixed in with those of her family.

I don't think any of us knew the price my father would pay for listening to her. Maybe he had. He hadn't let me come with him up top the wolf-mound to lay her body down. I'd been big enough to make the climb. I maybe even could have helped him, but he'd climbed up the rocky ledge with my mother's body thrown over his shoulder. I think he wanted to be alone, and it was probably just as well. I'd been able to hear him sobbing from the ground below.

If you've never heard your father cry, you can't understand how it feels. And if you have heard it, then there's no point in me explaining it because you already know the unique type of pain that spreads in your chest when it happens.

My mother had fed Niyi with her body, and when the baby was full and sleeping—that's when she cried. I think she'd known it was the last time, and she'd wanted to drag it out, to savour it a little longer. But the baby was asleep, so it was over.

She fed Kid as well, which wasn't that unusual; he'd still taken milk from her some evenings when he hadn't been sleeping well. But then she fed Preah too, and I became uncomfortable. Preah was too big to be taking milk like a baby. I'd turned my head so I wouldn't have to watch and feel the strange mix of disgust and shame I'd been feeling... or maybe it had been so my mother didn't have to see what I was feeling; I still don't know.

My mother asked me to come to her when Preah was done, but I couldn't—it was too strange a request. Again my father's voice began to rumble, and again my mother calmed him.

"But it's most important for you to drink," she said. "More than the others."

Still, I shook my head, my father shooting spears at me with his eyes. I think he hadn't wanted me to disobey her then and there, as she was dying. But why hadn't she asked something easier of me? Even my father took milk from her.

I had to look away again, unable to bear the sight of it. Now I wish I hadn't because when he finished, my mother told me to take the kids outside. I knew what they were thinking of doing. As I've said, they weren't so secretive about the things adults did when children weren't around.

I gathered the little ones up and wrapped them in furs and tried to get outside into the dreamy late afternoon light before my parents began moving together beneath the sleeping furs, before the sounds of them could be heard. I remember sitting out near the fire as it leapt and crackled, my eyes open but not seeing. The world grew dim and then dark around me, but I hadn't seen any of it. When enough time had passed that I was able to come back in, she was dead.

I'd missed out on my last few glimpses of my mother living because I'd been shy and full of shame. That was the sort of thing that couldn't be fixed or forgotten—it would float just behind my head forever, waiting for a quiet moment to slither out and remind me of my mistake. That was just how it was.

I waited for her spirit to show itself. I'd been told my whole life that a person's spirit looks like a bird for four days after their death, and then it became whatever happened to a spirit next. I'd been told that a person could see the bird flying away from someone's body after they died. There were even stories about heroes chasing after bird-spirits to catch them and bring them back to the body, trapping them inside again. I didn't see her spirit and I guess that was a big part of me growing up. I decided that the stories I'd been told weren't true, or if they were true, they didn't happen to normal people like me.

As I begged my mother for forgiveness in my thoughts, a thin spear of red-tinted light rose up from the floor to the icy wall. A single star stretched out across the ice. It was my father's invention. I've already said he was clever. He'd figured out a way to cut through the ice and hide a disc inside, so it caught a bit of the light from above and reflected it down to us beneath the ground.

Each day, the stream of gold would wash across the ice so slowly that it didn't look like it was moving, but if I shut my eyes and opened them again, it would be in a different place, fading into grey in the western corner before dissolving for the night. It was because of this ghostly light that I was able to measure the passage of time.

I could also use the shred of captured sun to see the slightest bit; I could hold up lichens to the ray and make sure they had nothing growing on them before I gave them to Preah and Howl. I could keep one eye open and then close it, and at the same time, open the other eye to make the beam dance. I could move my hands in front of the light, making shadow rabbits and wolves when Preah got whiny. I'd always start with the wolf chasing the rabbit, but just when he thought he'd gotten his dinner, I'd move my rabbit fist far from the light so the rabbit would get bigger, big enough to chase after the wolf. Preah always giggled a little at that part.

As far as I knew, no one in all of Kettin had such a luxury. Light in the wintertime? Below the ground?

It was unheard of. Sure, everyone had hollowed-out bones that let fresh air down but a source of light? It was my family's little secret.

Yes, I could have shared the idea. I maybe could have even charged people a few discs to set it up for them... but they didn't deserve it. Maybe Hallen did, but none of the others.

In a way, it wasn't fair to group them all together. It was probably only a few people who'd clubbed my father until he stopped moving. Still, I'd bet that most everyone knew who'd done it. And not one of them had tried to stop it, or warn him, or tell me the truth of what had happened. So I hated the lot of them.

I hoped lakerunners were digging into their tunnels right then and eating them. I couldn't hear any screaming, so that was probably unlikely. Besides, from what I'd heard, lakerunners weren't often around in the daylight. In all the stories, they liked to cross the frozen waters in the dark and sleep all piled on top of each other like walruses during the day. There'd probably be more of them coming for weeks as the different waterways froze over. No one was taking the time to break it up anymore, so dozens more paths would be forming and staying solid for weeks, maybe months. Until the warmth of spring came and they migrated back to their side of the lakes.

So yeah, I wouldn't be sharing my father's genius with the villagers of Kettin. I wouldn't share any of my own ideas with them either. I wasn't as clever as my father, but I had a few thoughts about building, about how lodges could be shaped and filled. This was something I liked to do when I had an odd moment of quiet and no work to fill it with; I liked to imagine new ways of building lodges.

It wasn't so much the actual labour that I fantasized about; I mean, sometimes I did daydream about that too because me and my father had always had a good time building together (and afterward, we'd sneak and share a skim tea even though my mother hated the stuff and didn't want it around her at all). It was more the little details I envisioned: the seabirds that could be carved into pieces of whale bone and pressed into the ice around the entrances, the way spare lichens could be twisted into intricate rhythms like the inside of a snowflake, then frozen so that the ice walls would be full of curious green spirals. I could save red algae and violet pasque flowers from the two weeks each year when things bloomed and fill the ice with those too. Crimson bear berries, purple star-shaped petals from saxifrage blossoms, sunny baby poppies...

It wasn't just how I'd fill the walls I dreamt about. No one in Kettin had more than three rooms: the one above where people lived in the usual months and two below: one for living and one for shitting and pissing that had to be shovelled out every spring. But I imagined having four or five domes with stories etched into the ice, stars carved into the top, and bears and foxes and wolves carved onto the sides and how I'd make the top a little flatter so there would be a place to sit on sunny days. I tried to stop myself whenever these fantasies pulled at my mind because they were a waste of time. I'd never have the hours to actually see them come to life. In the winter, there was darkness, and in the other seasons there would always be more work to do.

SIX

THE LONGER I STARED into the darkness, the more it seemed like something was staring back at me. Something with big round eyes—the size of my fists, maybe—that didn't blink enough. They had a greenish-yellow glint to them, sort of like when you can't see a wolf or a fox out on the tundra until the light catches their eyes and reflects back.

At first, the eyes frightened me, especially when I thought I could see a smile spreading beneath them. I looked away and told myself they'd be gone when I looked back. Sometimes this was true, but other times it wasn't. I started swiping at the darkness where the eyes were because, as terrified as I was, I was the closest thing to a grown-up in the tunnel. If I didn't check to make sure there wasn't some sort of gruesome creature waiting to devour us, no one else would.

But then, by the time a few weeks had passed, and my body was recovering from my injuries and my arms and legs had stared hurting from how little I moved around in the dark, I got used to having the eyes near, and when they weren't there, I'd look for them.

They were watching every time I let Niyi cry a bit too long, hoping that if I ignored her, she'd stop, and I could sleep a little longer.

They were watching when Preah dug into the lichens for the third time, and I slapped her, screaming, "We have to eat it slowly! Don't you understand?"

But they also saw how I tied Niyi to my chest and pulled Preah along the walls, feeling around until we found the slippery tunnel that connected us to the world above. I pushed her up the icy slope so she could slide down it knowing how much I loved doing that when I was her age. Her ear bothered her so much that I don't think she could fully enjoy it; she was constantly miserable and always sniffling, tugging at her ear with all her might.

"Tell me what it is," I'd say, trying to be comforting but probably not managing it because I was never good at the gentle stuff; that was my mom and Kid, not me. No matter how soft and warm I tried to make my voice, she didn't seem soothed. "Show me what's bothering you; take my hand and show me."

She would pull my hand to her ear as she whimpered, and I would feel stupid because I didn't know what to do. I dragged her to the shred of light each morning to peer into her ear, forcing her to tilt her head to the side as she squirmed and kicked me. It seemed fine from the outside and from the little bit of the inside I could see, but I knew that bodies were more complicated than that.

I myself had terrible stomach pains every time I ate, no matter which meal it was or how well I chewed, or whether I had water with it or tea. When I ate, it felt like my meal was burning my insides as it moved through, so I hated eating. I would hold off until the pain of my hunger was too much to bear, and then I would eat and exchange one type of suffering for another. There was nothing I could do about my stomach or Preah's ear or Niyi's tongue, (though I wasn't sure the blue tongue was so much a health problem; Niyi didn't seem to mind it at all).

The eyes saw how I kept the girls fed and scraped Howl's frozen shit off the ground and tossed it into the secondary room behind a leather flap. It didn't matter that the room had a wide hollow bone reaching to the surface to let in fresh air; it still smelled so rank that I had to cover my mouth and nose when I went in (which I had to do a lot because even though I wasn't eating or drinking much, I was scraping shit off Niyi's furs in there several times a day).

And when Preah had to go, she would poke me, and I would push Niyi under the stool in the corner so Howl wouldn't step on her while I was gone and walk with Preah into the back room, trying not to breathe while she did her business, keeping two fingers on her tiny shoulder so she would know I was close by.

I could remember being scared of the backroom too as a kid. Little me had figured that because the air tunnel was bigger and my parents weren't back there guarding it, something bad could get in more easily. Every time I'd lifted the leather flap, I'd expected a giant toothy mouth to chomp down on me. Being older and figuring how smart animals were, it seemed like a lakerunner would know not to dig toward the smell of piss, so probably the back room was safer than the front one. The back room is where I'd shove the kids if one did burrow down to our hiding spot.

The eyes narrowed with glee whenever Niyi seemed like she was floating away from me, which happened more than makes me sound sane. I promise I'm not crazy; I was just stuck in the dark for too long, or at least, that's what I figured was going on. If I didn't hold the baby tight against me, she sometimes seemed to be hovering. I'd get her firm and safe in my arms and then fall asleep and wake up to the sound of her giggling, to the feel of her weighing nothing against my shoulder as she lifted up and away. Sometimes I'd wake up, and she'd be so far from me it seemed impossible; she could crawl a little, but I'd wrapped her up so tight her arms and legs couldn't move enough to push her one way or the other.

"Niyi?"

She made that phlegmy, rolling purr sound, and I scrambled toward where it came from. But she wasn't there.

"Niyi?"

She rolled a shrill *rrrrr* off her blue tongue from behind me, and I jumped and crawled in that direction, setting my limbs down as light as possible to be sure I didn't press a knee into her little body.

She giggled just as I was about to reach the wall in my search, and somehow, she was behind me again. I spent a fair amount of time playing find-the-baby with the blackness, wondering if I was finally going mad, telling myself that it was only the dark playing tricks on me.

❄ ❄ ❄

Then we had our bad day below. That day, I woke to the sound of Howl grunting and chewing, heaving father-sized breaths out her nose. Niyi was sucking on something: her fist or her sleeve maybe, making spitty slurping sounds. And Preah wasn't crying anymore.

Thank the wolves, I thought, taking her silence as a good sign, thinking that maybe her ear was healing, and she was finally getting a proper night's rest.

I was just about to let the soothing rhythm of it all lull me back to sleep when Niyi spit out whatever was in her mouth and gargle-screeched, which is what she always did right before she cried.

I almost laughed. No, I wouldn't be going back to sleep.

I yawned and moved groggily through the darkness on my hands and knees, feeling around for the milk skin that I'd fallen asleep holding, that would certainly be in the last place I looked because that was how things always seemed to go.

My palm came down on Preah's cold fingers. She didn't cry out from the weight of me. Her breathing didn't change. She didn't jolt awake or flinch or react at all.

I knew.

Then, in my heart, I knew, but I had to make sure.

I pushed my fingers forward into the darkness, finding her arm and feeling along it until my palm met her neck. I held my hand out in front of her mouth. I set my head close to her lips and listened. I dragged her to the sliver of milky light that was just beginning to appear.

She was dead.

SEVEN

I SHOULD HAVE CRIED or shouted, but I didn't. I sat on the floor and stared at Preah's cheek, the only sight illuminated by my father's invention.

Of course.

That's what I thought: *of course.*

She'd been complaining about something being wrong in her head for months, and nothing I'd done had really helped. We were unlucky orphans, and I was the sour Crab... good things didn't happen to us.

Of course.

What else could have happened, really? More than anything, I felt stupid for thinking that I could do it, that I could get us all through the winter unscathed. That wasn't how the world worked. Once something bad happens to you, it makes you sticky, and more bad things keep coming and getting stuck to you until you're smothered by them.

I looked for those big eyes in the darkness, and after a few moments, I found them. They looked sad, too; they might even have been crying.

I moved Preah to the wall farthest from where we slept and tried to set her hands nice, but no matter which way I moved them, they felt wrong in the darkness. I gave Niyi and Howl all my mind for what felt like a day before realizing my next problem. Preah's body couldn't stay below with us until springtime... the rot would make us sick. It was the type of scent that you know is poison, just by how it smells.

I thought about putting her into the second room below, but I didn't want her left where all the waste was. I didn't want to be tossing shovels of Howl's shit where Preah's body lay or pissing next to her. That was too horrible.

I had to take her up top.

It took another day and a half for me to build up the courage, and by then, her form was the wrong firmness. I can't explain it. If you've touched a dead body, you'll understand, but if you haven't... it's sort of like rocks made out of skin? It makes you want to hurl, the roof of your mouth tickles, and every muscle you have fights against you. You tell your hands to touch the body because that's what they have to do, and they refuse, and it takes a long time for you to be able to do what you need to.

I waited until it was midday—or at least, as close to midday as I could guess with only a wisp of light to guide me—and I crept up the icy tunnel toward the bone gate and listened. I listened for a long time, maybe an hour or so. I couldn't hear anything moving around above, which meant that it *might* be safe.

The silence didn't make it any less scary. My knees shook as I pressed up against the bone grate, and my heart slammed into my back so hard I couldn't hear properly. It was tough to lift—I'd grown weak sitting in the dark from moving around so little, and the grate was covered with a fur full of snow, and everything had frozen in place. I had to prop myself up in the tunnel with my boots and press against it with my back, straining so hard I grew dizzy.

There was a crack, a creak, and then a flood of blinding light. The shock to my eyes and mind made me lose my grip, and I slid down the tunnel. For many moments there was only white, even with my eyes closed. The brightness hurt, almost like countless hands were pushing against my skull from every direction. Even when I was able to open my eyes, I couldn't see properly. Everything was white or a strange blueish-green—the colour I imagined drial tails to be. Nothing was black or brown... there were no darker colours at all.

The light let me find my mother's spear—I'd bring it up with me, just in case. I mean, it wasn't like I actually knew how to use it, but if there was something up there, maybe it wouldn't know that. Maybe it would flee rather than face the sharp spike.

I thought about bringing Niyi up too, tied to my back, but I decided she would be safer below. I made sure the furs around her were tied so tight she couldn't move and pushed her beneath the stool my father had made.

Then I scrambled back up the tunnel, peering over the ledge to where our lodge used to be. The collapsed chunks of snow had been blown nearly as flat as the tundra.

I moved my gaze slowly, sweeping from the east to the west, making sure that I took in each and every detail before me, waiting for any sense of movement—any hint that there was something else living or roving about the village. It was one of those days where it was too cold to snow, and there wasn't a single cloud in the sky. The world was only vivid blue on top and pristine white on the bottom—there were no footprints or dog piss spots or ashy chunks of ice near fire pits, no sign of people or animals at all. Just clean emptiness.

When I was sure there was nothing waiting to eat me, it came time to pick up Preah, which, as I said, was harder than I can explain. I tried not to look at her or smell her, forcing air in through my mouth, trying to keep my nose closed, which, of course, didn't entirely work. I gagged and choked, and no matter how I gritted my teeth, it didn't get any easier.

To make things even tougher, the tunnel was slippery. I pressed my boots against one side and my back against the other, holding Preah's body on my lap, as I shifted up toward the light in teeny, shuffled movements. I kept my neck bent too, so I faced the sky instead of looking at the tiny body draped across my knees. I had to keep quiet, so I didn't draw lakerunners, even though each movement—each breath—felt like being whacked with an oar in the chest. For every three or four upward shuffles, I slid down some, grunting under the weight of her. All the while, I struggled to keep my mother's spear balanced on top of her body without looking too hard at it because I didn't want to see what I was doing. Or think about it, really.

When I reached the top, I shoved her over the ledge and heard something awful—some sort of snap. I didn't look because if I'd broken something on her rigid body, I'd break too, and if I started bawling, I'd never get her out of our hole. I could cry later once the bone grate and snow-covered fur were back on top and me and Niyi and Howl were safe.

Still, the sound made me gag and dry heave—maybe I would have thrown up if there was something in my stomach, but there wasn't. I didn't know where I would leave her either, but I knew I couldn't take her up to the human mound where my father's bones were or to the wolf mound where my mother lay. I couldn't leave Niyi for that long. I'd only be able to take her outside the lodge lines; anything more was too dangerous.

With the wind howling in the background, I tied my mother's spear to my back to make for easier movements. I took a deep breath and rolled my sister's body on top of the snow-filled fur I'd used to cover the grate. Once she was on, I grabbed hold of the fur's edge with mittenless hands and tugged. It was easier than carrying her, but the scraping noise it made as it slid across the frost-covered dirt made me want to throw up, and I nearly cried while choosing where to stop and leave her. She didn't belong on the ground like that, waiting to be picked apart by animals. What if the lakerunners came and ate her body? If they didn't, the wolves would come, and the birds after them.

There was a squawking from behind me, and I jumped, my heart slamming into my shoulders. For a moment, I remembered sitting in the snow, waiting to see my mother's spirit in bird form, and I wondered if Preah's spirit was what made the sound, but then I turned to see Preah's blasted owl.

I ignored the bird's piercing yellow eyes as I lifted one edge of fur up into the air, doing my best to roll Preah off gently. The scratchy sound she made as she slid onto the ice made me cry out because it didn't sound like a body hitting the ground at all—it sounded like rocks sliding down an icy hill. I clenched my teeth to muffle the groan, and this worked. Only then I looked down. I didn't mean to, but I looked down and saw her all solid and grey and not at all like a little girl should look. I fell to my knees, retching up a few drops of green water.

I spit a few times to get the taste out of my mouth, then wiped my chin with my wrist. I sat back on my heels, trying to catch my breath as I frowned hard enough that my tears knew they weren't getting out, that they should go back where they came from and leave me alone.

The sun reflected off the snow, making the whole world gleam as I stood up, being even more careful not to look at Preah all dead and stone-coloured.

It was sort of good that I took my time walking back toward the tunnel because, if I hadn't, I would have been trampled when Howl burst out of the hole, white powder streaking through the sky. My legs were moving after her before I realized what was happening—that Howl was close to getting away. Could you blame her for trying? She wanted to be above ground, in the light where people and animals are supposed to be, but she couldn't be; I needed to keep her for Niyi.

She gave me a pathetic trial, and I almost felt sorry for her, for how little she could muster. She ran out of my reach once and then stopped to catch her breath because she was weak from being below so long. She bolted again when I came at her, but only at half the pace. I stopped chasing and moved slow, holding a clenched hand out to her like I had a something yummy hidden in my palm. I clicked and made whispery sounds to keep her from taking off until I could get close enough to grab her thick fur.

Maybe because I was so messed up about everything, my imagination gained more power in my mind. No longer was Howl the brown, hairy, horned creature that my father had brought home to save the baby; she *was* my father. I pressed my face into her furry side, and it felt like his beard.

"I'm sorry," I whispered. I'd started with three of my father's children to care for, but now I had only one. I buried my forehead into Howl, trying to build up the courage to turn around and lead her passed Preah's stone-like body, back into the darkness below.

I grasped the leather strap around her neck and guided her toward the tunnel, trying to keep my eyes on the sky so I wouldn't have to see Preah again. Only I had to look back to the earth because there was a sickening sound.

A laugh.

But not the normal sort... a high-pitched, gleeful snicker.

I froze, and so did the little blue man.

You heard that right. *So did the little blue man.* I told you this story was weird.

There was a tiny, blue-tinged person in front of me. He'd been trying to sneak out of the lodge tunnel without me noticing.

Yes.

He wanted to get *out*. Which meant he'd been inside.

He was nearly naked, except for a grimy leather knotted around his middle—even his big flat, hairy feet were bare. He had a wispy beard and was maybe only as tall as my waist. I was aware of all these oddities in the back of my mind, but two things pulled my attention with the force of lightning and demanded my focus.

First, there were his eyes. They were big and round and familiar, maybe the size of my fists—he'd been down in the dark with us. It was this wrinkly, tiny man who'd been staring at me for weeks. How had he gotten in without me noticing? Had he gone down before the horn had been blown and waited? Was he a winter sprite?

He must be, I decided.

And then I saw what he was covering with his arms and chest by keeping himself turned away from me. It was Niyi. The little man had Niyi in his arms, and the second I noticed this, he giggled and took off running. Not back into the lodge. Not deeper into the village. Toward the lakes, to the other side where the lakerunners lived, chuckling as he went.

I didn't think, even if maybe I should have. I took off after him toward the lands I was forbidden to enter.

Across the ice.

EIGHT

I'D NEVER STEPPED ONTO the ice without hesitation, but I did that day. There was no space in my mind for the things I should have been thinking. There was only Niyi. And that strange little man who held her in his flabby arms as he ran, hopping over bigger chunks of ice, his floppy feet slapping against the frozen lake.

My boots thudded against the ice sheet as I gained on him (pretty quickly too since my legs were longer than his). But when I reached out in front of me, trying to grab his thin white hair, I heard, "DON'T!" from behind me.

In the second it took me to look over my shoulder and see nothing, I nearly tripped over a cleft in the ice, and the teeny man ahead of me swerved, giggling as he did. Because I was running my fastest, I couldn't change my direction quickly enough. I slid across the ice as I tried to slow and turn, ending up spinning on my hands and knees while the man bounced away.

With a grunt, I was up again, charging at the old, nearly-naked man whose beard was so long it dragged on the ice. When I gained on him a second time, I didn't reach out; I dove for him, hoping to get my arms around his legs or torso, knowing Niyi might get hurt if the three of us crashed to the ice, but choosing to do it anyway because I couldn't let him run off with her.

He veered left just in time for me to fall face-first onto the sharp, solid cold; my fingers, cheeks, and chin were shredded by the shards of ice left jutting out from where the waves beneath pressed up against their frosty cover.

It didn't matter that there might be lakerunners about. I was up and running and screaming. There was no way everyone hiding in their stupid holes couldn't hear me. They heard and didn't come up to help. Like Hallen had said: fuck them.

Other things were happening too—things I would have thought about if the wee man wasn't stealing the only family I had left. Howl was chasing after me. She did this often when I went to hack ice, and in another situation, I would have made sure she didn't step on the ice because she was so heavy the chances of her falling through were pretty big. Preah's owl was trailing after us too, squawking as her shadow floated alongside me.

When the tiny man was a little ahead of me, he turned around and stuck his tongue out with an impish, "Neeee–he-heeee."

I got close and ready to dive for him again (trying to make sure it didn't look like I was about to tackle) and he darted right at the last second. I screamed as I slid and tried to veer after him, and he seemed to think this was especially hilarious because his laughter got deeper and louder.

I urged my legs to go faster, taking the biggest steps I could, but he was always just out of reach: his saggy, flat feet with giant yellow toenails slapping against the windswept ice. Short, quick, creepy breaths escaped his hairy nostrils between snickers.

I could hear the ice beneath me as well, straining as my boots slumped into it. Groaning. I was probably heavier than the little man and Niyi put together, but I ignored the squelching that came whenever my feet landed on places where the ice was wetter than it should have been. I'd seen enough wolves stalking elk to know that whoever gave up running first lost.

That was the only rule in nature.

Something else began to happen as we ran, something that made me feel like my eyes weren't working right or my head was messed up somehow: he got bigger. The little man grew as he ran. I didn't notice it straight away as I was too focused on Niyi. But suddenly, he wasn't as tall as my knees; he was as tall as my hips. And then he was up to my shoulders. And then he was nearly my height. And if that sounds odd to you, I'll let you know now it's nowhere near the oddest thing that happens in this tale.

At least being bigger seemed to slow him down; I gained on him. Quickly.

But then he was taller than I was—by a lot. When he was maybe two or three times my height, he stopped and turned around, a deep, slow, "Heh-heh-heh," coming from his throat.

I tried to stop, but the ground was too slippery, and I slammed into his bare, sun-spotted shin, collapsing back onto the ice.

He smiled, and my heart sped even more. His mouth was big enough to eat Howl in one gulp. Each crooked tooth was bigger than Niyi—his giant fist was closed around her, hiding her from my view. I hesitated for a moment—because he was massive and terrifying—but I had to try something, so I clamoured to my feet and started loosening my mother's spear from my back. It had iron in it, so I thought maybe it would scare him or hurt him some.

As I fumbled to untie the thing, he laughed at me and fell backward onto his rear. Hard.

I couldn't ignore the sound the ice made then. It was cracking beneath us—I could feel the echo through my boots. The ice screeched and stretched and moaned, and the little man—who was now a giant man—knew it was breaking too.

He was up and running, and I realized that he'd been going a lot slower than his fastest—maybe as part of a cruel joke?

As we ran, I could hear the ice snapping apart behind me, but I didn't think about how I'd get home again—the thought never even crossed my mind. It's kind of funny how focused you can get when you need to be.

The giant-little man took stupidly large leaps, and I think part of me knew I couldn't keep up with him, not with me being as tall as his knees—each of his steps equaled ten of mine. But another part of me couldn't think about that. There was only Niyi and not being the first one to stop running.

He made it to the land on the other side of the frozen lake and then, I made it too. We were somewhere in the blurry white across the lakes from

Kettin, in the forbidden wild where the lakerunners lived. In the open.

I didn't care. I kept chasing him.

There was something massive in the distance, only I didn't really see it until we were closer because I was watching the giant with my baby sister in his palm. He was still getting bigger too, but I'd stopped paying attention to that, maybe because I didn't want to get too scared to do whatever I was going to have to do.

From across the lakes, it looked only like the hint of a hill, but it was much more than that. A mountain of bluish-green basalt rock capped with a perfect trine of sparkling blue ice. It was so smooth it didn't seem real—precise and flat and composed of many different ledges—a perfectly symmetrical mountain? I'd later learn that type of building was called a pyramid—a stepped pyramid if you want to get specific. But I couldn't understand it back then, or why, when the giant got to it, he climbed up instead of going around it. I didn't realize it had been built by someone; I thought it was a funny rock, a fluke, never to be repeated by nature again.

The first ledge reached just below the giant's armpit, and he was able to pull himself up the mound with one arm and a little jump, keeping the hand with Niyi in it high above his head. I tried to catch onto his hairy, calloused feet, but he pulled them up too quickly.

He peered over the ledge at me and laughed again, his big, round eyes the size of a lodge.

I screamed and tried to climb up the wall before me, but like I said, it was perfect and smooth, icy too. There was nothing to grip onto. I untied my mother's spear from my back (which miraculously hadn't been lost in the run despite me trying to untie it right before the ice started cracking), then I dug the iron into the frozen stone. It stuck deep enough for me to pull myself upward some, only there was nothing to help me move farther up once I did. And also, my hands were a bloody mess of shredded skin from falling on the ice, which made the spear slippery.

It was around this time that I began to feel my pains, my chin especially. I'd come down hard on the ice at one point, and my lungs needed a break. They couldn't make use of the cold air when I breathed so quickly and screamed so much. The corners of my vision swirled grey.

The giant watched me struggle to find some way up the wall to where he sat, but as my attempts slowed with exhaustion, he seemed to grow bored and began making his way up the next ledge.

Finally, I did pray.

In my thoughts, I said, *Skyfather, if you hate me, that's fine, but don't hate Niyi. Don't let him take her.*

The Skyfather didn't answer, and the giant climbed over another ledge out of sight. My eyes frantically darted around for something that could help me climb up to where Niyi was. It was then I saw that Howl hadn't been swallowed up when the ice behind us collapsed. She was nearby, tufts of white breath spiralling out of her nose, breathless but otherwise completely fine. I had so much breathing to catch up on I almost couldn't walk. My shoulders heaved forward and backward as I struggled to find enough air to keep my mind sharp; the edges of the world sank into darkness. Was I going to pass out?

No. Not until I got Niyi back home safe.

I made my way to Howl slowly, so I didn't scare her off. I couldn't understand how the muskox had kept up with us or how she'd managed to avoid falling into the frigid lake when the ice had started breaking apart.

Papa, I thought as I pressed my face into Howl's fur. *Papa, I don't know what to do. Niyi is up there with the giant, and I can't get up.*

I was about to cry, thinking for the first time that I might not actually be able to get her back. I probably should have thought this earlier, but I hadn't.

Before I lost it completely, Howl ruffled her furry shoulders, and I got an idea. I led her to the wall or the ledge, or whatever it was: the icy stone thing that the giant climbed up. I looked into her eyes and tried to tell her with my expression: *If you're really Papa, you won't move.*

None of us had ever climbed atop Howl before, and I wasn't sure how she'd react. No one back in Kettin rode muskoxen that I knew of, which must have meant that it couldn't be done.

Forgive my stupidity here. At the time, this was how my thinking was. I didn't understand that things could be done differently than how they were done. Or maybe I did know that, only I figured everyone around me was a lot smarter than they were and had tried all the other options and did things one way because it was better. Either way, you know, and I know that this understanding of the world is absurdly foolish. I'd maybe go so far as to say if everyone's doing it, it's probably wrong, and there's almost certainly a better way.

I climbed onto Howl's back, and she did move, but not so far that I couldn't keep a hand on the ice wall. I stood slowly—really slowly—because Howl was a lot less stable than I'd imagined she would be, and I was sure that, at any moment, she'd take off, and I'd be landing on the ice one more time that day.

My legs shook. In part, because it was hard to balance atop a muskox (again, if you've never done it, there's no way to explain it... just know that it's hard) and in part, because I'd been running my fastest for far too long. I set my bloody fingers that were burning from the cold against the stone wall and stretched. There was no way I could reach the ledge, even standing atop Howl. I'd have to think of something—use the spear or maybe move one boot atop Howl's head—I was sure she wouldn't let me do that without kicking about and hurting me. Maybe I could grab onto the ledge if I jumped...

I got myself ready, and just as I was about to leap, Howl shifted. I slipped and cried out, coming down on the tundra, managing to land in a way that wasn't too painful. Only my toes hurt, and that was mostly from the cold. I coaxed Howl back into position and climbed up a second time, readying myself to jump once more.

"But how will you get up the next ledge? You won't get the muskox up there. You'll be stuck."

I wasn't nearly as surprised as you would think. The day had exhausted me in a special kind of way—all the surprise my body could create had been used up by the little blue winter sprite—so a strange voice didn't unsettle me at all. I turned, trying to figure out where the voice was coming from.

There was nothing and no one.

"Ah. Up, up, up."

I tilted my head back, and I saw her. It was Preah's fucking owl. She was standing on the ledge above me. Talking. I maybe would have listened to anyone else, but I wasn't about to have a conversation with the lousy bird. I hated that bird.

I set myself on jumping, and, this time, I did leap. Howl moved wrong before I'd finished the motion, and I came down on the frozen earth below. Hard. So hard that the air was knocked out of me.

I'd had this happen once before when I climbed on top of our lodge as a kid, so I knew that the pain was going to pass, but that didn't make it hurt any less. I gasped and made that whispery-sucking noise that people make when their lungs stop working for a moment, and the stupid bird laughed at me. She made it seem like she was trying not to laugh, but I knew she wasn't really trying in the way that I knew Equah's "sweet voice" wasn't actually her being sweet. She wanted to humiliate me or hurt me—as if my life hadn't done that enough already.

I pushed Howl back against the wall as soon as I could breathe again.

"A clever girl would try something new," said the owl.

She sounded self-righteous, like one of the girls in Kettin who knew they were pretty and that their parents had a lot of discs hidden away somewhere. One of those girls who knew she would get her pick of husbands or wives when the time came.

I had no patience for the bloody owl. "What do you suggest?" I said.

"I'll go and get her for you," the owl said.

"You couldn't lift her."

"I could." She took a few wonky owl steps to the side and tilted her head. "All I'd need from you is the furs you wrap yourself in. This way, I can grip her with my talons without cutting her baby skin."

It made more sense than I wanted to admit.

I was used to haggling, so I knew it was better to state exactly what I expected so there wouldn't be any surprises later. "So I give you my coat, and you'll fly up there and wrap her up and bring her back down?"

"Yes."

"And if she's still in his hand?"

"I'll wait until he falls asleep. Full-sized winter sprites sleep a lot. It won't be long."

"Okay," I said. I hopped off Howl and unlaced the furs tied around me, thinking for the first time how Niyi wasn't wrapped up properly for the cold.

"Be quick about it," I said, holding out the fur toward the owl. It wouldn't take too long for me to die waiting for her to return. The cold was beneath my skin instantly.

"Very well, we'll agree on a price when I get back."

She swooped down to grab my coat with her talons, but I ripped it away. "Price?"

"Yes. For my help."

I didn't have time for her games. "Name it."

"Well, what do you have?"

I had nothing. I had Howl, but I needed her to feed Niyi, so I couldn't give her away. That being said, I knew that the owl wouldn't have spoken of a price if there wasn't something she wanted. My tone couldn't have been harsher. I spit out each word like it was rotten fish. "Just tell me what you want."

"Te-he. You're a salty one, aren't you?" She flutter-skipped closer to me, her yellow unblinking eyes so round and focused that I felt nervous. "Hmmm. I haven't had guests at my home for many years. Would you—and the child, of course—come over for dinner? I can tell you all the wonderful things little Preah told me as we eat."

It was a trick of some kind. I knew it. It was a silly thing to ask for when she could have asked for anything. Besides, owls didn't have lodges or dinner as far as I knew. And the way she'd said *little Preah*... it was like she was teasing me. Dangling in front of me how much closer she'd been with my sister than I'd been. But what else could I do?

"Deal," I said.

The owl took my coat from my hands and disappeared over the ledge above.

NINE

SO THE OWL LEFT with my coat in her talons. I knew that you usually couldn't count on people to do the things they said they were going to do unless they were family or you were paying them a lot, and I figured owls were probably the same as people in that regard, so there was a good chance she was just stealing my coat. I mean, I was stupid, but I wasn't *that* stupid.

Besides, I hadn't forgotten that I'd been a little rough with her in the past; I couldn't remember how many times I'd chucked a stone at her or shooed her or sent hateful thoughts her way.

The more I thought about it, the more confident I was that the owl was fucking with me. Still, on the off chance she wasn't, I had to let her try, you know? My coat was worth maybe getting Niyi back.

I can manage without it, I told myself. *I can press myself against Howl or dig a tunnel like Papa showed me.*

Of course, I wasn't going to sit still and wait on the unlikely chance that the owl would come back. I needed to keep trying to get Niyi on my own and keep moving to stay warm. *I've got Howl*, I thought. *And mom's spear. And...* I felt around in my hair. I'd tied it in a tight bun that morning, but the day's running and falling had messed it up, leaving a curly, red lopsided knot. By a rare stroke of luck, what I was looking for was there: my mother's arrowhead.

My mother had taught me that trick. It was what she'd done when she went on whale hunts before she and my father had gotten married. She'd hide an arrowhead in her hair in case any of the other hunters tried anything.

It was a silly habit to keep up with in the dark—tying the thing into my hair—only I liked the feeling of doing it, of hanging my head upside down and gathering up my wild hair and twisting it around, then hiding the stone piece inside. I'd started doing it after my father died and it became my responsibility to hack ice with the grown-ups. My mornings didn't feel right without it.

So I had a stone arrowhead, a spear, and Howl.

I looked around me, trying to figure out if there was something else. Anything at all. Maybe there'd be enough snow on the next level that I could pile it up and make a ramp of some kind? *Here's hoping*, I thought, setting the arrowhead between my lips as I retied my bun, pulling the knot so tight the skin on my face was pulled taut too. Then I brought Howl to the wall again.

The beast made a cute, muffled noise and shook her head. I imagined my father's voice saying: *But the owl's gone to get her; you can rest.*

"She might not come back," I said, and Howl seemed to understand that because she stayed still, or at least, still for a muskox.

I climbed atop her once more, the arrowhead still between my lips and the spear in my hand. I was breathing heavy on purpose to heat the arrowhead because it was so cold that already the skin on my lips was sticking to it. The blood coating my fingers was frozen and crumbly, and my hands were so numb that I kept using the wrong force with them, realizing my mistake when a dull pain shot through my wrists. My hands would have to deal with it. At least until I got Niyi back. When she was pressed against my chest again, then I could sort out my hands. And it was cold enough that I knew I didn't have to worry about infection. So there was that.

My fourth attempt at digging the spear into the ice that coated the pyramid wall worked. As I clung to it, Howl wandered away, so I was left hanging there, unsure what I was supposed to do next. I managed to swing my legs and get one ankle up and over the spear, willing the spear to stay lodged in the ice with all my heart.

I pulled myself up, and it wasn't graceful at all, but at least I was doing it. I sat atop the spear stuck into the ice wall and prepared myself to stand up on the thin shaft. My legs trembled, half in exhaustion from the day's running, and half because I was up at least two of my own height and balancing on a skinny spear. It felt like I was going to fall any second. I held my breath and stayed as close to the wall as possible, thinking that would encourage the spear to keep its hold for some reason.

I tried forcing the arrowhead into the icy surface above me so I could use it to pull myself up higher, but I couldn't press hard enough to get it in. It was also so small—smaller than my palm—that I wasn't sure I'd be able to pull myself up by it. I thought I got it in once or twice, but then I put a little weight on it with my fingers, and it toppled out. I caught it the first time it fell, but not the second. It bounced on the ground below me, and Howl wandered over to sniff at it. So I was stuck halfway up the wall with no tools

apart from the spear that I was standing on. Not great, I know.
Maybe I'm close enough to jump?
I set my boots right—or at least, in a way that felt right; I'd never attempted anything like this before, so there was no saying whether my instincts were correct or not.

I took three or four deep breaths to calm myself and then jumped.

I managed to grip the ledge above me with my right hand (which was my better one), but it was icy, so I couldn't hold on (it also hurt my sliced fingers so much that I probably couldn't have held on even if there hadn't been ice). I came down on the spear, and the force of my fall plucked it from the ice.

That was the day I learned that falling from a big height feet first isn't a good idea. There was an awful snapping sound, and I was a little confused because the ground was so hard and cold, and my mind was sliding around in my skull while stars twinkled at the sides of my vision. The second I looked down at my legs—the left one, to be exact—I wasn't confused anymore.

A bone slick with blood was sticking straight out from my shin.

I moaned and gagged at the disgusting sight, choking on the overwhelming pain of it for a nice chunk of time, feeling insane with the ache of it. But then realized that I had to do something besides wail because I was alone in the lakerunner's wilderness except for Howl, and Niyi was still stuck up top with the sprite, and maybe Preah's owl was going to get her, but probably she wasn't. Also, by then the sun was nearly half hidden by the grey horizon, so I knew things were about to get infinitely colder.

I had to do something.

I reached out for the spear which had fallen not too far from me, thinking I could use it to get myself up and moving, but each stretch of my arms somehow pulled or pushed at my leg and a new bolt of pain came for me. It took a long time to drag myself along the snow with only my arms and the toes in my right boot to help me, grimacing as I left a trail of pinkish blood in the clean white snow. As I slithered, I picked up my mother's arrowhead, and with the spear, I propped myself up on my right leg and hop-waddled over to where Howl was laying. I tucked myself against her because I wasn't about to freeze while I figured out what to do next.

I thought about dying. Of course, I did. If the owl didn't come back or if the sprite returned looking for a meal, if I wasn't able to move because I got too cold and then starved, if my injury slowed me too much and I froze, if I bled to death because there was A LOT of blood pooling in the snow around my shin...

In a way, it was a fitting sort of end. Maybe I would have welcomed it if Niyi wasn't somewhere in need of my help. She was probably cold and crying, and I knew she was too little to be broken like Preah. Niyi would expect me to come for her.

I also knew I was supposed to rip some of my undershirt and wrap it tightly around where I was bleeding heaviest. I knew I was supposed to press against where the blood was coming out because blood listened to hands. What I didn't know was if it were wise to remove more clothing. What was more important? Staying warm or stopping the bleeding?

I made my choice almost randomly, more bothered by the grotesque look of my shin than how cold I was, so I tried ripping my sleeve, but it was far tougher than I thought as it was animal skin, so I had to take my shirt off—completely off, in the cold—so I could cut it with the arrowhead and then rip it once there was a tiny hole.

The piece I ripped off was too small, so I had to rip another and then put my shirt back on, wincing as grains of ice trickled down my back and melted against my skin. I tied the strips together using my teeth more than my frozen fingers, and then I tried to wrap up my shin, but it hurt so much that I couldn't do it. I couldn't pull the fabric tight against the bone without losing my vision for a second.

I howled and tried again, taking a few quick breaths to psyche myself up for the pain that was coming. And then I screamed in frustration because the cloth wasn't going around properly because, as I said, my bone was sticking out.

I grew dizzy. Woozy. The world spun, and it was suddenly colder, if that were possible. The sun was nearly hidden by the lake, making everything a dusty purple, except for the puddle of my blood. That was still vibrant and red. My mind slowed, and along with that, things turned grey like the world was growing fuzzy.

Maybe I *was* dying. Maybe that's what dying feels like: the colour slowly seeping away from the world. Around the edges first and then in the middle.

"I can't die," I said to no one in particular. "I have to get Niyi back from the giant."

The pool of my blood was beginning to freeze; dainty pink snowflake patterns crept along its edges. It was almost pretty.

Everything was a little funny to me then. I don't know why or how, but I laughed. I've been told that sometimes when something is too painful, your body turns off so you don't have to feel it. Maybe that's what happened then.

The glee didn't last long. Panic slammed into my chest. *I can't die*, I thought. I was only seventeen (maybe), and Niyi needed someone to save her and take care of her, and one day Kid might come back to Kettin and look for me, and I had to be there. The fear jolted me up, and I pulled the cloth tight around where the blood seemed thickest and screeched as my whole body convulsed from the pain. I couldn't see for a second; that's how much it hurt.

And then there was the most irritating sound of all, only I was relieved to hear it because it meant that maybe things would turn out alright after all. Preah's stupid owl screeched. "Te-he. You're not too smart, are you?"

I wasn't really listening. There was a furry bundle in the owl's claws; it looked to be the right size and weight, and I couldn't believe my luck.

"Give her to me!" I said.

"Hold your horses," the owl said. She laughed, setting the bundle down onto the snow just out of my reach. It wasn't moving or making any noise, and my heart stopped. I didn't even think to ask what *horses* was.

"She's fine," the owl said.

"I want to see her," I said, reaching for the furry ball.

"Darling," the owl said, nodding at my shin. "What have you gotten yourself into?" She laughed again, and as she laughed, she stopped being an owl.

Her body cracked and snapped and twisted, and it was honestly so gross that I wasn't the least bit impressed.

Her big yellow eyes moved farther apart, giving her a horrifying expression, like her head was being split in two. And when the eyes came back together again, they were still yellow and round, but they were human. Before me, there wasn't an owl. There was a beautiful woman with snow-white hair and salmon-pink lips.

TEN

I COULDN'T REMEMBER WHAT happened next. All I know is, I woke up somewhere unfamiliar: a lodge but not built out of snow with a round dome to hold in the heat like the ones I'd seen before. It was square and dark and hard like bones with greyish-brown walls. I thought maybe it was made of wood, but trees were so rare it seemed impossible to have so much in one place. There were only a few big pieces of wood in all of Kettin, and each one was used either for a skiff or an ice-hacking pillar.

I sat up, expecting a shock of cold as the furs covering me slid down to my waist, but the shock didn't come. The air was warm—impossibly so. And something was tugging on my hair.

I flinched and looked up, thinking something was grabbing onto me. Hanging above where I'd woken were long strands of something dried and pale green like lichens. They swayed a little as the wind whistled through cracks in the walls, giving off a warm and itchy smell that made me want to sneeze.

The whole room was filled with dangling, twisting trinkets: bones from animals I didn't recognize, skulls too—tiny faces with horns and big, black holes where the eyeballs would have gone, and jagged little teeth. Rocks and pebbles in all different colours sat on ledges that ran along the walls. Some were so beautiful and shiny and clear that I wanted to pick them up and hold them, the greenish one especially—it was richer and deeper than the best spring moss but somehow also clear.

"They're gemstones, darling."

Her voice came from nowhere; I turned, and there was the woman who'd come from the owl... or maybe the owl had come from her? She was standing in the archway, her arms crossed with long, red fingernails digging into her skin as an orange fire-glow flickered behind her.

I couldn't understand what made her so beautiful. She shined like the moon, but it was more than that; every part of her was smooth and glossy and just a little rosy. How did a woman get to her age and have no scars or bruises or filth that stayed caked into her skin no matter how much she washed? She was maybe the cleanest person I'd ever seen. Even her hair had no oil in the roots, so instead of sticking to her scalp, it was lifted—light and flowing.

"How are you feeling?" she said through her widening smile.

At first, I felt a little worried because it wasn't a good smile. I mean, she was still pretty; her mouth got big and wide, and her perfect white teeth gleamed, but her eyes didn't change to match it. She also hadn't blinked once since I'd seen her. But then I felt guilty for judging because maybe that was just how her face was.

"You know, if you frown like that, darling, you'll get wrinkles—the bad kind." She raised her brows, and since they were already too arched and round for her face, they looked like one of Kid's drawings in the snow.

I should have disliked her for saying that, but she said it in a playful kind of way, and then I was fully awake, and my thoughts went straight to Niyi.

"You want to see her?" the owl-woman said.

I nodded and, without thinking, got up to follow the glowing woman, only as I moved I felt the weight of something on me, and I remembered I'd broken at least one bone (there had been only one that I could see, but that didn't mean there weren't other broken ones that had stayed inside my skin).

My shin was wrapped in a thick, white cloth that wasn't animal skin or fur or yak wool, so I didn't know what to make of it. But I could tell, even with the wrapping on, that my shin was smooth again, that the bone must have been back inside... or... could it have been removed? I dared to feel along it with my wrapped fingers. It hurt, but only a little, and no place was softer than it should have been, so I decided whoever had patched me up mustn't have taken the bone.

The woman laughed at me once more and said, "Are you hungry?"

I was. But I was afraid to admit it. I didn't like people knowing about all the ways I was failing as a person; I didn't like them knowing how badly I wanted or needed things.

"I'm about to eat," she said. "You could join me."

Never had anyone outside my family offered to share a meal with me, to let me eat something they'd caught or dug up and cooked. Yes, Hallen had left me fish, but me and the kids would eat that alone, and I still had to cook it (and don't think I didn't appreciate it; there were many nights that Hallen's fish had made all the difference, only being invited to share a meal was something different is all I mean).

"Maybe," I said, still trying to act like I wasn't desperately hungry. "A little."

"You can walk," she said. "But best be light on the one side there."

I stood slowly, my bare feet pressing into a deliciously soft rug and found that she was right. My legs held, but the left one felt weak. I tested it gently before feeling confident enough to hobble to where my boots sat, just beside the pretty rug. I shoved my toes back where they belonged, stopping to dig my socks out of my boots as that was where they'd been left for me.

I shuffled after the stunning woman whose hips swayed with each step she took into a bigger room with walls made from the same material as the first room.

It is *wood*, I realized. I could tell by the smell. But then I saw her.

Niyi.

Niyi was bundled up in furs, in a grass basket near the fire. The fire was probably the most confusing part. There was a section of the wall that was stone, and inside it was a big carved hole and inside *that* was a fire. Inside the building! I thought it was marvellous. I'd never imagined for a second that there'd be a way to have your fire inside.

I would have gawked at it if I wasn't rushing to pick up Niyi and press her to me.

She was making spitty baby noises, and I didn't care that she was drooling all over me, not in the

least. Suddenly the air wasn't pressing down on my shoulders with so much force I wanted to crumple to the ground and die under its weight. Suddenly it was easy to stand up and take a full deep breath.
One thing.
One thing was right again.
And for the moment, that was enough.
Torn between searching every part of Niyi to make sure she wasn't scratched or hurt and pressing her into my neck, whispering to her, "Hey, hey baby girl," (that's how my mother had talked to her), "How are you? Are you okay? I missed you. Did you miss me?" I switched between examining her and squishing her so fast that I was doing neither properly. Water pressed against the back of my eyes, but I frowned it away. She was okay. All her toes and all her fingers were there, no black frostbite on her ears, no cuts or scrapes.
"You can put her down and come eat. She will be there when we're done."
I wasn't ever going to put Niyi down.
"Has she eaten?" I said, finally getting past the initial rush of relief and starting to examine every part of Niyi properly. Her skin was a good colour and felt warm to the touch. Nothing was bruised. She seemed completely unaware of the danger she'd only just been in. Though as she babbled, she opened her mouth, and I could see that the blue colour of her

tongue was brighter and deeper than it had been before. It was spreading too. The inside of her cheeks, her gums, maybe even the back of her throat (it was hard to see that far in) had turned blue.

My heart began to pound against my back. What if the glowing owl-woman had seen? Blue was forbidden. I turned Niyi's face toward my chest so the woman wouldn't notice if she hadn't already. And I looked around for my mother's spear or the arrowhead. *And where's Howl?* I thought.

"Would you like to hold her while we eat?" the owl-woman said.

I nodded, trying to look pleasant and not give away that I'd decided to figure out where all my belongings were and then maybe run, just in case.

I thought I could see where the way out was, but it was good I didn't run just then because I'd guessed wrong.

The owl-woman led me into the room that I thought would lead outside, and there was no entrance other than the one we'd just walked through. She sat down on something that was kind of like a stool but very odd looking because the back of it came all the way up to her neck, like it was hugging her from behind. Yes, this was a chair. I hadn't seen one before. In Kettin, we had stools.

I sat across from her when she gestured to another stool-that-wasn't-a-stool. And there in front of us, on her table, were bowls of something steaming that smelled so good I wanted to laugh and cry at the same time.

I took a seat and lifted the bowl to my mouth.

"There are spoons if you'd like," she said, but I was already drinking the warm, rich... whatever it was, it was good.

"I tried to make it soft so the baby could have it without too much trouble," the woman said, stirring her own meal with her spoon but taking none of it to her mouth. "Though she didn't take as much as I think she needs. You could try feeding her; maybe she was nervous because she didn't know me."

I didn't respond right away because I was too happy to be feeling something so warm and savoury in my stomach.

But when the woman's words settled in my mind more fully, I took the spoon from the table and dipped it into the rich stew. When I took it out, I blew on it many times to make sure it was cool enough and brought it to Niyi's lips. She squirmed and made sad, mumbling sounds, and the more I tried, the harder she resisted. This went on until she was really crying, and I gave up.

"She's not had real food yet, except for what you've given her," I said, trying to explain away Niyi's moodiness, not wanting the woman to think we were rude. "Where's Howl?" And then I realized that the owl-woman probably wouldn't know Howl's name, so after I swallowed another starchy mouthful, I said, "The muskox that was with me."

The owl woman smiled and said, "Darling, I know who Howl is." Again she smiled, but it wasn't quite right. "Howl's outside—she wouldn't fit through the door, I'm afraid. But it's not too cold tonight. She'll be alright, I think."

Of course, she knew Howl. She had been around watching us and talking to Preah for the last three months at least. I stood to make my way outside, only I didn't know where my coat was or which direction to go, so I stopped and stood awkwardly.

"What are you looking for, darling?"

I didn't like her calling me *darling*, but I didn't say anything as she'd shared a good meal with me and also saved my baby sister from a giant sprite. "My coat."

She smirked. "It's hanging up in the room you woke up in."

So I hobbled back to where I woke up, feeling like my mind was a bit... lazy? I thought, *Maybe my brain is tired since I was so scared for nearly a full day straight.*

It took me a long time to find my coat, even though it was hanging right in front of my face when I walked in. The room was so full of shiny, pretty trinkets that it was hard to focus on any one part. I put Niyi down on the bedding, and she giggled, which she hadn't done before. I turned to look at her, a big smile on my face.

She gurgled, and something kind of like soil or dust—but it was blue—floated up from the floor in twisty, swirling streams. I spun around, looking at the spirals of teeny, tiny dots wafting around my ankles, sparkling like the sea did when the sun hit it straight from above.

"It *is* a little fabulous, isn't it?"

"The floor?" I said, a little bothered that I hadn't heard the owl-woman coming, that she'd suddenly been right beside me without me knowing she was near.

"No darling, the baby."

I frowned. "Niyi?"

"You're really not very clever, are you? Preah figured it out months ago."

ELEVEN

I WANTED TO ASK more questions, seeing as the owl-woman had just implied that there was something mysterious or whatever about baby Niyi, only she'd mentioned Preah's name, and my chest started aching. Plus, I didn't want to admit that she knew something I didn't know. I decided to act like I already knew what was so "fabulous" about Niyi.

"There's no need to be ashamed, darling—*Crab*—that's your name, isn't it? *Crab?*"

My stomach tensed. As far as I knew, Preah was the only person in Kettin who'd spoken to her, and if she called me Crab, that meant Preah had called me that.

I didn't take my eyes off her as I stuffed my arms into my coat. This woman had pushed my bones back in place and wrapped me up—even my hands were bandaged—*and* she'd rescued baby Niyi from the sprite. Really, I owed her a lot. So why did I feel so... slow and fuzzy?

"I'm Ilona," she said. "If you were wondering."

I decided not to make trouble, so I said, "Thank you... for getting Niyi and for fixing me up."

"You're welcome, darling. Do you want dessert?"

Dessert. Another word I didn't know.

"You'll like it, I promise."

I kept Niyi tight against me, closing my coat around her so only her little face was showing, running my arms up and down her sides, trying to soothe her even though she wasn't the one who was feeling off.

I wanted to see Howl and have my spear back and my arrowhead, but I knew Ilona might have left my mother's belongings at the foot of the sprite's pyramid. Both might be gone forever.

So I sat back at the table and discovered that Ilona had been right; dessert might have been my favourite thing I'd ever eaten. It was sweet and fluffy and sticky, and I ate it up like it was my last day to live, trying my best not to glance at the shiny white and red bowl in the middle of the table that was full of rosy sweetness. I wouldn't ask for more, no matter how bad I wanted it. I knew it was always best not to ask for the things you wanted, because then no one would know how to bother you.

Ilona laughed. "Here, darling." She scooped three more big lumps into my bowl.

Niyi got a little fussy as I jammed mouthfuls of the creamy pink into my mouth, and I knew I should feed her.

"You got a bucket?" I said, covering my mouth with a bandaged hand so Ilona wouldn't see the dessert splashing around inside as I talked. "Or even just a small skin?"

Ilona smiled in an amused sort of way, like she couldn't wait to see why I wanted a bucket, like she expected it to be entertaining.

She pointed (which felt like an odd way to answer), and I went to where she directed into another room that was way hotter than the first few I'd seen—uncomfortably hot.

There were lots of buckets and vessels and skins and a giant iron cauldron as well, blacker than night. I went and touched it just to be sure it was real. I'd never seen so much iron in one place before. It was one of the most valuable things there was—even more precious than discs—because you could melt it and make it into shapes, so your tools and blades would be better than everyone else's and your work would be easier.

There was a thin shard of iron hidden in the blade of my mother's spear, but she'd carved a piece of bone to fit around it so no one would know and try to steal it from her. Only if you looked straight at the pointy end could you see the little black dot. My mother had always been careful to dry it if it got bloody or wet from fishing—she said if the iron turned red, this was *rust*, and if we got it in our food, we'd get sick.

I needed to find the spear if it was in Ilona's lodge. But first, I'd sort out Niyi. I took one of the buckets that didn't seem like it would be too leaky and smelled the inside of it just to be sure it was clean. When I came back out, Ilona was still watching me and smirking.

"I've got to milk Howl," I said. "For Niyi."

Ilona's expression didn't change, and she didn't blink any either. She seemed to be having fun, and my cheeks flushed with inexplicable embarrassment. Maybe she actually did just want guests? Like she'd said before? People to have around and talk to? I understood that plenty.

She pointed to an archway that I hadn't gone through yet, that maybe hadn't even been there before? I was feeling a bit disoriented because all the rooms looked the same, walls covered in ledges stuffed with all sorts of distracting oddities: a cluster of golden balls that jingled when the wind blew through the lodge, a clear bowl with a grey, miserable-looking fish inside of it, a disk that showed me my own face with my chin all bandaged up and my forehead and cheeks scratched raw—at first, I thought it was another girl, and I flinched, but it was only me. *Is there water inside the disk?* I wondered. Water was the only thing I knew of that reflected like that.

Each room was made distinguishable by one big thing in the middle. I'd just come from the cauldron room back into the table room where Ilona was, and I thought I was going through an archway to the outside, but it was only to the room with the soft, lumpy bedding that I'd woken up in. I hadn't noticed before how there was a hole in the wall that was covered by some sort of clear stone so I could see outside without getting cold. What a marvel that was! I had to stop and examine it.

If I ever make my own lodge, I'll have to find a pane like this, I thought. My breath left steam marks on it, and—as I wiped them away (because I didn't want Ilona to think I'd made her home dirty)—I saw Howl outside, grunting as flakes of snow fluttered down from the night sky. *That's right*, I thought. I wasn't studying how Ilona's lodge was designed; I was going to milk Howl. But where was the bucket?

I scanned the room, finding the vessel near a bear skull with little bird skulls set into each of its eyes and teeny red stones in the bird eye sockets. All the eyes followed me no matter which way I walked. I hobbled forward and back, watching the six sets of eyes chase me until Niyi squirmed in my coat, and I remembered I was going outside to milk Howl.

I went back to the table room, promising myself I wouldn't get distracted again until Niyi was fed. I saw what had to be the way out, and I walked up to what I now know is called a door, only we didn't have those where I grew up, so it was foreign to me (we used a flap of stretched leather to cover the way you got in and out of our homes). I pressed my wrapped hand against the rough wood, meaning to push on it (I hoped that's all I had to do to open it), only just before I did, I remembered the spear and thought that it might be better to take it with me in case there were more little men around or something.

So I turned around and scanned the room, my eyes getting stuck only briefly on an ice ball with mountains and trees inside.

"Darling, what are you looking for?"

"My spear. I had it when I fell—"

Ilona pointed me into another room, and it took me a long time to find it even though it was right in front of my face when I walked in because I was too busy staring at a miniature ship with teeny fox figurines wearing what looked like human skin doing the sailing. And this worried me a little, but I ignored it because Niyi was getting grumpier, and I wanted to feed her.

I went back to the entrance with a bucket, my mother's spear, and my coat on already, and then just as I was about to go outside, I thought that I might want to leave right after milking Howl, so maybe I should grab my arrowhead as well?

And the exact same thing happened again.

I wandered around until Ilona asked what I was looking for, and she pointed, and it took me way too long to find it, even though it was somewhere really obvious. I should have been suspicious, to say the least, and I did comment. I said, "I've had the same moment three times now."

"That doesn't make any sense, darling."

"No..." I frowned. "It doesn't..."

But I didn't think it was strange because I was caught in something sort of like a dream but also like a knot, which is hard to explain if you've never been inside one before. But part of the trap I was in, I think, is that I didn't fully notice I was in it.

I just kept going about my business, trying to leave and remembering a reason why I couldn't or being reminded by ever-smirking Ilona of something I should do before I left and getting distracted or confused along the way. Once when I was about to step outside, she said that I should at least let her brush my hair before I went out, and I refused at first because it was a strange thing for her to suggest.

"I insist, darling."

I listened to her. And not even that felt odd to me. I sat down and let her brush my hair, and she put that big reflective disc in front of me.

"I love this colour red," she said, pulling on one of my frizzy curls. "Could I have this piece to keep?"

"A piece of my hair?" I scowled. "No."

"Please, darling."

AND I LET HER CUT OFF A PIECE OF MY HAIR.

And even *that* didn't seem strange to me because I was in this woozy dream-daze. But when she took the curl she'd cut off and set it in a small clear vessel with a brownish plug and put it on a ledge, I did start to feel weird.

First, because the whole wall was full of these little vessels—small enough that you could close your hand around them and no one would be able to see what they were—all of them clear, like ice, and all of them with hair inside. Red hair and brown hair and yellow hair and black hair and every colour in between. I knew then that something was unusual. That there'd been others, like me, that had come to Ilona's home and had their hair cut off.

Second, my stomach was beginning to ache since I'd eaten so much. *Ache* really isn't a strong enough word. It was burning, and I had to clench my teeth and breathe slow to keep myself from making noise.

Poor Niyi still hadn't eaten. I had my spear and my arrowhead, and Niyi was in my lap still. So I twisted my hair all together, but I didn't put the arrowhead in while Ilona was looking at me, because I didn't want her to know that's where I usually kept it.

There was a wide smile on her face—too wide.

"I really want to check on Howl," I said, trying to give her a reason to stop staring at me so knowingly.

She rolled her eyes. "Darling, you're even more foolish than Preah said you were."

The idea of Preah thinking I was foolish and then telling her owl stung like the blunt end of a dagger jammed into my chest. And then I was thinking about Preah and her little hands and how she'd follow me everywhere when she was small, putting her teeny boots into my bigger boot prints in the snow so I hurt in another way too.

"Let me make it clear for you, darling. You can't leave. It's quite impossible."

I frowned, considering how silly some of the reasons I'd stopped leaving were, how many times I'd walked to the entrance and went to push on the door and then stopped. Had I been at this for hours? Longer?

I decided it was too nonsensical, so I went to where I thought the way out was, and then I stopped, certain I was forgetting something. Something really important. Something I couldn't leave without. I turned around, running through my meagre list in my head. Niyi. Spear. Arrowhead. Coat. Boots. Howl was outside. Milk bucket was near the door. There was nothing that was missing.

"Watching this is getting boring. I have other things to do, you know. Why don't you make yourself useful? Maybe sweep the floors or something?"

I hadn't seen a broom at this point in my life or heard about *sweeping*, but my hands started moving on their own and my legs too, and it was horrifying, to say the least. I set Niyi down in the grass basket near the fire and took Ilona's broom and began sweeping the floors: the dust and dirt and teeny pebbles piling up into a tiny mountain. I was scared in a way I'd never been scared before because I had no control over my body, and I was missing pieces of my mind. And since she still hadn't been fed, Niyi was crying.

As she wailed louder, the clouds of dust I was sweeping changed colour—growing bluer and bluer.

They began to move, making shapes and swirls before coming together into a tight ball.

Ilona smirked as she watched me struggle to stop myself from cleaning her home, but after Niyi had been crying for a minute or two, she grew frustrated. "For light's sake, child, stop."

Niyi cried louder.

"STOP, I said!"

She pointed right at Niyi with a long red nail that was as sharp as a blade. Niyi didn't listen, so at least whatever Ilona had done to me hadn't worked on the baby. I didn't have time to contemplate the idea and whether or not it could help me any, because the owl-woman turned to me and shouted: "Make her stop!"

My bandaged hands dropped the broom and picked up Niyi and held her close. The ball of dust that was growing bigger the louder Niyi cried tumbled all together and stretched and tied around itself sort of like a rope, and when the knot was pulled tight, it stopped being dust. Instead, there was a skin. The skin floated to me, right into my hand, and I smelled what was inside.

Milk.

I tasted it, and it seemed fine. And I wanted to give it to Niyi, but I was scared it was another trick. My hands didn't care; they were still following Ilona's orders, so I fed Niyi the dust-milk, and she stopped crying.

Ilona cackled. "See! See! What a voice! It makes no sense. Why a poor baby from an ice village—Kettin of all places—why her? In all my days, never have I seen such an unimportant child with such a gift."

That also hurt. Niyi wasn't unimportant.

I wanted to tell Ilona that, but I knew there was something more important to focus on. I had to do something—get away from the tricky owl-woman somehow. Panic was stirring up my blood, and it only got worse when Ilona said: "Give her to me."

I didn't want to, but my arms did it.

No. No. NO, I thought.

My thoughts made no difference. I walked to the glowing woman and put Niyi in her arms. My muscles ached because I was fighting so hard to have them do what I wanted. I was almost crying...

"Don't cry," Ilona said. "I hate listening to children cry."

Even my tears obeyed her. *What's happening?* I thought.

"Darling, you've eaten my food. You can't leave, and you must obey me now. This is how it works."

I choked, not because there was something in my throat but because I was so scared. I tried to look brave as I swallowed away the choking feeling and said, "What do you want?"

She smiled. "I want you to sit down over there and be quiet."

So I sat in the corner and couldn't talk anymore. No matter how much I told my legs or arms or mouth to move, nothing listened to me.

Ilona didn't hold Niyi for very long. She set the baby back down in the basket by the fire and began to brush her own hair, looking at herself in the giant disc for a long time, tilting her chin to one side and then the other, enjoying the sight of herself so much that I felt embarrassed for her. When she was done, she looked over at me, her round brows sliding up her forehead like she'd forgotten I was there.

"Darling, don't look at me like that. It's going to make you even uglier."

I felt my cheeks moving. My brow relaxed. And—I'm not joking—I smiled.

"That's better." Ilona moved one of her strange stools over and sat right in front of me, smiling in the most menacing of ways. "By now, you're probably thinking of all the times you threw stones at me."

I hadn't been thinking that, but as soon as she said it, I was. And I knew by the twisted cruelty in her flashy smile that she meant to make me suffer for it.

I tried to say, *do whatever you want to me, but Niyi never did anything, leave her alone.* But of course, I was still being quiet because that's what Ilona had told me to do.

I think Ilona could see my struggle, even though my body wasn't doing anything other than what she'd told it to, because she laughed. And I think Niyi could feel it, too, because she was crying again. Ilona rolled her eyes and went over to where the baby lay.

"How do you put up with this noise?" she said. "How did Preah do it? All day?"

I couldn't answer.

"Darling, go to the kitchen and fetch me the jar. You'll know which one."

I stood and walked into the room with the big black cauldron, and I looked at the different vessels and buckets and containers.

I did know.

I knew exactly which one Ilona wanted me to bring.

I groaned and wailed as my fingers moved toward it. *She didn't say how fast I had to go,* I told myself, but my hands didn't listen. They knew what Ilona had meant, and they picked up the jar full of little blue tongues and ears, and I was carrying it out to her, my heart battering against the bones in my chest. I set the jar on the table.

"Good girl," she said.

I tried to beg her, but I was still being quiet because that's what she'd ordered me to do.

"Now, put the cauldron on."

My body knew what she meant before my mind did. I went back into the cauldron room to the big iron vessel. I dragged the hunk of metal to the fire, which I shouldn't have been able to do because it was so big and heavy, but because of the curse or whatever she'd done to me, I could. And once it was sitting atop the fire, the instructions seemed to wear off a little. I ran back to where Ilona and Niyi were still sitting, next to the jar full of blue tongues, and I dove for my mother's spear, hoping I was faster than Ilona.

I wasn't.

"Stop!"

I was still. Frozen completely. My arms were left reaching out for the spear. My legs were still at the angle they needed to be for running (sort of running, it was still more of a hobble). My whole body was slanted wrong—I should have fallen to the ground, but I didn't. I stayed, kind of hovering, with my head and chest out in front of my hips and legs.

"Tsk, tsk," Ilona said. "You are the stupidest child I ever did see. No wonder Preah hated you so much."

There was a lot of pain, all different kinds of it. *She's lying*, I told myself. *She's just angry because I kicked at her a whole bunch.*

"You don't believe me?" She raised her perfect, round brows. "She told me all the time how much she despised you. She was planning on running away with me, to get away from you. Always shouting. Slapping. Ordering her about."

I tried not to believe her, but I couldn't help it. Of course Preah had hated me. I hated me. Kid probably did too. Tears formed behind my eyes, but I couldn't give her the satisfaction of seeing them, so I fought them with everything I had in me.

And then, whatever was holding me steady let go, and I fell to the ground. My chin slammed against the hard floor as she laughed at me again. I scrambled for the spear and proper footing, but deep down, I knew there was nothing I could do. You can't compete against someone whose every order you must obey. It's impossible.

"Now, Crab, into the pot you go."

My legs spun around, and I walked back to the iron cauldron, which was sitting over the fire, where I'd left it. Empty.

I climbed inside.

The metal was thick, so it wasn't hot yet, but I knew that would change soon.

Ilona followed and set the lid atop me, clicking some sort of latch into place, and once again, I was in the darkness.

TWELVE

I'D NEVER SEEN WHAT happened to a person who'd been left inside a pot over a fire, but I figured it was the same crispy, sizzling thing that happened to anything else. It was maybe the worst death I could think of.

So, by the time Ilona's orders wore off, things were getting warm, and I was pretty panicked, as you can probably imagine. I was so scared, I felt like I was dissolving, like my mind and skin and all the rest of me was blurring together into one thoughtless, terrified feeling that tasted and smelled sour.

In a frenzy, I tried pressing against the tepid lid. It didn't budge.

I lay on my back and tried to kick the lid off with my boots. I tried crouching and pushing up with my back. I tilted my head and pressed my shoulder against the cover, straining my legs as I groaned. The lid moved—lifting off the rim of the pot just a bit—but there was some kind of latch keeping it from coming off entirely.

I stuck my trembling fingers through the teeny opening and grasped at the latch, trying to pull and push it. I did everything I could think of except calling for help because I didn't want Ilona to come back and order me to sit still and be quiet, because then I'd be cooking to death and not even able to scream about it.

I was sweating—because it was hot and I was terrified—and I was grunting, getting more frantic the longer I couldn't get out. You wouldn't think I could hear what was happening outside because the metal was so thick, but I could. Maybe she planned it that way to make everything worse for me. I don't know.

I heard Ilona humming, and then I heard her stop. I tried rolling myself into the side of the cauldron, hoping to tip it over by knocking it off balance. And when that didn't work, flashes of Ilona eating me once I was cooked took over my mind. I imagined her saving up what little fat came out of me in a vessel and gagged.

Niyi started crying, and in my heart, I knew something terrible was about to happen because it wasn't her normal cry, you know? It was that terrible baby wail that comes after a long intake of breath, the sort of cry that happens when a kid gets truly hurt, not just an everyday bump or tumble. I did start shouting then, thinking about the jar of little blue tongues, hoping Ilona would put Niyi down and come to me, and maybe I could... I don't know what I thought I could do. But there would be a few more moments without Niyi suffering and that was something.

Ilona didn't come, and Niyi screamed in a way I'd never heard a baby scream ever. I slammed myself again and again into the metal that was getting warmer by the moment. Niyi's scream turned into a shrill, eerie squawking. The piercing chirp of a little bird in terrible, terrible pain.

I pushed against the cauldron once more, screaming "No!" as scalding tears burned the back of my eyes and my shoulders felt like they were splitting from the pain of slamming into iron.

The cauldron pushed back.

Not because of what I was doing, but because of something happening outside. It wobbled and rumbled and suddenly I was the wrong way up, knocking my head against the side of the pot, my mind rattling inside my skull as it rolled. And whatever had knocked the cauldron off the fire, loosened the lid. It popped off and rolled on the floor, round and round, slower and slower until finally it fell over onto its side.

I crawled out of the cauldron into a stark blue light that turned everything a deep, shady colour. My head throbbed so intensely I couldn't open my eyes fully. I tried moving forward, but my mind was still spinning from how I'd been rolling in the cauldron, and I kept crashing into the floor on the right side. I pulled myself forward on the floor as my mind spun, desperate to get to the crying, chirping, sorrow I'd heard. My mind caught up, and I pushed myself off the floor, my eyes immediately finding the ball of Niyi's furs on the table.

Suddenly, I couldn't walk slow enough. Niyi's furs weren't the right size or shape… they weren't moving right either. I knew I had to look, but I thought *I don't want to do this, I don't want to do this, I don't want to do this* as my feet led me to the pile. I lifted a flat piece of fur and a teeny blue bird fluttered out, trying each corner of the room for a way out before it zipped out the door with a terrified shriek.

No.

Niyi wasn't the only thing changed by whatever had knocked the cauldron over and coated the house in blue light. Ilona was there too, shrunk down to the size of my thumb.

I didn't think. I only acted. I grabbed one of the little hair jars Ilona kept on her wall and picked up the shrunken owl-woman. She bit me, but it felt like the faintest prick, and even if it had burned with the full force of an oil fire, I don't think I would have reacted. I pushed her in the jar and put the stopper on and stuffed her in my pocket. I grabbed my mother's spear and charged out the open door after the bird. Whatever Ilona had done to Niyi, could be undone. I'd seen Ilona transform. Niyi could too. She would have to. And I was a giant now compared to Ilona. I was sure I could hurt her enough that she'd do as I asked. I just had to catch Niyi first...

Howl was outside Ilona's lodge, and she huffed and followed me, but I paid her no notice. I only had room in my mind for the little blue speck fluttering many paces ahead.

THIRTEEN

"NIYI!"

I'd seen which way the bird had gone and shouted myself hoarse as I followed, moving as fast as I could with my bandaged-up leg and the tangle of roots on the ground—Ilona's lodge was nestled in a forest, it turned out. Ancient and gnarled and dark as night apart from the few beams of light trickling down through the trees.

Niyi didn't listen. Maybe she couldn't hear me or, while she was a bird, she couldn't understand me or recognize my voice. Far off in the distance, I could see the frantic fluttering of her little wings.

I ignored the agony of throwing my whole weight onto my wrapped-up shin and the sharp throb of my lower back each time I sent a boot as far ahead of me as I could without stumbling. I ignored how each knee felt like it was about to split in two, and the burn of every frigid breath that I sucked into my lungs, and the speedy thrum that meant my heart was going to burst. All I had to do was keep running, and things would be okay. I'd get Niyi back.

I kept my teeth clenched and chased that bird out of the forest, into terrain I was more familiar with— an expanse of white. I chased that bird until it got farther and farther ahead of me, beginning to blend into the haze of grey clouds above.

And then there was nothing except Howl and me and flat whiteness.

"She'll rest," I said, kind of to Howl and kind of to myself as I thrust air in and out of my exhausted lungs. Spirals of white breath floated away from my face. "If we keep moving, we'll catch up with her."

I didn't take my eyes off the sky where I'd lost sight of Niyi as the wind whipped my cheeks with flecks of ice and the cold burrowed into my sweaty skin, freezing the salty water that coated my forehead and eyebrows. I didn't let myself think. I didn't let myself question. Of course the bird was Niyi—she could transform like Ilona could; she was magic after all. Or else it was her spirit, and I could catch it and bring it back to her body and keep her close for the rest of my life. There were no other possibilities.

I jogged until my legs trembled and lost all feeling. Then I walked until they didn't feel so numb. Then I ran again, one hand dug into my side where the muscles screamed at me to stop, my other hand still gripping my mother's spear. I could've run faster with it tied to my back, but I didn't want to stop and waste time tying the knot because I was telling myself Niyi was close—just out of my vision—and I didn't want to lose what distance I'd imagined I'd gained. I knew that running on the tundra caused blood to gather inside your lungs, and then the blood would freeze, and your lungs would burst.

The sooner I find her, the sooner I can stop running.

As if making a morbid joke, the wind stirred up and raged against me, lifting waves of snow and tossing them around, blurring any sight more than a few paces ahead. I kept my head down to protect my face from the blast and hugged the spear to my chest, tucking my cold-seared fingers under my armpits because my father had told me that bodies heat limbs better than anything else.

By the time the blizzard swallowed the sun, I was going a quarter of the pace I should have been—maybe half the pace here and there. The cold slowed my muscles and burned my nose, but still I kept moving.

Even though my hood covered my ears, and the wind was screeching like an animal, I heard the thump.

I looked behind me and saw Howl's collapsed body on the snow, her mane coated in icy white. She was groaning, and for the first time, I saw how thin she'd become. I got confused, because I felt like it had only been a day and a night—maybe one more day—since the winter sprite had taken off with Niyi. But I had no idea how long I'd been asleep at Ilona's lodge. Or how long I'd been awake and trying to leave.

Howl looked like it had been a lot longer that it felt, but we didn't have the time to stop—she needed to carry on, at least until we got to Niyi. After that, I could sort out Howl and then myself because I wasn't feeling great either.

I pulled at How's collar, and she got up, moaning in protest and lumbering slowly as I pulled her along. She made it only a few more steps before she came down again, even harder this time, tufts of white floating out of her nose from her laboured breaths.

"We don't have time for this. I need you to feed Niyi," I said, wiping at my eyes with my sleeve and grabbing her horns and pulling with all my might. "She went this way, so *we* have to go this way. If we keep going, we'll catch up to her. We have to."

Howl didn't budge.

"Please!" My voice cracked. "Niyi needs you. Papa..."

Howl lay on the frozen ground, deep, uneven breaths sputtering out of her mouth, her wide eyes rolling back into her head as she suffered. When her droopy black eyes met mine, I could see it; I could understand how much she was trying not to give up but how much she was failing.

Because we weren't running anymore, the cold crept into me. My teeth chattered. I shivered. "No. No. NO."

I tried to drag her. I tried to push her, grimacing under her weight as she twitched and panted, struggling to pull herself up on her wobbly legs. Blood dripped out of the corners of her lips.

"Enough of this! Come on!"

I couldn't move her. I knew it, and she knew it.

"Gah!" I kicked at the snow and then frowned really hard, hating myself, hating the thought I was having, but needing to have it anyway. "I have to leave you then," I said, choking on how awful the words were. I pressed my forehead to hers, feeling her thick, scraggly fur on my face, knowing no apology would be good enough. I would just have to add Howl to my long list of things to cry about later. I whispered. "I have to find Niyi..."

And just as I stood up straight, preparing myself to leave her behind, she died.

Papa.

The whistle of the wind drowned everything out as I prodded her, knowing she was dead but wishing I was wrong. I turned and took a step in the direction the bird had gone, but I didn't make it very far. My tears wouldn't be swallowed so easily this time; they blurred my vision, and my shaking legs gave up on carrying me. I know it shouldn't have been Howl dying that finally beat me down—that wasn't as bad as Preah dying and getting all gravelly, or having to tell Kid he was going with the sailor, or having no parents, or Niyi being stolen by something I couldn't understand—but for some reason, that was the point when I couldn't hold back the tide anymore. I was frozen and tired and bruised and bloody and completely, entirely, totally alone.

I frowned as hard as I could, trying to force my tears away as I urged my battered limbs forward. The sound of my sniffling was covered up by the howling of the wind. I thought of Niyi and ran. My ankles ached like they'd been bashed with a club, but I ran.

When my ankles gave out, I crawled, noticing that I couldn't feel my hands or feet at all. My muscles were rigid and hard, and it took all my strength to force them onward.

And then, the cold won, and I stopped moving.

My limbs were exhausted and stiff, and my eyes burned in that itchy way that happens when your body has decided you're going to sleep whether you agree with it or not. I knew that if I stayed and slept on the frigid ground like that, I'd die because the ground steals your warmth. But even knowing that, I was too tired and cold to get up. I stayed there, nodding off, lying to myself, saying that I was just going to sit for a moment until my legs warmed up some and I felt ready to keep going. One or two minutes maybe...

My breathing slowed, and eventually, I fell asleep.

FOURTEEN

I DON'T THINK I slept for long. Maybe I did. There's no way to know for sure. Only I *did* open my eyes again, and I was alive when I did, so I'm thinking it couldn't have been too long or my heart would have slowed from the cold and frozen in my chest and this story would have been over right there on the tundra. Maybe that would have been better. In fact, I'm sure it would've been, but it's too late for that now.

What you need to know is that I didn't wake up—I was *woken* up. Not by a person either—by a thing.

My mother's spear.

It knocked into the side of my head, right where my ear was.

I pushed it away in a half-asleep daze, but then it hit me again.

It hit a third time, and that was when I opened my eyes.

The sun was high in the blazing blue sky, and the wind had settled, so the snow stayed on the ground, gleaming in the brightness of the sun. Thank the thaw I'd fallen asleep with my face against my arm and not the tundra or I would have been frozen to the earth by the skin of my cheek. My limbs were a little stuck, but when I jerked them, the thin stitches of ice that had formed while I slept, shattered.

Everything was quiet. The snow takes the sound out of the air, if you didn't know that, meaning things like your breath that you can normally hear are swallowed up. So it was quieter than silent.

I blinked several times to get the crust of snow off my eyelashes, and that was when I saw my mother's spear. No one was holding it, but it was standing upright almost like someone was. The spiky part reached toward the sky, and the flat end rested in the snow, except when it moved.

All on its own.

It hopped like a really skinny one-legged creature. And then it struck me again—a nice hard thwack on my temple.

"Whhagaft?" was what came out of my frozen mouth. Apart from the clouds of dust that had floated around Niyi back at Ilona's lodge and the milk skin that had come from thin air when she'd cried, I hadn't seen an object move on its own before. I felt mad and like the world was impossible, but then I remembered more of my waking life and none of that mattered.

Niyi.

I was on my feet faster than you would think, given I was nearly frozen and numb in a lot of places. I was sure that if I took my boots off, I'd see my toes were black, which meant I was going to lose them. Probably patches on my face, too. And because I'd been crying, there had been snot coming out of my nose when I'd finally grown still. It had frozen to my face in an itchy glob, so I scratched it as I took a step in the direction I remembered the blue bird flying. Instead of the icicle on my upper lip coming off by itself, a chunk of my skin came off too, stinging so much that my eyes watered.

I moaned from the piercing pain and from the ache in every bone in my body but knowing how cold I was made me sure Niyi was suffering too. Probably more because small things get cold faster than big things.

The spear struck me right in the forehead, knocking me back and jumbling up my mind.

"Hey!" I shouted, not sure if spears could understand people.

I lunged forward, and again the spear gave me a whack, right in the stomach this time, causing me to bend over as my organs adjusted to the pain. I already warned you; this story gets weirder and weirder. Where I was—that wasn't a place people went often, and there were lots of things that happened in the world when humans weren't there to see them.

I growled at the stupid stick, grabbing it with my hands and trying to throw it, only it wouldn't leave my grip. It pressed against my chest, trying to force me backward. I tilted, letting the thing roll off my less sore shoulder, and then I took off running, only to have a hard wallop hit my shins, just low enough to the ground that I tumbled over it.

I screeched at it, "WHAT DO YOU WANT THEN? HUH?"

It lay in the air horizontal-like and pointed to the east.

Maybe because I was so tired and nearly dead, or because I was used to speaking with Preah and Niyi and neither of them talked back, I didn't have trouble understanding it. The spear wanted me to walk to the east.

"I have to go after Niyi," I said, pointing west. *She's all I have left.* And even then, I didn't have her. I'd lost her. Just like I'd lost everyone else. And once I found her, I still had to figure out how to feed her now that Howl was gone.

She must be so hungry, I thought.

The spear pointed again, with a bit of an aggressive shake included this time.

I nodded like I was going to listen and even turned my boots the way the spear seemed to be telling me to go, but at the last second, I took off toward where I was pretty sure the bird had gone. I got a stick to the throat, which left me sputtering on the ground for several minutes.

I looked up at the spear as I gasped, wondering what was making it move and promising myself that I'd punch someone in the throat the next time I was really annoyed because it felt AWFUL.

When I caught my breath, I got up and looked at the enlivened spear a little more closely.

I said, "Mom? Is that you?" And to this day, I'm really ashamed of that because it's such a silly, childish thing to say. Like an orphaned animal trying to find a replacement mama, only a spear can't be a mother; it's a piece of sharpened bone with leather tied around where the strain is greatest when fishing.

Instead of answering me, the spear simply leaned to the east and bounced the smallest bit, like it was nodding in the direction it wanted me to go.

"Niy—"

The spear pushed into my back, forcing me east, and no matter how I tried to get away—rolling or shifting or ducking or jumping—it was preemptively adjusting, moving in exactly the right way to keep me going the way it wanted. I shouted and cursed and used all the tricks I could think of (which weren't really that many), only it made no difference, and I did eventually give up. Or at least, I *acted* like I'd given up.

I walked the way the spear was pushing me, but in my mind, I was scheming.

I was thinking of a way to outsmart the thing and go the direction I wanted. I was also counting my steps so I could get back to where I'd gone off track more easily. You learned things like this if you grew up where I did, where everything looks the same and the wind blows away your footprints just about as fast as you made them.

When I got to thirty-nine, I started all over again, only I bent my little finger into my palm, so I knew I was on my second counting. And on my third, I bent my finger next to my little finger in, so I knew I was on my third counting. When I was on sixteen in my eighth counting and beginning to worry about what I would do when I got to my tenth counting and had no more fingers left to curl in, I saw where the spear was leading me.

There was a caribou herd just ahead, and I knew by the way their heads were dipped and by how they were gathered together, tugging at the ground with their hooves, that there were lichens to be had. I should have been a little cautious around them, as they could be dangerous, but my hunger took over, and just like when Ilona forced my limbs to obey her, I had no control over my body. I pushed through the caribou. Most of them weren't bothered at all by my presence, but some of the younger ones rushed to the other side of the herd to get away from me. I threw myself to the ground among their hooves, digging with my elbows (because my hands were far too cold), and stuffing my mouth with the thick, mossy meal, hardly chewing at all before I swallowed, clumps of soil grinding around in my teeth. Raw lichens would be hard on my stomach, and the taste was disgustingly bitter, but I didn't care.

I realize that, so far, I've not been a very grateful person, and I guess that's true of me for the most part, but at that moment I was so grateful I almost cried.

Thank you. Thank you. Thank you, I thought as I ate. I was thanking the spear and the caribou and the Skyfather and the ground, and still, it wasn't enough. I wanted to thank everything that was and everything that would ever be and had ever been, and still, that wouldn't have been enough.

You're welcome.

I shot up from among the caribou, peering over the brownish-grey bodies in all directions, trying to gain a sense of where the voice had come from. It wasn't like anything I'd ever heard, and it terrified me because it sort of shook my bones, but also it warmed me up and filled my chest with a pressure that was kind of... pleasant, I guess?

I couldn't see anyone, just caribou and snow and my mother's spear, which was still holding itself upright.

"Who said that?" I said. It had sounded like a man.

There was no answer.

My heart pounded, and I can't really explain why hearing that voice was so much more unusual than anything else that had happened to me so far, but it was. Maybe because it felt kind of nice? And I wasn't accustomed to nice things happening?

Then the spear hopped off to the south, and I felt like it might be smart to chase after it. The spear had brought me to food, so maybe it would also bring me to Niyi. Maybe it knew better what was happening than I did. How else could it have known to go east?

I took one step and stopped. It could just as easily be another trick, and I was done with tricks.

I stared at my boots as I thought. There was no way for me to know. There was no extra information. I was just going to have to make a choice and deal with it.

The only thing I shouldn't be doing is wasting time, I thought. *Niyi could be nearly frozen by now.*

I decided to count to three and choose the first route that came to mind when I got there, following the spear or going back the way I'd come and going the direction the bird had been flying when I'd lost sight of her. *Even then, I probably won't find her,* I thought, my heart sinking into my stomach.

No. I banished the thought as quickly as it had come.

One...

Two...

I stopped counting because I could see something strange in the snow.

A little spot of blue—maybe the size of a drop of blood or a wad of spit. Almost like the sky had leaked onto the snow.

I crouched down to look at it more closely before noticing more blue out of the corner of my eye.

When I lifted my gaze, there was another drop of blue.

And another after that.

I pushed the caribou away, crawling through the hoof-mashed snow, and found another after that. I didn't realize then that the drops of blue were leading me in the same direction as the spear. I wasn't thinking much of anything, other than Niyi had blue in her some way. Somehow. She had a blue tongue and had made blue dust appear and now she had blue bird feathers, so maybe she also dripped blue. I don't know, I was exhausted and frozen and delirious. Blue meant Niyi in my mind.

I scrambled after the drops, probably looking like a fox following a scent, scurrying around on my hands and knees in an aching, wincing frenzy. The blue drops became blue smears and then swirls. Beautiful, complicated patterns, zigging and zagging and twisting and dancing all together atop the snow. No line had a beginning or an end. Instead, the beginning was the end again.

I clamoured back onto my feet and followed the trail of blue, catching up with my mother's spear, rushing along the cerulean path with the sound of *put-put-put* as the spear hopped beside me.

I didn't find Niyi at the end of the trail.

But I did find Elken.

Of course, I didn't know his name at the time. All I saw was a boy, maybe my age, maybe a little bit younger, kneeling on the ground, dipping a brush into a vessel of blue and dragging it across the icy snow with meticulous care. He was frowning with concentration and so absorbed in the precision of his work that he didn't notice me at first.

I reached out for the spear, ready to use it if I had to. I figured there was no good reason for anyone to be alone so far away from any villages.

The spear leaned away, just out of my grasp.

The boy looked up at me with wide eyes and then, almost a full second later, he jumped. His reaction time calmed me a lot because I knew for certain I was quicker than he was. A lot quicker.

He stood, his eyes still round in either confusion or fear or maybe both. "Are you a hag?" he said.

"No," I said. And then I added, "What's a hag?"

"Like a witchy sort of woman. Do you curse things? Cast spells?"

I frowned.

"You've got yourself an enchanted spear." He pointed to my mother's spear with his painting tool as if that explained everything.

"I didn't make it like that. That's just how it was," I said in an abrasive voice because I felt like I should be offended for some reason... only I wasn't sure why.

He lifted his eyebrows. "You've come to mock me then? Call me crazy?"

"No." Though at this point, I *was* beginning to think he was a bit off. I mean, why would he assume I'd come to see him? I reached once more for the spear, but it pulled away again, just out of my reach.

He said, "If you mess up the snow, I'm just going to paint it again. You can't out-patience me. I'm warning you now. I'm more patient than pretty much anyone."

"I don't care about your stupid snow," I said.

And then he tilted his head to the side, scratched his chin, and I'm not joking, he said, "Wait, you're not… are you turning blue by any chance?"

FIFTEEN

ELKEN.

SO, LIKE, I knew this part of the story was coming, which means I should be more prepared to tell you about it. But I'm not. Because Elken is... well, he's a lot of things, but one of them is that he's hard to describe.

I can tell you what he looked like (lanky with sandy hair and the kind of smile that takes up half his face). Or I can tell you things about him, like how he walked (like he was never going anywhere in particular, like he had endless time, like he almost didn't know he was walking). I could tell you how he had a gap in his back teeth on the left side, so every time he finished eating, he poked at it with his tongue to make sure no food was stuck in it. But none of these things capture him, what it was really like to be near him, to breathe the same air he was breathing. To have him look at me.

Already I'm regretting saying any of this. I guess the best way I could describe Elken would be to say that when you looked at him, and he was looking at you, you could tell that he really understood. That he could see the things you were hiding, and he wasn't bothered by them any. As for the rest, I'll just have to tell you what happened, and you can make up your own mind about him. And about me, because I have a feeling you're going to change your sense of me real soon. Don't feel bad when you do. Everyone does. I'm used to it.

When Elken asked me whether I was turning blue, I didn't say yes or no, or that Niyi's mouth was blue, or that Ilona had a jar full of blue ears and tongues. (I did reach into my pocket to make sure she was still there though, because I still wanted to squish her once I'd found my sister and figured out everything else). I crossed my arms, trying to make it seem like he was annoying me and said, "What kind of question is that?"

I think Elken knew I wasn't actually offended. He got this big, silly grin on his face and said, "I don't know. I just had a feeling blue was coming next. Why else would she have me painting the snow like this?"

He gestured to the dizzying swirls of blue on the frosty ground. The marks were beautiful—they felt like flowing, like whispering, like teeny, little promises all stacked atop each other. To be honest, I had to force myself to look away.

When I did, Elken was still staring at me, still smiling, his head tilted a little to the side.

I decided he *was* crazy. Why else would he put so much time into something so useless?

He shrugged and laughed AT HIMSELF and said, "Maybe she wants to teach me to stop coming to conclusions. It wouldn't be the first time—"

Being laughed at was one of my least favourite things in all of life, so I couldn't imagine doing it to myself. I cut the whole conversation short—actively ignoring whoever *she* was. I said, "I'm looking for a bird," because as much as I'd learned to keep my mouth shut, I figured maybe this weird boy had seen something.

"A blue bird, perchance?"

My heart skipped three beats in one go. "Have you seen one?" I hardened my gaze, trying to threaten him with just my expression. I studied him, waiting for a hint of a lie or some sort of recognition as hope fluttered inside me and warmed my aching shoulders.

"No." His eyes flicked down to my boots which had begun to turn dark grey from the dampness.

"You could use some warming up." It wasn't a question; it was just him knowing the truth. Elken was like that. He knew what people needed. And maybe you think I'm foolish for saying this since it's pretty easy to guess that someone who's come out of the tundra needs to get warm. But you'll see. As things go on, you'll see what I mean. Elken was... there maybe aren't words that can explain what he was.

"How about we sit you down next to a fire, and you tell me all about this bird? Any help I can offer, I will."

I shook my head. As tempting as the idea of heat was—and as weirdly calming as this boy was—I didn't want to get lured into sitting for too long. Already I had no idea how long I'd been asleep, how much time I had to make up for.

My throat grew scratchy, letting me know tears were moments away from forcing their way out of me. "Are you sure you haven't seen a blue bird?" *I have to keep looking*, I thought, turning back to where I was pretty sure I'd come from, just in time for my mother's spear—which I'd sort of forgotten about—to whack me in the stomach so hard that I hunched over and thought I might vomit in front of the weird paint-boy.

"Whoa, whoa," Elken stepped toward the spear with his hands raised as if he were trying to ease a skittish animal. "There's no need for any of that."

Strangely, it seemed like my mother's spear understood him some. It hopped back two little leaps, giving Elken space to come closer to me

"You all right?" he said, crouching next to where I was slumped over and groaning in the snow.

"Fine," I choked out, even though I wasn't fine at all. Every part of me hurt or was numb, and my stomach was already burning from eating the lichen back at the caribou herd, and what was left of my family was fluttering farther and farther away every second that I stood still, if she hadn't frozen already.

Elken seemed like he was going to reach out and touch my shoulder, but a single glare from me left his fur-clad hand hovering in the air between us. He smiled and it felt like warm stew. He truly had the least frightening face I'd ever encountered. He said, "I can see that it's real important for you to get where you're going, but you'll get there faster if you've warmed up a little."

Go with him. The voice again surged through me, heating me, holding me, driving me mad with confusion.

My voice cracked as I said, "I can't stop." I wasn't sure if I was talking to the boy (who was making too much sense), or to the strange voice that made my chest feel like it was swelling with a big wave from the sea, or to the spear that was bouncing up and down making it clear another thwack was coming if I didn't obey, or my own shaking legs (which were so sore they were threatening to give up on me). My voice had sounded like a pathetic child's whine instead of like someone who had the energy and determination to carry on forward, and this embarrassed me, and then I felt stupid for being humiliated because why did it matter what anyone thought of me?

All I have to do is not stop running. That's all I have to do…

I clenched my teeth and heaved my broken body back up on my ankles, taking one more step before the spear came down, only the spear didn't hit me, it struck Elken's knuckles, because the stupid fool had stuck his hand out. I could tell by the sound that it hurt. A lot.

Elken opened his mouth in shock, shaking his hand several times, and then he laughed. "She's got quite the bite, doesn't she?"

My mind stopped working for a second because why would this stranger have reached out to take the spear's beating from me? It made less sense to me than the spear moving all on its own.

He was still smiling. "I don't think she wants you to go. I don't either, really. I know you said you're fine, but it doesn't look—I mean, you're pret—" He cleared his throat. "Are you sure you're well?"

Listen to him.

I started to worry that the voice I was hearing meant I was losing my mind because the boy next to me (who was reaching out his arm, offering to support me, by the way) didn't look like he'd heard anything unusual. I thought of Amlap, the furrier back home, who'd gone crazy after his daughter had fallen through the ice. Instead of crying like a normal person, he'd started babbling to foxes and trying to train them instead of skinning them. He'd growl to them and yelp and whine until one day he wasn't able to talk like a person anymore. He'd even held his hands up to his head like fox ears and perked them or wiggled them around. He'd been found dead on the tundra with his face bashed in and all his fingers gone, teeny fox nibble marks on his cheeks.

I stood up without taking the odd painter-guy's arm, my knees aching terribly as I did.

"At least let me patch you up some before you carry on," he said. "You've got a lot of blood on you, which means wolves probably or a bear or them speckled land-fish things—what do you call them? I never saw them before coming out here or heard anyone talk about them, either. Those—" He waddled a bit with his fingers curled up near his lips like tusk-teeth.

I knew he meant sabre-toothed seals.

"I had a nasty run-in with one," he said. "You can imagine my surprise—I thought sea creatures stayed in the sea and land creatures stayed on land." His big grin again.

I didn't smile back even though part of my cheeks wanted to when I thought of this lanky, foolish guy seeing a sabre-toothed seal pop out of the ice for the first time.

"Come back to my camp for a minute. Get out of the wind and the cold. I'll get you sorted, and you can tell me about this bird, and maybe we'll get your spear to calm down some. You're bleeding a bit too much for me to feel okay just letting you go."

I nodded, hating how right he was. My heart felt like milk that was souring right there in my chest. I would draw animals soon with so many open wounds, even if they were clotted, and I'd be no good against a pack of wolves hobbling as I was, and then I'd be eaten and Niyi would be alone and then she'd die because she was only little, and she needed me.

And maybe he has something worth taking, something that could help. It was a mean thought to have, but I had it. I told you; I'm not the sort of person people like.

Elken didn't wait for my response; he picked up his paint vessel and started leading the way. At first, it was quiet except for the squeaky snow sound beneath our boots and the little *putt-putt* the spear made as it hopped alongside us. But then, in the quiet, one of us started speaking. And it wasn't the one you'd think. It was me.

I said, "What would you do? If I *was* blue, I mean?" I couldn't help myself; he'd asked such a specific question, and he'd been painting the snow blue, so he must not have been as afraid of the colour as the folk back in Kettin. Maybe he could tell me something about how to take better care of Niyi. Maybe he knew all about blue people.

"Uhh, I don't know," he said. "She hasn't given me that much... Not so far ahead, I mean."

I couldn't ignore his mention of another person a second time, especially not since we were walking to his camp. "She?"

He laughed again, only his cheeks went all red, so I knew he was embarrassed. "The uh... you know, the green goddess."

I didn't know. I had no sense of what he was talking about. I put together that a goddess was a girl god, but I'd never heard of one of those. I didn't know girls *could* be gods, so I kept quiet because I didn't want him to think I was stupid.

I had just turned my focus to how he'd expect me to pay for him "patching me up"—because I knew things like that weren't free—when we came up over a sparkling, snowy knoll and I saw Elken's "camp."

It wasn't a camp at all but a bluestone structure maybe as wide as all of Kettin and taller than at least three adults, maybe four, with one part that was even taller and pointier than the rest of it rising out from the centre like a narwhale horn. I could feel my mouth hanging open in awe. Arch-like carvings dripped off the sides of it, almost like wings, like the whole thing could lift itself up and fly off into the sky where it belonged.

"Don't be too impressed," Elken said, smirking. "It's not really mine. I'm only borrowing it for a while, and it's none too warm—"

"Whose is it?"

"I have no idea."

"Who said you could stay then?" I was worried it belonged to another blue man, like the one that stole Niyi or an owl-harpy, and at any moment, one of them would pop out of nowhere and steal something.

"The green goddess. I'm supposed to wait here for the others, only it's been three years—" He scratched the back of his head. "And you're the first person I've seen."

He kicked at the snow, making me think that even though he was smiling, he wasn't pleased with his loneliness.

He said, "I got spaces set up for everyone, I think, you know, depending on how many end up arriving. But I don't know—"

As we got closer to the building, I stopped listening entirely. In the corner of my vision, I could see Elken's mouth was still moving, and I think he mentioned the structure was "a temple at some point" but I couldn't pay attention. All of my mind was mesmerized by the sight. I'd spent a fair bit of time dreaming about building something special, as I've said, but never in my wildest imaginings was anything so spectacular. There were arched holes cut into the stone and filled with a pane of material I couldn't fathom. It was clear *and* colourful, kind of like the gems at Ilona's lodge. And all the colours formed images that probably had fascinating stories behind them: people with funny haircuts and clothing that certainly wasn't made from fur, with boots that didn't cover their toes but only the bottom of their feet with lacing tied around the ankles. The most impractical footwear I'd ever seen in my life. How did their toes not turn black from the cold and fall off?

I stopped gawking when I realized that Elken was watching me, smiling that stupid smile of his.

"Even if you're not turning blue," he said. "And you're not staying very long, it's nice to have someone here."

I didn't know what to do with that, so I frowned.

He laughed and said, "All I mean by it is you're welcome. Stay as long or as little as you'd like, and maybe once you find your bird, you could come and... I don't know... visit or something."

And I still had no idea what to say to this strange guy who lived in a glorious rock lodge alone in the tundra, who seemed to say exactly what he was thinking, even if it was too embarrassing or truthful to be said aloud.

"You'll be needing fresh bandages?"

He asked it like a question, but it wasn't. I followed him inside, through giant wooden doors with sea-green stones pressed into them that swung on iron hinges. I might have fallen over backwards from the sight of inside if I wasn't worried about what I'd look like in front of this weird guy. I kept still and quiet and made sure my face didn't reveal how in awe I was as he shut the door behind us, the thud echoing through the giant building.

"I'll just grab—" He didn't finish what he was saying as he walked away, or maybe he did but I wasn't listening? I was staring up at the roof, which had the most intricate scenes laid out across it: people crying, people dying, people laughing. Animals I'd not seen before. Lichen-like things that came out of the ground and grew taller than the people. I couldn't understand any of it, but that almost didn't matter. It was overwhelmingly beautiful. The highest roof I'd ever seen, with long, skinny wall holes with panes in them like at Ilona's lodge only way bigger. More light captured inside a building than I'd thought possible.

Papa would love this, I thought. And then I ached because Papa wasn't seeing or loving anything anymore.

Elken brought a stool and a bucket of hot water, and lots of material that was cloud-coloured and not at all like fur or leather. He had a bone needle in his mouth, and he gestured for me to sit down.

"You're not stitching me up with that," I said.

My father had told me once that I should never stitch a wound with a needle that hadn't been burnt clean with fire.

Elken laughed and took the needle out of his mouth. "I thought in case what roughed you up tore any of your clothes—"

I glared at him so hard he stopped speaking and set the needle on the ground. "Okay then, no needle," he said.

I sat down with a lot of difficulty because every part of me was stinging or numb. He cleaned my face first, and the hot water burned like nothing else for a second before it felt like dessert. Better than I can explain. Like my face was coming back to life. Only I couldn't feel it when it got to my nose, and I knew that meant my nose was probably frostbitten because that happened to people who were out in the cold for too long. Their noses died and fell off, and seeing a person with a big flat hole where there's supposed to be a nose is one of the spookiest things. I bit my cheek in disappointment; I was already ugly enough. I didn't need to be scaring children, too.

"You needn't worry," Elken said. "I don't think you're going to lose anything."

And that was odd, you know, because I hadn't said anything.

I probably *would* have said something, but Elken pulled one of my hands out of my sleeve where it had been tucked and balled up in a fist for most of the recent time I could remember.

I cursed in horror. Every part of me sinking in despair. The tips of two fingers were black, and I knew I was going to lose them—the ends of them at least.

"I can fix this," Elken said.

I didn't believe him, but he rubbed my fingers between his and brought them up to his mouth. He blew hot breath on them. That left me feeling… something confusing. I hadn't been so close to someone since I was down in the hole with the girls and instead of feeling good, it stung. A little reminder: *this is what you won't have anymore if you don't find Niyi.*

When Elken took his hands away, the tips of my fingers weren't black anymore. All the bloody, raw skin was gone. Healed. Completely.

"Ah!" I jumped, not sure if I was about to cry from relief or shock or fear.

Not even any scars, I thought, turning my hands over.

"Not all scars are visible," Elken said.

And I knew I should be really freaked out because this was the second time he'd seemed to guess what I was thinking. Also, he'd just healed my hands, and my recent experiences had led me to be suspicious of beings I met in the wilderness, especially magical ones. But my fingers weren't aching for the first time in a while, and the relief was overwhelming.

My eyes darted around the room to where my mother's spear was standing. I was going to run. I decided then and there. There was no way I could afford to pay for his services. I was going to wait until he'd finished healing the rest of me and then I was going to run with all that I had.

"The bird you're looking for—it's important to you?" he said, taking my other hand out of my sleeve and drawing my mind from my plans.

He said it so innocently that I almost started to nod. Don't worry, I caught myself. The less he knew about me, the better.

"I'm not doing anything—other than waiting, of course, which I guess... that is something. Maybe one of the most important things, really, but maybe the green goddess wouldn't mind if I helped you look.

The trees know I've given her enough of my time lately, and she really likes you. I can feel that already—how fond of you she is."

I stared at the strange boy's face as he ran his healing fingers over my wrist that had been scratched up at some point. Maybe from slipping on the ice back when I'd been chasing the man who'd stolen Niyi.

Elken crouched and took off my boots. My feet were far worse than I'd imagined, worse than any frostbite I'd ever seen. I didn't want him to touch them as they seemed so gross to me, swollen and black and purple and oozing some yellowish gunk from under one of the toenails, but he knelt before me and rubbed my feet between his hands and blew on them, his lips almost touching my toes, and when he took his hands away, every part of me that had rotted was returned. And then Elken rolled my pant leg up and ran his hands along my shin and calf before unwrapping what Ilona had put on, and even that was healed.

"Or if it's one of those searches you've got to do alone, you could just tell me how to find you, in case the one you've lost... in case she comes this way, I can let you know that I found her."

I slid off the stool and backed away from him, pulling my arrowhead from my hair and pointing it at him. *Her.* That's what he'd said. He shouldn't have known that it was a girl I'd lost, and, for some reason, it was him mentioning Niyi that let my awe morph back into fear.

I stuck my left hand into my pocket and pulled out the little vial with teeny Ilona inside. For a moment, I was worried he was the owl-woman tricking me in another way. I needed to see she was still in there and not taking the shape of the guy in front of me.

Elken backed away with his hands raised a little, which made me feel better because it seemed like he was afraid, which meant he probably didn't think he'd fare well if we got into a proper tussle. I also didn't think he'd put up much of a fight.

And before I could demand he explain everything spooky that he'd done in the short time I'd known him, he began to talk.

"A few years back, I felt like I was being told things. Or... rather, not told. That's not right, more like... I suddenly just knew things. I could feel them. Just because. And around that time, my chest got... well—" He took off his coat and opened the front of his undershirt, and it was something kind of familiar to me but completely new at the same time.

Like Niyi's mouth had gone blue, Elken's chest, right around the heart, was green. And the bigger veins leaving the area were green as well; I could see them through his skin.

"At first, I thought I was dying." He laughed. "But then she made me know that I had to come here, that I had to wait for the others, you know, get it ready for them. You feel blue to me. I can't explain it, but you do. I think you'll change colour soon too. I think you're supposed to wait with me."

It was an outrageous and bold thing to say, but it was right in a sense because I calmed down.

"It's not me. It's my sister who has a blue tongue."

"Tongue?"

I nodded.

"And she's what you've lost?"

I nodded again, pressing my teeth together so hard my jaw creaked. I didn't like admitting it. It cut into my heart to think of her all little and alone.

Elken came closer to me then and said, "May I?"

And I didn't know what he meant, but I was emotional and kind of flattered that he would ask my permission at all, because no one asked my thoughts about anything, so I nodded.

He set his hand on my chest (over my clothing, just beneath the neck where the collar bone is—don't make it weird. But also, don't feel too bad because I also wondered for a second what he was up to before I saw his expression change).

He was listening.

The air around us seemed to grow a little more alive—wiggling or waving or dancing as Elken closed his eyes and slowly began to frown. Finally, he opened his eyes and said, "I can't find her... She should be connected to you, but I can't feel her anywhere."

He took a step back from me and closed his eyes again, raising a hand in the air as he listened. The air swelled again. He frowned and then relaxed his face, his eyebrows lifting. You don't normally get to see someone's face like that: all relaxed, without them looking back. His mouth was a little wide for his jaw, but in a pretty sort of way, and his eyebrows were closer to his eyes than normal and tilted down near his temples, making his empty face seem a bit sad. He wasn't as dorky looking as I'd first thought. Not at all.

His eyes shot open, and he looked straight at me, his whole face full of sadness. He said, "I'm sorry. You're not going to find her."

And that felt like another sick, twisted, evil joke. So I slapped him right across the face, even though he'd just healed me. It shouldn't have made me so angry; he was just a strange, stupid guy who could do some sort of healing trick. I probably wasn't actually any better. Maybe he'd just messed with my eyes some. But I think it bothered me because, deep down, I felt like he could be right. How could I find a bird in the tundra? What if she'd changed direction since I'd last seen her? We'd already been apart for so long... How could she not be dead like everyone else?

The more I thought about it, the more I realized he was probably right, so I slapped him again.

SIXTEEN

MY FINGERS STUNG FROM how hard I'd slapped Elken.

I didn't care.

He stood in front of me, looking stupidly confused, blinking while I stuffed my feet into my boots. I heaved those big doors open with a grunt and stormed out of that gorgeous lodge, my mother's spear speeding after me. It nearly whacked my forehead, but I was lucky for once and stooped just in time to avoid the hit.

I made it ten paces before the voice came again.

He's right. You know this.

My mother's spear stopped and stood in the frosty cold, almost as if it expected me to take what

I'd heard seriously, like it didn't think I was insane for hearing a voice at all.

I kept walking, tucking my chin into my chest because the cold wind was already stinging my face.

I didn't want it this way, either. But it's done now.

"Shut up!"

LISTEN.

The voice vibrated into my bones, shocking every part of me all at once. I fell to my knees in the overwhelm of it. The ground was frozen, so it hurt and that was extra annoying as I'd only just been healed.

I guess that's the way it is, though, isn't it? You get these little pain-free moments that last just long enough to remind you what you're missing before the next pain comes.

Go back to the boy. Listen to him; he will help you. Rest. You need to be rested for what comes next.

"I have to find Niyi," I said, trying to sound like I was tough but knowing that I sounded whiney.

She's with me.

My heart stopped. I didn't want to ask what that meant, but I had to. "And where's that?"

Child, a baby blue bird cannot survive out here anymore than a baby human. I am sorry.

My entire body heated in an instant, making the frigid wind feel like nothing on my skin. I shouted at him—the voice, whatever it was. I said, "I hate you!"

Even though it didn't really match with what he'd said before, it was the perfect thing to say because I did hate him. I hated him for telling me something so horrible as that.

Sometimes I hate me too. But that doesn't change what I need you to do.

I scoffed. I wasn't going to do anything for anyone. Ever. Not again—

I didn't want you doing it either, child. It was supposed to be Niyi; that was my plan. But you'll have to do.

And then there was only silence. The empty sort that happens in the snow when the cold sucks all the sound out of the world, and there's just nothingness.

I clenched my teeth and told myself the voice had been lying. Or mistaken.

What does he know? I thought.

I looked around at the vast, empty white to the north, the west, and the south, to the expanse of icy wasteland behind Elken's borrowed temple. I didn't know which way to go to find Niyi. I'd lost sight of her to the west some, but it would be easy to overshoot and miss her if I went too north or too south. I might accidentally take myself farther away from her if I made the wrong choice.

"You need to be clever," I told myself. *The reason this has gone so wrong is because you've been stupid.* "What would papa do?"

My mother's spear stood next to me, swaying a little in the wind. I crouched and thought so hard that my brain hurt. I could figure this out. I was Niyi's sister... I'd know where she would go.

Child, she's gone home. You will not find her on this plane.

The voice's words clawed at the back of my neck so aggressively that I pushed my hood off to let the cold numb it. The wind whistled and licked my scalp and neck. My mother's spear leaned against me, gently nudging my shoulder.

I can show you if you don't believe me.

I choked on the air. Of course I didn't want to see. But at the same time, I had to know.

"I don't believe you," I said, my voice quiet.

Take a deep breath, child, said the voice.

I didn't. I stopped breathing entirely. *Take a breath* was a bad warning; it was the sort of thing an elder said before they pulled out your tooth.

And suddenly, instead of seeing the endless, glittering white before me, I saw a little blue feathered ball coated in frost as the wind washed snowflakes over it.

"STOP," I said.

The vision stopped.

I didn't want to look long enough to know if the blue ball was Niyi. And, if I'm being honest, I didn't need to.

"How can I know it's not a trick?" I said.

If you remain in one place, I'll have the wolves bring you the body.

My jaw felt like ice just about to crack under too much weight.

Go back inside. Your ears are already numb; the boy won't harm you.

The sun was really bright and reflecting off the snow, stinging my eyes, confusing me because it seemed like the world should be dark and miserable just like me. I stood, the wind writhing around the neck of my furs, crawling in through the crevices, chilling my back.

"What am I supposed to do now?" I said.

You're cold. You're exhausted. Child, go back inside. Sleep. I will stay with you.

All I could think about was the little dead bird. Cold and frozen and hard. *Dead.*

My mind emptied into nothingness, and I had no idea what to do with my arms or my legs, so I listened to the voice.

When I came back in, Elken was near the door, lacing up his boots like he was planning on going outside. Knowing him, he'd probably been on his way to find me because he wasn't the sort of person to figure out that if a stranger comes into your home and slaps you after you've tended their wounds, they're probably not the sort of person you should see again if you can help it.

He let go of his bootlaces and stood up straight.

There was a long moment where we just looked at each other, and I was too hollow and floaty-feeling to be bothered by his staring. Normally, I didn't let people look too long without saying something salty because I wanted them to know they didn't get to look at me just because they existed. But my mind was elsewhere—drifting across the tundra like the wind. Why hadn't I considered the idea that Niyi was... well, you know... before? She was a baby. Grown-ups died on the tundra all the time. Babies couldn't even keep themselves alive in a warm home filled with milk and whale meat.

"I drew a bath for you," Elken said finally.

I was too empty to know what that meant.

"It'll take some of the day off you. You'll feel better after."

My thoughts were gone, gone like Niyi. Gone like Preah. Like my parents and Kid. So when Elken started walking down a dim corridor with splotches of colour on the stones from the sun shining through the clear-coloured panes, I followed him. The bath was tucked in a shadow-filled alcove with three little oil lamps set on the floor. Orange flickers of light pranced on the walls and mixed with the steam that rose from the tub.

"You can just use that there to dry off," Elken said, pointing to a fluffy brown cloth. "And I'll go. Like I'll go to the other side of the temple, and I can— uh, I'll hum if you want me to, so you'll know that I'm not near and, you know, watching."

He also gave me "fresh" clothes to wear, which was a new concept for me. I'd never known anyone with enough discs or spare time to end up with two sets of clothing. But this strange guy had two, and he gave one to me, so I didn't have to wear my bloody torn-up furs once I washed.

He set the bundle of cloth into my hands before unhitching a leather that had been tied to the side, so the alcove was closed off and private from the rest of the temple.

And the bath did feel good, I think. But my mind was empty—or maybe it was really full—that was sort of the same thing sometimes. The water grew cold without me noticing the time passing.

Elken hummed off in the distance as he'd promised. I dried and dressed in his clothes that were a little too long in the arms and legs for me but thick and warm and smelling like new snow. And then I came out of the bath-alcove and down the corridor to where Elken was sitting. Waiting. Just waiting for me. That was another thing about him that, depending on my mood, was lovely or terribly annoying; he had more patience than anyone I'd ever met. A stupid amount of patience. Maybe even a dangerous amount of it.

When he saw me, his brows lifted, making a concerned expression that I probably would have brushed off as a tricky performance if I wasn't so depleted.

"You're tired," he said, standing.

I nodded. I *was* tired, so exhausted my eyes were burning as he led me to a room that had a soft, lumpy thing to lay on and several furs.

"Just call out if you need anything," he said.

I nodded as I crept into the furs, burrowing under them as if the warmth and softness could ease the brutal hopelessness at the edge of my blank mind.

"I'm Elken, by the way," he said quietly as he stood in the doorway, just about to close the door.

And I nearly said, "I'm Crab," because that's what I'd been called for so long. No one but Kid had called me by my real name since my parents died.

"I'm Katya," I said.

SEVENTEEN

I THINK IT WAS one day, but it could have been two or five or ten that passed in the hole that was my emptiness; my brain was too numb to count them. If your mind hasn't shut off before, it's kind of like leaving your thoughts out in the cold for too long. They get slow and don't make sense anymore, starting and trailing off before they get where they're going.

Elken, for the most part, kept to himself.

I stayed in bed, in the hewn-stone room on the southeast side of the temple. It had a flower-shaped hole carved into the wall above where I slept, with the same panes that the main room had, only instead of scenes depicting people with poor footwear choices, it was full of blood-red flowers, their stems all wavy and twisted together in a never-ending circle. As the sun moved across the sky outside, the teeny red petals of light crept across the stone wall.

Elken brought me something to eat—lichen and herb stew in a wooden bowl.

I didn't touch it. No way was I about to accept food from someone I didn't know. Not again. Besides, I wasn't hungry. And even if I were, I didn't want to feel the burn in my stomach that would come from forcing myself to eat.

"I can make you something else if you don't like it," he said when he came to collect the first untouched meal. "As long as it's something I can find out here. That isn't much I'll grant you, but..."

I said nothing, keeping my eyes shut like I was asleep.

It's safe to eat, child.

Still, I said nothing.

"You'll let me know if you need something?" Elken said the second time he came, another bowl of stew in his hands. "I'm just in the main hall there, making paint."

The third time Elken entered the room, he brought a bucket of steaming water and a rag and started scrubbing at the impossibly large blue-grey stone slabs that made up the cold, smooth floor.

The squishing sound of him ringing the rag out and pressing it into the floor disgusted me and I reached my hands out of the thick tuft of furs, scrounging around for my boot which I threw at him.

He picked up his bucket and the rag and darted out of the room quicker than I'd seen him move yet, so quickly that if I weren't a hollow shell, I probably would have laughed.

He didn't try cleaning the room I was staying in again, but I watched him cleaning the hall through the open door, sweeping and then scrubbing on his hands and knees, my mother's spear hopping behind him eagerly, like it preferred being his pet more than mine. Which was probably fair; I mean, everything I'd ever tried to take care of was dead or sold, so...

Elken looked up at me as I watched him, and I quickly shut my eyes. He didn't need to be getting any ideas about me finding him even the least bit interesting.

He hesitantly came in again sometime later. I was facing the wall, but I knew he was hesitating because his steps stopped and started a few times before he spoke, his voice quiet and gentle, like he was trying to be delicate. "I've got fresh clothes for you, and a bath... if you want—"

I said nothing and didn't get up because I wasn't really a person anymore. Knowing someone you loved isn't living—that's bad. But knowing you maybe could have stopped it if you'd been more clever or quick or strong or hadn't eaten the hag's food—that was a different type of suffering.

"Do you need anything else?" he said.

I need papa back, I thought. My father wouldn't have eaten Ilona's food. He would have known.

"Does anyone *else* need anything?" he said.

I rolled over, prepared to yell at him for being stupid, but then I caught his gaze, his golden-brown eyes full of concern, his brows pushed together in concentration. I glared at him until he backed away.

When Elken came back once more, he had that hardened sort of expression people get when they're about to demand something—like an outrageous price for a scrawny fish—when they've decided they're going to get their way whether you like it or not. His fists were balled up at his sides, but he spoke gently.

"I would like to see the woman," he said.

I shut my eyes, not really caring if he believed I was asleep or not.

"She's suffering," he said. "I can feel it no matter how far away I'm sent to paint."

I sighed. "I don't know what you're talking about. Are you sure you're not just crazy?" I knew that was the right thing to say because I was good at being mean. One of the first things he'd said to me was something about people calling him crazy. I could tell it was something that stung him extra, like when people said I should fix my face.

He blinked, I think a little surprised by the hurt I'd caused him, before he frowned, trying to look firm but mostly failing. "The woman in your pocket. She's starving. It's hurting me to have her like that."

Now, given all that I've just told you, I probably should have been a lot nicer to Elken, seeing as he was a stranger who was taking care of me even though he didn't have to at all. And not only was he taking care of me, but he was doing it better than maybe anyone ever had. Even me. Again, I wasn't a person at this time, so I wasn't nice about it. I told him off in every way I could think of. Seal-fucker. Whale-crust. Bear-slack. All the names.

He huffed, and I could tell by the sound he was working himself up to make his demand again. "Let me feed her at least, and then she can go back in your pocket."

Not a chance, I thought. Ilona deserved to go hungry—it was kind of perfect actually; she wanted to cook me in a pot and probably eat me. Hunger was a fitting punishment.

"She's going to die," Elken said.

It was my turn to huff because as much as I loved the idea of Ilona dying, I kind of wanted her to live a little bit longer. However much it was my fault that Niyi was gone, it was Ilona's fault even more. I wanted her to starve, and I wanted to squish her; I couldn't have both those things. But I also knew that when my mind was going quick again, I might have a better idea of what to do with her—a way to make it worse for her, as bad as possible, as scary as possible.

I sighed and dug around in my pocket, plucking the vial out and presenting it to Elken.

He reached for the little glass bottle, but I pulled it back with my brows raised. "You can feed her right here in front of me before I put her back."

Elken let out a big breath, nodding before rushing away to prepare something for Ilona. When he came back, he sat at the foot of my bedding and took the little vial from me gently, clearly trying his hardest not to shake it or hurt her in any way. He sprinkled tiny, chopped lichens inside that he dipped in water first.

As Ilona ate and drank, Elken's jaw relaxed; his shoulders settled.

Before I opened my mouth, he answered my question.

"Sometimes."

I was going to ask if he felt what other people were feeling.

"Why don't I keep her for a while?" Elken said. "I won't let her escape, not until you're ready—"

"No way," I swiped the vial back in the time it took him to blink. He closed his hand far too late, making me a touch sad. His reflexes were slow, way too slow for someone living alone on the tundra.

I jammed the stopper back on the vial with Ilona in it and tucked it into my pocket, making sure to shake it as I did, hoping Ilona slammed her head off the side of the vial just like I'd hit my head on her stupid cauldron.

Elken's mouth compressed into a straight line, his brow furrowing.

Sorry, I thought, remembering what he'd just said about feeling other people's feelings. I wasn't going to apologize out loud. I didn't want this skinny guy thinking he could expect kindness from me; I didn't want to owe him anything, or at least not any more than I already did.

He swallowed; the bob in his throat was just beginning to show like a grown man's. He looked miserable, maybe even a little sick, and I grew embarrassed. "Can you... or... how I'm feeling right now..."

Elken nodded, clenching his teeth so tight that his jaw looked square. "It would—I mean, you've got to go at the speed that you've got to go—but if you stopped, um, pushing the feelings away from you... that would help. A little."

I frowned, not knowing at all what he meant. *No way,* I thought. No way could I feel responsible for Elken's sadness on top of my own. That was stupid. And not how the world worked. Even though I thought this, I felt guilty. A bit. Like the smallest shred.

"That bath still hot?" I said.

And when I was clean and dressed, I came back to the domed room to find Elken in the middle of washing the furs that I'd been nesting in, dunking the thick bundle into a bucket of steaming water, scrubbing at it with a little brush, his knuckles glowing red from the heat of the water as steam spiralled into the cold air.

Liar, I thought. There was no way he could manage that work if he felt the same way I did.

"I've had practice," he said, without looking up at me.

I'm not going to feel sorry for you, I thought.

But I did. I watched him wash the bedding and ring it out and hang it up to dry near the fire, noticing how often he winced, thinking, *What are you doing you idiot? You really shouldn't be this nice to people. You're going to wind up at least robbed. Probably dead.*

Seriously, why was he washing my bedding? That's an outrageously kind thing to do for a stranger. Especially one that had been acting the way I'd been.

When he was done, he turned and looked at me with a sigh—not a frustrated one, a friendly one. He said, "I was going to go for a walk. Do you want to come?"

I told myself to say no, but I said, "I guess."

We bundled up into our furs and wandered in silence, the ice crunching beneath our boots as the wind blew sheets of glistening snow around our ankles.

I moved slowly, exaggerating my steps because my legs were sore and tingly from spending so much time lying down.

Elken kept pace with me even though walking faster would have kept him warmer. The spear hopped after us in a lazy way, like she (I don't know why, maybe because it had belonged to my mother, I felt like it was a *she*), but she moved like she wasn't too worried about anything going wrong. I wasn't worried either, really.

"I'm going to climb the ridge there," Elken said, stopping and pointing to a rocky outcrop where a few stiff branches poked out of the glittery snow. "To check for herbs."

I snorted. "Good luck with that." No herbs would grow this time of year. *This guy is going to die out here*, I thought. Even the stupidest child in Kettin knew to conserve their energy for things that actually might produce results. It took a lot of energy to keep a body warm.

The corners of Elken's mouth perked up. "You don't have to come."

I scowled. "Don't tell me what I do or don't have to do."

His grin got bigger.

I watched as Elken wandered toward the outcrop, becoming a little grey speck in the snowy white before clamouring up in a clumsy, sporadic way, slipping several times, my mother's spear standing next to me, almost as if she was watching him as well.

Yes, I thought. *He's definitely going to die.*

The back of my neck prickled.

The voice said, *There is a lot we need to speak about.*

EIGHTEEN

THE WIND WHIPPED MY dry cheeks as I squinted into the blistery cold, looking for any hint of where the voice had come from, my mother's spear planted in the snow beside me. I was finally rested enough to really think for a moment about what the voice was, about what it had said to me before.

I need your help, it said.

I don't care, I thought, realizing suddenly that I had a lot to say to this voice. My mind had been dull when we'd spoken last, but it was sharper now, and I could remember stories my mother had told me. I could remember what the elders had spoken about.

"You're the Skyfather?" I said, my voice full of salt.

The voice sounded amused. *If you want to think of me that way, you can, but not really, no.*

"But you're a god? Like, you're in the place where people go when they die?"

Sort of.

"But you can *do* things. Like fix things or change them?"

Again, sort of.

"And you picked Niyi, but you still let her die?"

I don't choose what people do. What animals do. Or plants or clouds or water or stone.

I could feel the vibration of his voice in my ribs. It felt like he was climbing inside me somehow—trying to comfort me—and I didn't like that at all.

"But you're supposed to know things, right? Why'd you pick Niyi? If you knew how it was going to go? And WHAT ABOUT PREAH? It wasn't an animal that did that. It wasn't anything!" It felt good to yell at him. No one deserved it more, I thought.

Preah did that. She put things in her ear to stop what your mother did. Blame isn't worth anyone's energy, but if you want to blame someone, it would be your mother, not me.

I hated him so much I felt sick to my stomach; it was like simply holding the thought of him in my mind was poisoning my blood.

I chose your mother because... she was the easiest route. She was close to death, partly here with me, partly there with you—I only touch what is here with me. But she sensed what I did to her. She knew what she could pass on, and instead of giving it to just Niyi, as I'd expected, and perhaps Hemi if I needed a second, she gave it to Preah and Hemi and your father. Everyone but you.

I knew then that he was talking about the hours leading up to my mother's death and how she'd fed everyone with her body. And how I'd been the only one too shy to agree.

Preah's ears were—you don't have words for this yet— Preah's ears were like Niyi's tongue. And she didn't like being able to hear so well, and that's why she stopped talking. She didn't like how her own voice sounded once your mother changed her ears.

"And Kid?" My heart began to race just thinking about him. The dimples in his cheeks when he smiled.

Ha. He's... you needn't worry about him. At least not now.

"But he's living? And he's well?" Hope expanded within my chest like a flower opening up for the four days each year when it was really and truly sunny.

Better than well. He's eating dinner right now. A thick soup. He's laughing with the captain. One of the men on board thought he saw a mermaid, only Hemi saw it too, and he called it a fat-sea-wolf, and the captain liked this.

I clenched my teeth. It shouldn't have hurt to hear such a lovely thing, but it did. It made me feel alone but also worthless because I'd not really laughed with Kid that much nor fed him as much as I'd wanted to, and I was happy he had nice things, but I wished I'd been the one to give them to him, you know?

"Where is he?" I said, swallowing to keep my voice from sounding teary.

I'll go to Kid, I thought. *That's right. That's what needs to happen.*

Best leave him be, the voice said.

"What? No. He's... he needs me."

No. He doesn't.

I wasn't even fully paying attention. I'd started back to the temple hoping Elken had some preserves I could take before leaving. I had no idea how big the sea was or how to look for someone on it because ships didn't leave tracks as far as I could tell, but I could get back to Kettin and wait for Kid to find me. All ships came back to land. He'd want to see me—

He won't go back to Kettin, child.

"What? Why?" I screamed into the sky, having completely forgotten that it was strange to speak to something you couldn't see.

To hear about him. *Kid*. To picture him laughing. My body felt like it was mine again.

Because I need you here. You'll be safe here. Protected.

I wasn't going to listen—the voice said he couldn't choose what people did. I kept walking.

I said I don't *choose what people do. I never said I couldn't.*

That stopped me for a moment.

"So you *could* have saved Niyi then? But you didn't?"

Save is the wrong word. If anything, saving people would be bringing them here to be with me.

I'd had enough.

Where are you going?

"Away from you!" It was a childish thing to say, but I couldn't think of anything else.

Stop.

The power of his voice made my blood ring and vibrate. My jaw tightened as the tension of it pulsed through my ears, down my neck, grinding into my spine. His words somehow created real force in the air, like ice bricks stacked atop my shoulders.

Please, child, you've suffered enough. Just do as I ask.

"And what's that?"

Wait here for the others. Take your sister's place. When they arrive—

Of course, I didn't listen to him. I hated him. I hated everything.

Please, you won't like what will happen next. I have vowed not to interfere.

My mother's spear gained on me, moving to block my path, pressing against my shoulders as the rumbling voice that came from everywhere made my teeth feel like massive caverns full of echoes. The spear slowed me, but that didn't matter. I'd go slowly if I had to, digging my toes into the frosted ground and pushing forward. Digging again and pushing again, the spear gradually moving in the direction I wanted to go.

I was done with it all. Everything that had happened. I'd go wait for Kid, and then something would be alright again.

Or at least, that was what I thought would happen.

Instead, the sky began to fall.

Not as in the actual sky was coming down, clouds and all, but hail chunks slammed down with such a force that I could barely see anything a few paces in front of me. The whole world grew white in a cold, blurry instant. Hunks of ice crashed into my shoulders, my back, my legs. The whoosh of the wind circled around me, and the little clicky sounds that ice chips make when they hit frozen ground drowned everything else out.

My mother's spear struck me twice before I fell, and I think I shouted at her, but I couldn't hear my own voice over the drumming of it all. I curled up, unable to bear the pain of it, my arms crossing over my head to protect my skull.

And then I felt something I couldn't have expected, something that maybe changed how I thought about people and what they would or wouldn't do.

There was a sudden end to the pain. Not an end to the storm—I could still hear the rage of the sky, only there was something between where I was curled up and where the ice was coming from. It was warm, and its mitten-clad hands covered my head to keep me safe from the pellets of sharp ice.

It was Elken.

He'd been far away when the storm started. He hadn't needed to come looking for me. He could have bolted for the temple where he'd be safe from the stinging grazes of countless ice pebbles.

I couldn't understand it. We weren't family. He didn't owe me anything. Actually, I probably owed him quite a lot. It made such little sense to me that I was angry—I guess because it made me feel stupid to not understand something so entirely.

The storm ended just as quickly as it began, and Elken rolled to the side all slow and achy and groaning, no doubt sore from the ice beating he'd just taken.

"What did you do that for?" I shouted.

He looked at me, blinking twice as his eyes adjusted to the greying light that came after the storm, one brow already swelling from the battering he'd taken from the hail.

Elken winced as he poked at his bloody lip with a finger. "She told me to take care of you."

NINETEEN

MY HEART TWISTED IN my chest as I peeked around the corner.

Elken was sitting at the other end of a narrow hallway, my mother's spear standing attentively at his side, again like she was watching him. We'd separated once we got inside, so we could dry off, and then I'd followed the sound of him humming until I found him.

The entire western wall of the hallway was made from interconnected arches filled with ice-clear panes, and the sunset outside coated the stone floor in a pink colour. It made the sight of Elken at the end of the hall seem dreamy and magical and not at all like the beginning of a very annoying conversation that I didn't want to have but felt like maybe I should.

I took a breath and approached, trying to keep my steps from echoing, trying to draw as little attention to myself and this whole stupid situation as possible.

As I got closer, I saw that Elken was darning a rip in his furs, a rip that must have been the result of the ice pellets that hammered him during the storm. He was wearing only his under shirt, the sleeves rolled up to his elbows, a hint of green showing near his collarbone.

When I got close, I crouched and crossed my arms over my knees. "Thank you... er, for coming to get me in the storm or whatever."

Elken kept his bruised face pointed down, staring at his work. "You're welcome," he said, in a tone that was just a little too smug for my liking.

I rolled my eyes. "Don't feel too good about yourself. It was still a stupid thing to do."

He looked up at me, fighting with his smile for a moment, the corners of his mouth lifting and then being forced down, like he thought what I'd said was funny but he didn't want to laugh at me because maybe he knew I wouldn't like it. His need to smile sort of dared me to smile and it took some effort to keep the scowl on my face.

"Did you know you could do that?" he said.

I frowned. *I only said thank you. That's not such a big thing.* I was capable of being polite. I just didn't have the energy for it most of the time.

"The storm," he said, his eyes narrowing playfully as he watched me react to his words.

I glared at him, hoping to make him feel as foolish as he was making me feel.

It didn't seem to have any effect; Elken kept being Elken, all enthusiastic and friendly. "You made the storm, didn't you?"

"No."

"Huh... it just didn't feel... Like it wasn't a normal storm. It felt blue... kind of like you." Elken scratched the back of his head as he frowned, chewing on the corner of his mouth, the light growing dimmer by the moment, the sky through the panes outside turning purple.

"I think it was the Skyfather," I said.

"Who?" said Elken.

It wasn't me, said the voice.

I sighed. "The man people think lives in the sky. The one who ignores us when we need help."

Elken frowned. "Never heard of him."

And that made me feel better than I could remember feeling in recent days because it seemed to me the Skyfather wasn't worth hearing about. And it was nice that something actually was the way I felt it should be, you know? That didn't happen a lot.

You can keep calling me Skyfather if you like, but I know the name makes you angry because of Equah. You can call me something else.

"But you can do something, right?" Elken said. "Something other people can't do?"

He was even more foolish looking than usual that night—one eye was swollen and bruised, almost certainly from being struck with a ball of ice on my behalf. His cheek was scratched up as well, leaving the raw sort of skin that makes you feel a little sore yourself just from looking at it. As I stared at the jagged pink flesh, I wondered why he hadn't just healed it, because that was something I'd seen him do.

"She doesn't want me to," Elken said.

I still was nowhere near comfortable with having my feelings addressed when I hadn't said anything aloud, so I scowled and said (aggressively), "What?"

He shrugged. "She—the green goddess, I mean—she doesn't want me to heal myself."

"Why?" I said.

He shrugged again. "I didn't ask."

That made things a bit awkward because I couldn't understand why he didn't ask. I know now it's called faith and has to do with how much Elken trusted the green goddess—his belief that the way she wanted things was the best way for them to be. But I couldn't make sense of it back then, being so doubtless, I mean.

I looked around the hall, tapping my fingers on my knees, fighting with myself about whether I should make fun of him for it or not.

I settled on saying, "Well, don't you think you should have?"

Elken smiled and the smile made me... I don't know. It made me feel better about myself. I know that doesn't make any sense, but it felt like he was enjoying me, enjoying hearing what I was saying even if I was basically criticizing him. And I guess that makes sense because he'd been alone for so long. I probably should have ignored it, but it wasn't the sort of reaction I was used to getting from people, so I couldn't. My cheeks got a little warmer.

"Maybe," he said. "But I have trouble being so direct, I guess... I can feel her, only it's not words we use. Well, you know already; she's reached out to you too, right?"

I looked at him in confusion wondering if all that time I'd spent with slow, frozen thoughts had permanently damaged my ability to follow a conversation. "Why would you assume that?"

Elken pointed to his neck as a way of drawing my attention to *my* neck. He said, "You've got—"

I felt around my throat. There was nothing unusual as far as I could tell. Just cold fingers touching slightly less cold skin.

"No, you won't feel it like that, I don't think. At least, I don't. But maybe it's different for different people or different colours. You're turning blue a little. On your neck there. Were you given no guidance?"

You were near death. When you slept on the tundra, the voice said. *I gave you this—*

I leapt up and marched to the clear panes—I'd already noticed I could see myself in them at night. Of course, the sky outside was growing a darker violet by the second, so all of me looked indigo in the reflection, which defeated the point. I stuck my chin up and gazed down my cheeks, studying my reflection.

There was a bit that was a little darker than the rest—my throat and the very edges of my jaw—but I knew I wasn't getting a real sense of what colour it was. I saw my messy orangish-red curls bursting out of my bun, frizzy rings sticking out all over the place and dangling across my brow, and my almost-invisible eyebrows, and my way-too-big wind burnt cheeks. It sort of felt like being jabbed in the chest. I know it doesn't really matter what you look like—it's more important to be good at hunting or fishing or be the kind of person that other people can't push around too much. But at the same time, it hurts to not look the way you want to look.

"You've had no like... knowledge shared? About the blueness?" Elken said with what sounded like genuine concern in his voice.

Elken was easy to talk to. And even though I wasn't the sort to explain myself, I was a bit overwhelmed by the voice and the non-stop terror of the last little while.

"I heard a voice," I said. "It said to stay here and wait for the others."

Elken's back went as straight as a spear. "You heard her voice? Like her *actual* voice? In your ears?"

I nodded, wondering if I should tell him the voice didn't sound at all like a woman.

"Did she say anything else?"

"My sister's dead."

It was quiet. I hadn't said it like that yet—out loud and so plainly—and even though it didn't feel as bad as I'd expected it would, I knew there might just be a delay in the sting of it. My father's death had been like that. I was too surprised to really feel bad about it until later.

"Do you want to talk about her?" Elken said. "Your sister, I mean."

I shook my head.

The wind outside whistled as it raced passed.

"So you'll be staying then?" Elken said, his eyes growing so bright with eagerness that it was hard to pretend I didn't notice. My mother's spear jumped a little beside him, like she was agreeing that it was a fantastic idea for me to stay.

And for a second it was nice that someone wanted me somewhere, but that faded pretty quickly. I needed to find Kid, or at least be somewhere he could find me, and that meant I needed to figure out how to deal with another storm from the Skyfather (because I didn't believe for a second that he didn't cause it). I needed to find a way to deal with my mother's spear as well.

I could just chop her up, I thought, knowing that I didn't want to do that.

But just in case the voice was listening (and maybe also a little bit because Elken's eyes lit up so sweetly when he'd mentioned me staying) I couldn't bring myself to say, "No," right to his face, even if he was old enough to know he shouldn't put his hopes onto a person like that. Especially a person he knew so little about. Especially one that had slapped him and brought a whole hailstorm to his door.

Instead of saying: *stop being so stupid and hopeful*, I shrugged and said, "I don't know yet."

I mean, I needed to be somewhere as I figured out how to withstand a god-voice-storm. Ideally a place that would keep me out of the wind and cold. I needed to eat and have a few more full night's sleeps. I hadn't had much of that since my father died and I'd been the one waking up with Niyi. But also, Elken was basically the only stranger who'd ever been nice to me, and I wasn't scared of him at all, so it seemed like a good place to wait while I figured everything else out.

Just for a few days, I told myself.

But I stayed a lot longer than that.

TWENTY

SO I WAS PLANNING on leaving.

And as I saw it, I only had two things to figure out before I did: my mother's spear and whatever-his-name-was—the voice from the sky that was maybe the Skyfather but maybe not. I'd already made peace with Elken, or as good of a peace as was needed to keep him from interfering. Maybe he'd even help me. He seemed stupid enough to waste his efforts doing something that didn't benefit him at all and actually would probably make things harder for him because then he'd be all alone again.

My stomach twinged.

I can't worry about this silly guy right now, I told myself. And even if I did, I knew it was still early winter. That meant things were going to get a lot colder, and Elken was probably going to die. I know he said he'd been living on the tundra for three years, but maybe the temple had been full of supplies when he'd arrived, or maybe he'd just been lucky so far. I mean, a fish once jumped right out of the water into my father's lap. And really, the only way a guy like Elken could possibly have lived this long out here alone was if he'd been lucky.

Focus, I told myself.

I'd been snooping around Elken's temple all morning, peeking into rooms, digging through trunks, looking for something that could help me deal with another hailstorm should the Skyfather send one my way when I set out.

It wasn't me, said the voice.

I was also ignoring the voice because I had enough problems, thank you.

And, at the same time, I was falling in love with the temple because it was even more cleverly put together when you started really looking at it. So, since this might be my last chance to study a building that was so magnificent, I wasn't going my fastest.

My mother's spear hopped behind me, the little *put-put* sound echoing through the corridors of the gorgeous structure. It felt like she was watching me, like she knew I was waiting for the chance to get away from her. But I'd noticed that she seemed mighty interested in Elken and sometimes let me get a little further away from her when he was near.

He'd left that morning to paint the snow saying, "Red is next, I'm thinking," and I'd said nothing because I had decided not to care about what he was doing, and mostly I was looking forward to being able to go through the temple without Elken seeing.

My mother's spear had watched him go, losing a little of the energy she had in her hop once he was gone.

"If you like him so much, why don't you go after him?" I said.

The spear said nothing of course, because it was a spear. And honestly, it was a bit ridiculous that I was talking to it at all.

I figured that once I had my storm supplies, I might have to play along with the Skyfather's game, so the spear would relax a little. Maybe if I seemed like I wasn't going anywhere, she'd follow Elken out to paint the next day or the one after that, giving me a decent head start. Maybe she'd settle enough that I could slip out of a room and shut the door behind me. I was pretty sure she couldn't open a door without hands.

I came upon one of my bone buttons that I'd left first thing in the morning with the suspicion that the temple was all connected inside like a big ring. I'd been right. I was back where I'd started my search, and while I'd found dried herbs, a little oil, four extra furs, and a shiny metal bowl that seemed too thin to carry hot food in without burning my hands, there wasn't as much as I'd been hoping.

In my search, I'd seen what I was pretty sure was Elken's room and had left it alone thinking it might be gross or weird and maybe it wasn't something I wanted to see. And whatever, maybe I felt a little bad about stealing right from the room he slept in, but now that I knew there wasn't much the temple could offer me (I'd really been hoping for a decent-sized piece of leather that I could stretch out and hold above me as I walked to keep the hail from battering my skull in), I knew I had to go in.

I peeked out of a paned window in the direction Elken had gone for his painting—south—and saw no sign of him returning across the wispy white land before going back to the room that I'd figured was his because it had bedding and a little sack in the corner.

The sack was threadbare and floppy, but I dug around inside anyway finding a human tooth, a green strip of cloth, and a wooden carving of a dog. Disgusted by the tooth, I put the sack back where I'd found it. Then I lifted the furs on his bedding, feeling along and under them for anything of value hidden inside. Elken didn't seem clever enough to hide something in his bedding, but I wasn't going to take the risk and not check.

If there's discs, I won't take them, I told myself, not really sure if that was true or not; I just needed to feel like I wasn't being extra horrible, you know? Only as horrible as I needed to be.

There was nothing hiding that I could find.

I spent a few moments trying to pull the furs as taught as they'd been when I'd come in, getting frustrated pretty quickly because it wasn't working.

I'd just stepped out of the room with my mother's spear close behind me and slid the door shut quietly when I turned and found Elken looking at me, a smear of red on his cheek, a brush in one hand, a bucket in the other, his gloves stuffed poorly into his pocket so that they looked ready to topple out at any moment.

"I—" There wasn't anything I could say; he'd seen me come out of his room.

His brows came together. "If you need something, you know you can just ask, right?"

"I know," I said, scowling.

And then it was awkward for far too long, or maybe it wasn't long at all, only feeling awkward makes a moment seem like it lasts a year? I don't know. Elken broke the silence.

"Are you hungry?"

I was. And I'd found the herbs and lichens and stock when I was scouring the temple, but I hadn't made anything with them because I was more focused on finding what I needed for my journey home.

"I was going to cook," Elken said. "If you wanted to join me."

So I sat on a stool as Elken cooked, and it's not that important, but it was really annoying, so I need to tell you that Elken cooked SO slowly. It was like he was in love with each part of it, like he wanted to marry cooking. Each cut he made into each single lichen strand, every herb he crushed or chopped was given his full and gentle attention. He cleaned between each step as well. So I sat on a stool beside the ledge he used to prepare things, being miserably hungry as he moved as slow as the moon. A few times, I even caught his lips moving as he did it.

"You're whispering to the lichens?" I said in a judgemental voice, wanting him to know that I thought what he was doing was embarrassing.

"I'm praying," he said, not looking up from his work.

"Praying?" I snorted. "For what? The ability to cook faster?"

He looked at me then, his face open and sincere and not at all bothered by my comment. "For each thing that had to die so we can live."

There's not really anything you can say to something like that, I don't think. So I said nothing, even as the brick of frozen broth he'd thrown into his pot melted into soup and my stomach roiled in desperate hunger.

Eating went probably exactly how you would imagine. I kept my head close to my bowl but my eyes on Elken. He ate ridiculously slow and kept looking at me and then away awkwardly, and I spent the whole time wondering if I was about to be ordered to die in some awful way because this was the first meal I'd taken from Elken. And I was sick with anticipation because I guess eating was now a scary thing for me, but I also knew that I wouldn't be able to move fast across the tundra if I didn't have at least a little energy.

"If you're going to stay…" Elken scratched at the table. "There's something I should tell you now, upfront, before too much time passes and it becomes kind of terrible that I haven't said anything—"

"What?" I sat up straight, looking directly at him, my tone hard as frozen rocks, but my chest feeling oddly light with relief. Of course there was something bad about Elken. No one was as nice as him. Or as strange. I pushed my bowl away from me even though there was still some soup inside and I really wanted it.

Elken set his elbows on the table and then he took them off and the longer he hesitated, the more certain I became that something awful was coming.

Elken cleared his throat. "Well, I've been... um, doing something that... if you were just passing by wouldn't have been too bad, but if you're here now for a while, you might not—"

"Just say it," I said, feeling my face go blank, preparing to hide whatever I was about to feel.

He took a breath. "Well, I've been taking away—or lifting your, uh, suffering, I guess. Like how I fixed up your hands, I've been holding your feelings so they're not so heavy for you."

"That's it?" I snorted. "That's your big secret?" I almost laughed. He looked *so* bothered by what he was saying. And what he was saying was complete foolishness; no one could help anyone else with their feelings. But I could tell by the look on his face that he really believed he was doing that. I said, "You can keep them. No charge."

"Well, that's... I mean, I can, for a while, but they want to go home. It's not going to get any better for you if they just keep being as they are, sort of ignored and... sad."

I frowned. "What are you trying to say?" I said, "You trying to rub in my face how sad I am?"

"What? No—"

"Really, cause it seems like that's what you're doing," I said. "Maybe you're from someplace warm where people are cheery all the time and all that, but here on the..." I almost said, 'lakes around Kettin,' but then I realized I didn't know where I was. "Tundra," I continued. "People have to struggle sometimes."

His brows lifted. "How'd you know I wasn't from here?"

"How could I not know?" I said. "You walk on the snow like you *want* to be blown over backwards. Like you've never stood on anything slippery in your life. *And* you said you got here three years ago."

Elken pressed his lips together. "Well... maybe you can help me with the snow-walking. I only wanted to say that I was sorry for messing with your feelings, because they're yours and I won't—"

"I don't care," I said. "If you want to apologize for something, you can apologize for wasting my time with such a stupid conversation." I don't know why I was this mean to him either. Maybe I was bothered because he seemed to think he wasn't as nice as I thought he was and maybe that meant I was foolish and in a lot more danger than I'd realized. I mean, I was, but not for the reasons I was thinking at the time.

He sat there quietly for a few moments, looking guilty. He stuck his hands into his pockets and leaned to one side, like he thought by changing which way his shoulders were pointing he could change the way our conversation was going. "But I guess you're right in a way," he said. "It is warm where I'm from. Only, you were wrong about the cheery part. People get sad everywhere."

And that's how Elken and I started talking about his home which was very far away from the sound of it. And I did pull my bowl back to me and finish the soup while I was listening, and when I was done and still hungry but not wanting to ask for too much because maybe what was in the pot was for tomorrow or the next day, Elken poured more into my bowl, and I finished that too.

That was the day I learned that there were different ways of doing things depending on where you lived. I'd never considered the idea before, but nothing in Elken's village was the same as in mine. Nothing. He said that where he came from it was always hot and everything was damp, but it never froze and it was all green, and to make music, people would jump on giant pots with the right type of leather stretched over them. The best dancers knew how to make perfect rhythms with only their boots.

"And everyone has at least one cat to scare away the mice."

I didn't understand what a *cat* was no matter how Elken explained it. Because to me it seemed like something that you shouldn't trust at all, let alone keep in your lodge. He even said, "They don't like humans, I don't think. They just use us for food and glare at us."

And even though I was confused by what he was saying, I was even more confused by what we were doing. I might have said more that night than I had in the whole year previous. And I couldn't understand why I kept opening my mouth and asking another question or where the questions had come from or why the answers seemed interesting to me, but it kept happening and Elken didn't seem to think it was weird that we just accidentally spent hours talking about nothing.

We moved to sit near the big oil lamp that he'd cooked over as the day got later and cooler and we were sitting pretty close by the end of the conversation. Closer than I think people who aren't family normally sit. Of course, it had been a while since I'd spent time with people my age with nothing to do, so I couldn't fully remember what was normal. I kept wondering if he wanted me to move away from him a little or if he wasn't that grossed out that we were sharing so much of the same air.

TWENTY-ONE

I'D WOKEN SOMEWHAT EARLY for the first time since I'd stopped sleeping with Niyi in the crook of my arm. Waking before the sun without her crying was sad and terrible and I wasn't quite sure what to do with myself without a baby to feed and no ice to chop, and maybe I was looking for Elken because why else would I go to his room? But I didn't *feel* like I was looking for him, you know? I felt like I was just moving around sort of confused as my mother's spear hopped lazily beside me.

Elken was sitting with his legs crossed and his eyes closed, his palms on his chest, right where his heart was. He was almost perfectly still, and even though I made noise when I approached and leaned against his doorway, he didn't react at all to me being there.

I said, "What are you doing?" and it seemed like I was judging him, but I didn't mean for it to sound like that. It was just how my voice came out of my mouth. Maybe because I'd been pretending I didn't like anything or anyone for such a long time, my voice didn't know how to be any other way.

Elken opened his eyes and smiled a little. "I'm... uh, listening I suppose. Feeling. Just being with the goddess."

"Sounds boring," I said.

"It's not," he said. And then he closed his eyes again and just sat there breathing slowly, looking completely unbothered for a bit. Finally, he said, "I can show you how, if you want."

I snorted which was really embarrassing. "No, thank you."

You might like it, said the voice.

I might like being left alone, I thought back at him.

"Have you noticed the floor kind of sinks in in the middle of the corridors?" I said.

"I expect it's from lots of people walking over it for a long time," Elken said, keeping his eyes closed.

"People's steps can't carve stone."

Elken shrugged. "Water can carve rock, water's softer than boots, right?"

I thought about this for a moment, because it made sense to me but it also still felt impossible.

"There were people here before us," Elken said. "A lot of people. I can feel them sometimes. And there will probably be people here after us."

I'd stopped listening because he'd said *us,* and I hadn't been included in a word like that in what felt like a long time. But I also knew I couldn't just stay there watching Elken do nothing, because even though I hadn't had any friends back in Kettin except for maybe Hallen, I knew it would be weird if I stared at Elken for too long.

So I left, wandering around in the temple, noticing that the archways had two different floral patterns carved into them and thinking that it must have been made by two different builders because the patterns weren't at all alike. Maybe even one builder worked with their left hand and the other with their right.

And then, when Elken had gone out to paint for the day and I felt even emptier than I had when I'd woken, I came across an alcove that I hadn't spent much time in yet because the only thing in it was one large stone square. I ran my fingers across the grey surface, enjoying how perfectly smooth it was, how unreal it felt because nothing in life was that smooth, except for maybe baby cheeks and arms.

I climbed on top of it and sat with my legs crossed just like I'd seen Elken doing earlier, putting my hands on my chest and everything. I even tried to make my face like his had been, but I wasn't doing it genuinely. It was more like I was making fun of him.

It is interesting you chose this place for this, said the voice.

My spine tingled. His voice felt so much louder and closer than usual. I could feel it vibrating in my teeth, in my shoulders and collar bone.

It was built for this purpose. For closeness. People used to pour animal blood onto the stone.

Even though I was a little impressed that a structure could make a voice sound louder, and a bit intrigued because the Skyfather sounded sad when he spoke about the blood, I couldn't show that to him.

I huffed. "Seems like a waste."

They thought it was what I wanted.

"But it wasn't?"

Not truly. I wanted them to know I was here; they thought they had to pay for that—

"And what do you want now?" I said, wondering if I was about to be offered some sort of bargain, if he was trying to make me feel sorry for him so he could get something from me. Pity never worked on me.

I want a great many things, but let us begin with something we have in common. It is my desire that things become easier for you.

I frowned. "So, you turned my neck blue? Because that's actually not—"

The voice felt lighter when he answered, like he'd just finished laughing. *I have done much more than that.*

I sighed. "Just tell me. Explain all of it—the green goddess, the blue throat thing, what we're waiting for—just tell me."

The green goddess?

"Elken's goddess, the one who made his chest green."

In a way, I am his green goddess.

"But aren't you a boy?"

Kind of. I am both and neither.

I had no patience for him or his fancy way of speaking. I moved over to the edge of the stone, ready to leap down and find some other room where he wouldn't be so loud when—

I have given my voice to you. Elken has my heart.

I sat up straight, suddenly VERY interested in what the voice was saying. And it was foolish and not the point of the conversation at all, but there was piece of me that really liked that Elken and I were part of the same thing. That we were connected somehow.

You have my ears too, only you don't use them very much.

I decided he was lying because who would give up something as important as that? Their ears and voice? And how was he living without a heart?

I leapt off the stone.

I've never been living, not in the way you think of it. But also, the way you think of it is incomplete. There is only sleep and awake. I have been awake since the beginning.

"But you're talking so you definitely have a voice—"

I'm not talking aloud though, am I?

Again, I grew still. Now that I was paying attention, his voice didn't seem to be coming from outside my head like other voices. My head started to hurt.

Be still, breathe.

"I don't have to listen to you," I said.

You do not. But you might like to. Elken might like you to. Because you have my ears, I can commune with you quickly. To share with Elken takes much longer.

I wanted to tell him to shut up, but I also figured he was right. Elken probably would want me to listen. And then I wanted to shout at Elken, because he was just a stupid guy, and I shouldn't care what he'd want me to do or not.

I sighed. "I'm not going to take anything you say seriously unless you give me a really good reason for why you'd give away such important things."

For something more important—

"Why can't you give a simple answer—"

Because it is complicated. He sounded frustrated, and I sort of liked that because it made him seem more real, more trustworthy I guess, because he wasn't pretending to be perfect in front of me. And also, maybe I'd been the thing to frustrate him and that was a comfortable idea to me.

It's delicate. There are pieces that mustn't be rushed. And ones that must be. There will be a great divide. When your kind begins to pull iron from the earth, this divide always comes.

I knew a little bit about iron. I'd once seen a man trade nearly a full whale's worth of meat—fat and all—for a single iron blade. It took the sailors four days to cut up the meat in a way that would let it fit onto their ship without tipping it.

Iron is in your blood. Your kind will always find it. But each time you lose it again—each time you forget all that has come before—the witches, most of the animals, the trees, and rivers—they try to hide the iron. They have realized this will not work. They will try something new this time. I will not intervene directly, but I am allowed to answer the questions of those who call for me. I am allowed to touch those nearest death. There is a great moment coming. Much must be prepared. The wolves cannot do it alone.

"I'm not working for you without pay," I said, crossing my arms with the most unimpressed expression I could manage. I'd heard my mother say those exact words more than once, and the more he talked the more certain I was that he had a problem he wanted solved. A problem that didn't seem to have anything to do with me. "And it'd have to be good pay because you're annoying."

He did laugh then. *I pay everyone, whether they do what I ask or not.*

I rolled my eyes.

Yes, there will come a day when I will ask for your help, but it will not be for some time. Use my voice. Play with it. Spend time with Elken. Maybe you'll learn something from him.

I felt like his use of the word 'maybe' was a little smug and I was still pretty certain we were haggling. "Just tell me what you want, and I'll tell you what it costs."

I told you. I want things to be easier for you.

There aren't enough discs in all of Kettin for that, I thought. But then I heard the small side door that Elken used creak open and suddenly I didn't feel like things were so terrible.

I hopped off the ledge and ran to Elken, my boots tapping on the cold stone floors.

"You won't believe it!" I said. "He... or the voice…" You'd think it would take a really long time to explain to someone that they'd been given a god's heart, but Elken understood it right away.

"So only you can hear her, but I can feel her?"

Yes, the voice chimed.
"Yes."

TWENTY-TWO

VERY QUICKLY—ALMOST INSTANTLY—Elken and I fell into a pattern that was pretty comfortable. He'd wake stupidly early and do his quiet-sitting, prayers, and cleaning while I slept. Then he'd go painting or gathering and I would tell myself I was preparing to leave, that I was digging up lichens for the journey home, but then I'd start feeling happy when it was close to getting dark and I knew Elken would be back.

We'd have dinner and talk, and he'd always ask me the same question to pass along to the Skyfather: "Is there anything you want Elken to know?"

No, he is right where he needs to be.

Sometimes I'd tell Elken things I'd figured out about how the temple was built just from looking at it, then he'd close his eyes and feel for the builders who he said lived a very long time ago and tell me whether I was right or not. He'd try to explain the contraptions they used to lift heavy stones up high, but he couldn't. And the whole time my mother's spear would watch us and the Skyfather would listen and answer questions when he was needed and occasionally Elken would encourage me to "be more welcoming to my feelings." I would then make a face that made him laugh, and we'd forget about it because I was sad a lot, but I was also not sad more than I was used to and that felt pretty special.

And then there was a day when Elken had come home early from painting because it seemed like a storm was coming. He laid out a whole bunch of instruments and herbs, and I came to watch what he was doing because I liked watching him. He was mixing powder into paint using a plant oil, which was something I didn't even know was inside plants. In my defence, it took a really long time to make it so it doesn't seem like the sort of thing a person could accidentally discover unless they were told about it. (If you were wondering, he made oil and mixed paint just as slowly as he cooked.)

He said, "I know we haven't talked about her much, but the woman in your pocket... she... do you think it's maybe time to let her go?"

Honestly, I'd mostly forgotten about Ilona. I knew Elken fed her when I bathed and left my outer furs in my room, but he always put her back when he was done and I *had* wondered if she was one of the witches the Skyfather had mentioned. But I didn't want to talk about her. I was too focused on how the toe of my boot was touching the toe of Elken's boot and wondering if he noticed that was happening because how could he not? But also, he didn't seem to be reacting to it at all so maybe he hadn't.

I felt my face going slack and stony, like I was bored out of my mind. My eyes glazed over in that disinterested, unimpressed way that usually got people to stop talking to me. But it was sort of frustrating to me that I made that face (I pulled my boot away from his too). I kept telling myself to stop scowling at him, but I couldn't.

Elken laughed and struggled to keep his mouth straight. "No, Katya. This isn't funny or... it's really serious actually." He cleared his throat as he fought his smile. "You're holding her prisoner, and nothing should, or...I've felt for her... like the energy of her... and prayed for her, and she's too small for us to hear her even if we entered into an agreement with her by going into her space or eating her food. That's how her enchantments work; she needs to be heard to do any harm. Nothing bad will happen if we just let her go."

I said, "It's her fault my sister's dead."

And Elken said, "There's no such thing as fault."

"That's the stupidest thing I've ever heard," I said, my voice gaining that ring that comes when you're not yelling but part of you wants to be, so you're warning the other person with the way your voice sounds to shut their mouth or deal with the consequences.

Elken's tone didn't shift the way mine did. "No, Katya. I mean, I know people *act* like every action is alone and unconnected to other things, and that makes it easier to... live, I guess, but no one chooses to be what they are, or they do, but they don't have the same options as everyone else."

"What are you talking about?" I said, raising my voice. I was offended in a way I can't explain. Maybe because it seemed like Elken was saying my whole sense of the world was wrong, or maybe it was because I didn't hate Elken as much as I was used to hating people and I didn't want that to change because he'd decided to say something stupid.

Elken put down the oil-slick rock he'd been using to press oil from a crumpled purple flower and looked at me, his eyes bright from the fire just behind me. "What happens to us changes the shape of us. Maybe what happened before life does too—I don't know about what comes before being born," he said. "But we give away what we're given. If we're evil or do horrible things... this means we've had horrible things given to us from someone else. But that person got it from someone else and that person—"

It was so foolish I didn't even know how to respond.

"You have a tooth in the sack in your room!" I said with a lot of accusation in my voice, sort of implying that he'd done something awful to the person who'd owned the tooth, like maybe they were dead or something. "A human tooth!"

Elken didn't say the obvious thing which was: "Why were you looking through my stuff?" he said, "Katya, it's mine. We were talking about the woman in your—"

"Why do you keep it then?" I said, making a disgusted face.

Elken sighed. "Because that's one of the ways hags can harm people, if they get a piece of a person, they can do enchantments. I wanted to bury it where no one would find it, but the ground was too frozen to get deep enough." He hardened his voice the teeniest bit, not in a mean way, more in a determined way and honestly it was kind of... I liked that he was someone who didn't give up on things, I guess. "The woman in your pocket—"

"If no one's in charge of the bad things they do or the good things, then there's no point in feeling anything about anyone; nobody's good or bad or anything," I said, feeling like I was maybe making a decent point, and I hadn't planned it or anything. I was just angry, and I wanted Elken to feel wrong for making me angry. "Nothing that we do matters—"

"No." Elken hadn't interrupted me before and my cheeks burned with irritation. "What we do matters more because it's either giving pain or relieving it. You can make a person worse by hurting them or better by healing them. What we do is very important."

And then I got really mad because I felt like I was losing the argument, so I said, "And that's all you're doing with me then? Trying to make sure I'm not getting any worse?" As I said this, I thought of slapping Preah and how terrible that was because she was just a little girl with no parents. "That's all you're doing with me then," I said again, feeling sadder this time in a way that I couldn't explain to myself back then. Now I know I was hurt because I wanted Elken to be spending time with me because he wanted to, not out of pity.

He got still and quiet as he watched me, his head tilted to the side as his gold-brown eyes shimmered. Finally, he shook his head with a little defeated smirk. "No. I have no idea what I'm doing with you, but it's not that."

The air got thick when he said that, sort of like those foggy mornings by the lakes when the water isn't sure if it wants to be up in the sky as a cloud, or down on the ground like a puddle. I stared at him, and he stared at me, and I knew then. I knew that I was in some serious kind of trouble. And I got scared because I didn't like the feeling of it at all. The wanting. The needing. The wishing.

He set his hand on top of mine, weaving his fingers through mine, and at least thirty-nine different responses flashed through my mind at once. I thought about pulling my hand back and saying "Eww," because I knew that would be really hurtful. I thought about slapping him and telling him to keep his hands to himself. I thought of glaring at him until he took his hand away. I thought about kissing the stupid smile off his stupid face. I didn't do any of the things I thought of. I just sat there, letting our hands be together.

"Fine," I said after a long time had passed. "You can keep her in your room and take care of her or whatever, but I don't want her getting away." I still had to squish her once I'd dealt with everything else, which was slowly starting to mean dealing with Elken and the way he was looking at me more than dealing with my mother's spear or the voice-storm that would probably happen again if I tried to leave. Because I knew that the ships wouldn't be coming back to Kettin until the thaw, I could stay a little longer, but that might not be the smartest thing given how my heart was leaping around in my chest just like it had when I'd fallen from the pyramid ledge.

TWENTY-THREE

WHEN ICE SHEETS BREAK off from the mainland, they look like little islands that would support your weight. If they're big enough, they might. But most of the time, they'll tip, and you'll slide into the water where your muscles will harden from the cold and you'll probably die. That's the best way I can explain what was happening with me and Elken in the temple. I was trying to balance on this slippery thing that wasn't going to hold me up forever, and he was already in the water, waiting for me to stop pretending I wasn't going to sink. Or at least I think he was waiting, I can't say for sure what was going on in his head, only that he didn't seem as surprised by what came next as I was.

The day I fell in the water started like a lot of my days started: me watching Elken scrub the floors on his hands and knees even though he'd scrubbed them the day before, and I don't think either of us or my mother's spear even went down the corridor he was cleaning since he'd washed it last.

"Why do you clean so much?" I said, and unlike the other times I'd asked Elken about what he was doing, I don't think it came out smug or salty. It was just a question.

"Well... it's a bit," he made a face I hadn't seen him make before, and because I was good at being mean I knew the face meant that he was uncomfortable talking about it, probably because he'd been made fun of because of it or something.

"I won't laugh," I said.

And then he looked at me for a long time with his brows raised and there was so much happening in his eyes that I felt lost for a second even though I knew exactly where I was.

"It's part of keeping the temple healthy," he said, finally.

"Buildings don't get sick like people," I said.

"They can," Elken said. "Anything can get sick. The air, the sea, the snow..." he trailed off because I'd picked up a rag and dipped it into his bucket. I guess it surprised him that I'd try to be helpful, and that wasn't crazy because it surprised me a little too.

He went back to scrubbing as he talked. "And it's… well, feelings aren't how people think they are; when we feel something, unless we welcome it and respect it, we push it out from our bodies into the air and it floats on forever, coating everything it touches with that feeling."

Every part of me wanted to say: *you can't actually believe something so stupid as that*, but I kept it in because I didn't want to say that at all. It was a beautiful idea, and I wanted to believe it. I wanted to know that my mother's feelings were still in the air, that there was something left of my father and Niyi and Preah.

"Most people don't feel them," Elken said, dunking his rag in the steaming bucket again and ringing it out. "All the feelings, I mean. Well, I think they *can*, but they don't listen with their feelings, so they don't? And it can be good; it can be really beautiful, but it can also be horrible to feel all the pain and need. So that's why I clean, so I can get the feelings off everything and have a sort of normal morning, a few hours at least before you and the hag—"

I threw the sopping rag onto the floor and shouted, "You think I ruin the air?"

"No, no, Katya." He laughed. "I love… what I mean is, I wouldn't change it, and I wouldn't call it ruining. Anything you wanted me to hold for you. I would. Happily."

And no, I didn't let that one word slip into my mind. The L-word. It floated up into the ceiling, and I pretended I hadn't heard it. I pretended so hard that to this day I'm sometimes not sure whether he actually said it.

But it is hard on him, the voice said. *You could make it easier if you listened to what he is saying.*

"How do you know it's not just your feelings messing everything up?" I said.

Elken laughed again. "I mean, sometimes it is, but I try to greet mine and... direct them, so they don't have to—" he waved a hand loosely around the room, "—wander around homeless."

I almost said, "Feelings aren't things you can just talk to like people," but I guess Elken had worn off on me a little by then. I said, "How do you do that?"

"Uhh... it's not something that's easy to put into words. Maybe you could think of it... sort of like making space within? Like how you imagine building a great lodge all the time, imagine building spaces inside you. One room can be for being sad and you can imagine putting in all the things that you need when you're sad, like for me, back home everyone sleeps in hammocks and I always find the rocking really... well, it helps, so I'd put a hammock in my sad room. And I guess sadness and shoulders are sort of linked in my mind so I'd put that room in my shoulders, but you could pick whatever you want—whatever your sadness would like. And when something happens and you feel, you know, like crying, you can lead the part of you that's sad to the room inside and just... let it be what it needs to be—protect it kind of—and when it's done, it'll be on its way. But it'll be different."

I said, "You can't make rooms inside a body; they'd be all gross and bloody."

Elken pressed his lips together. "Yeah, maybe you want to wait a bit before you try. You might—"

I felt like he was implying I shouldn't be doing something and so, naturally, I wanted to do it, because I wanted him to think I didn't care what he thought. I glared at him. "I might what?"

"No... it's just... you've not mourned yet, not really, so there's a lot that has to come. And I think a lot of old stuff that's been waiting to be heard. It'll sting and, well, who knows how long we'll be here? You've got the time to wait until—"

"Until when? You don't think I can do it?"

"No, you can." He set his rag down and stared at me, his warm brown eyes heating my cheeks and chest. "I know you can. Just maybe you're not ready, maybe you don't want to feel all that just yet."

It seemed silly to try building rooms inside my body, but I did it because I wanted to tell Elken how silly it was, and I couldn't do that unless I'd at least tried it. I pictured a furry nest hidden inside the palm of my hand that a teeny version of me—the size of Ilona—could crawl into and hide in. In an instant, my whole mouth tasted like tears and my chest felt like there was an avalanche inside it, and I closed my fist and clenched my teeth and thought, *No more of that.*

When I looked back up at Elken, he was watching me and I felt certain that he understood, and rather than saying "I told you so," like I would have, he opened his coat, which he was wearing because it was pretty cold inside the temple, and somehow, I knew he'd made the space for me. I tucked my arms underneath his arms, and pressed my cold face into his neck and he closed his coat around me, and we just stayed there like that, on our knees, me wrapped up in his coat and arms as I breathed in the smell of him and felt the warmth of his chest through his tunic, and from that point on we were always together.

TWENTY-FOUR

SO ELKEN AND I started spending every second we could together, even if that meant being cold because his goddess had sent him to paint snow, or being quiet and just sitting together in a shadowy alcove because I was in one of my remembering-how-life-had-been-when-I'd-had-a-family moods. Usually though, it meant kissing until my lips were sore.

I know.

I'm stupid.

He's stupid.

But whatever, that's what we did.

What you need to know is that it was around this time that I began to understand what the Skyfather had meant when he'd said: *use my voice*. I hadn't really been thinking about it, other than maybe wondering if the Skyfather liked that I was speaking more to Elken because I never used to talk so much and maybe that was because I hadn't had someone who wanted to listen. But mostly, I was a little preoccupied with this guy who was sitting as close to me as it was possible for a person to sit, so I didn't really think about what my conversations with the Skyfather could mean. Only then Elken brought it up right in the middle of us trying to absorb each other through our skin.

For a second, I thought he was going to make fun of me because I'd made a noise, a humming sound that won't make any sense if you don't know what it's like to kiss and be kissed in a way that makes your whole body feel awake and alive and warm.

He pulled his face away from mine, frowning.

I said, "I'm sorry," because now that we weren't kissing, it seemed odd that I'd made the noise even to me.

"Her voice," he said. "You have her voice."

And I said, "Yes," and made a suspicious face because I'd told him that weeks ago, maybe even a full month ago. Normally Elken was a good listener, so it seemed strange that he'd reacted so late.

"No, it's more like… how I can sense things and heal things… just now, your voice—can you hum again?"

"No." I knew my voice wasn't pretty; people in Kettin had told me a few times and I always hated ritual days when we were supposed to sing as Equah blew incense into our faces because I knew I sounded terrible. I had always moved my mouth like I was singing but didn't let any actual sound out.

"Please?" Elken said, and for a moment I hated him because no one should be able to say one word and change someone else's entire feeling like that.

I sighed and pressed my lips together and made the shortest hum I could. And then I wanted to go back to kissing because kissing Elken was probably my favourite thing that had ever happened to me, but he took my hand and led me to where he cooked. He melted some snow in his big pot and put the water in a bowl, and he was moving pretty fast by Elken standards, so I knew something serious was happening.

He set the bowl on the table before me and asked me to hum again.

I rolled my eyes which made him smile, but then I did as he asked and when I hummed the water in the bowl moved. Little waves lifted and sunk, and then I said, "That's just the air I'm breathing out."

And Elken said, "I don't think it is."

So I backed away and hummed again to prove myself right, only I was entirely wrong.

Tell the water to jump out of the bowl.

My heart sped. "Jump out," I said.

A teeny tidal wave leapt over the edge of the bowl onto the table.

I'm pretty sure my mouth was hanging open and my eyes were big and round like a baby playing peekaboo.

"Jump back in," I said, and the water did just as I asked.

"Move," I told the table, and the table moved.

"Come closer," I said to Elken, even though he was already pretty close to me.

He hesitated. "I mean, I will," he said. "But I... don't think I have to? Not like the water..."

"Bend," I said to Elken's finger.

IT BENT.

My awe and confusion stirred together, and I think because I didn't know what else to do, I got angry with the Skyfather. "Why wouldn't you tell me I could do this?"

The voice laughed, and it was a beautiful laugh but I wasn't in the mood for it. I kept blinking because it felt like my eyes weren't working properly as what I'd just seen shouldn't have been something that *could* be seen.

I left Elken and hurried to the alcove with the odd blood-stone, feeling like if it could make the voice seem louder to me, it might make me seem louder to the voice. He was still laughing, and I could feel the vibration of it in my chest.

Don't be cross, child. You wouldn't have listened if I'd told you, wouldn't have believed. It would have taken longer for you to try it than if you'd stumbled upon it by accident. Besides, this was the more fun way. You haven't had much fun recently.

My heart burned a little in my chest because he was right. I hadn't had any fun at all since my parents died, except for the last little while with Elken. Also, it was really beautiful that the voice wanted me to have fun at all because I'd never thought that was something important before. But hearing him mention it made me feel like it was. It made me feel like maybe he was trying to take care of me. That he actually did want things to be easier for me. And then I had to fight really hard not to cry because I hadn't let myself realize how hard things had been, how impossible it had seemed that things could get better.

And then I prayed seriously for the first time ever, not just mumbling the words because Equah or the other villagers were looking, but because I had something to say, and I thought that I might be heard, and it might actually change things.

I said, "Can you make sure Kid has fun too?"

I can, said the voice.

TWENTY-FIVE

THE FIRST THING I did when I got comfortable with the idea that I could tell things how to be and they'd do as I asked, was plan a nice evening for me and Elken. I'd been pretty terrible to him after all, and sometimes I was still harsh or impatient or even just slow to be nice in return when he was being nice to me. So I made dinner for us that was like the dinners I ate back home—whale meat and the stew my father used to make. I simply asked our dinner to exist. And before Elken got home from painting, I told all the feelings in the air to leave and it would seem they listened because the first thing Elken said when he got back to the temple was, "It tastes… peaceful."

My heart hammered in my chest because I'd never been much good at making people smile, yet here I was, doing exactly that. It felt good, like it was something I could keep on doing, and it was maybe the first time I thought to myself that I could have a life that wasn't a constant struggle.

But the next morning, I got up when Elken did and told the air to get clean and Elken started washing everything by hand anyway.

"But it's clean, isn't it?"

"Yes," he said, smiling. "But I like doing it—the motion of washing, I mean. It's like... an act of love for the temple, for the green goddess. She brought me here. She gave me this place to take care of. I want her to know I appreciate it."

And that night he wanted to cook our food himself from things we'd gathered the slow way and have it be "real."

The next day, I called the clouds. I called to them, and they came. Elken and I were sitting on a ledge that connected two of the beams in the temple, looking out across the sparkling tundra, enjoying the few hours of sunlight we had at midday. I'd told the air around us to be warm, so it was comfortable, and then I'd told the clouds to come. They floated around us, making the whole world seem milky.

I was having a pretty good time. I think Elken was at first too, but then he got all... well... Elken.

"Do you think maybe you should send them back?" he said after a few moments.

I shrugged.

"Like maybe they were doing something up there we don't understand."

I rolled my eyes and sent the clouds back because even though his request was annoying, I didn't like making Elken unhappy because as far as people went, he probably deserved it the least.

But this sort of thing kept happening and finally we had a bit of an argument because we were going to take a bath together and I wanted to heat the water, so Elken didn't have to drag snow to the pot, heat it and carry it to the basin again and again and AGAIN until it was full.

I said, "Just let me do it. Take a break."

And he said, "Have you asked the green goddess about any of this? To make sure you're doing right with it?" And he was Elken, so his voice was soft and warm, but I could tell he was a little frustrated.

I hadn't.

"He said to wait here for the others. To use his voice—"

"Did she give you any instructions? Like things you're not allowed to do with it?"

I shook my head.

"Did you ask? Just to be sure you're not messing up something important? Like where does it come from? The stuff you make, I mean. When you ask a meal to exist is that someone else's meal you're taking? Or something like air turning into—"

"He told me he wanted me to have fun—"

"But do you not think you should ask, just to be safe?"

"I'm only filling the bath," I said, rolling my eyes. "This isn't a big thing."

"Do you not see how lucky you are?" Elken said. It was the closest I'd ever heard him come to yelling. His voice wasn't any louder, but it was firmer. "Thousands of people would give up everything to hear what she has to say. Just ask. Don't you think she might know better than you?"

The Skyfather laughed a little. *Don't be angry with him, child. He's right, in a way, only he's thinking faster than you. These questions will be useful to you, but these small games you're playing now are safe. When you begin playing with bigger things, we will speak.*

It was one of those discussions where you realize how wrong you are, but you don't want to admit it, so you get stronger in your wrongness. And by the end of it, my voice was raised, and I was telling Elken how annoying he was. I might have even said, "You're just jealous the green goddess doesn't want to talk to you."

Elken pressed his lips together and then he laughed. "You can be really mean," he said. "You know that, right?"

I don't know how he managed it, but he called me mean in the kindest way anyone has ever said anything. And then he walked away to be by himself, and I wanted to cry but I also couldn't let myself because that felt like losing even harder than I'd already lost.

So I sat outside feeling angry and telling the clouds to turn dark and grey, so they looked angry too. And when my anger finally cooled down a little, I started thinking about "bigger things" and what that could mean.

Immediately the Skyfather interrupted my thoughts.

So...

"So what?" I said.

Are you going to ask?

I sighed. Elken was so good I hated him sometimes. I mean, I love him even now, but he was so good it was irritating, you know?

I sighed. "Is there anything that I'm not allowed to do or make or whatever?"

Yes.

"Okay, what?"

You won't like it. But it is important to understand—

"Just tell me."

You are not allowed to change the past.

I'd never thought of anything like that. I couldn't even hold the idea in my head.

"What do you mean?"

You cannot order things to be different once they have come to be. It is too dangerous. I forbid it.

I knew. Then and there, I knew two things. The first was that I *could* change things that had happened a long time ago—why else would it be forbidden? And I knew that no matter what the Skyfather or the green goddess or whatever you want to call him said, I was going to do it.

I could get my family back.

TWENTY-SIX

"MAKE IT SO NIYI never died," I said to the air.

Nothing happened.

"Make it so I stopped the sprite from coming into our lodge."

Again, nothing.

"Make it so my mother never fell through the ice."

Silence.

"Ice," I said, thinking of the ice beneath my mother's boots the day she died. "Stay solid and strong."

That time something did happen. My mother's spear (which had been outside with Elken) hopped towards me and slammed into the side of my face, leaving my ear ringing.

I didn't know how to alter a day in the past. I'd never even thought about time as a thing that could be transformed or revisited after it was done tormenting me. And also, I had no idea what I was speaking to. When I told a rock to move, I was talking to the rock; when I told the clouds to come, I was calling the clouds. Was the past something that could be talked to? Moved or called?

Hours came and went with me huddled in a little ball in the dim below-the-ground room that had sort of become mine since Elken never went down there. If I was quick about it, I could get in and close the big heavy door before the spear realized what I was up to. It was cold down below, but I told the air around me to stay warm, so I didn't need to shiver too much. I whispered to the past and to the bones of my dead family. I murmured to myself from back then, "Littler Katya, please, listen."

Nothing came from any of it.

If you were wondering, I decided instantly that I wasn't going to tell Elken what I was up to. He was too good, you know? There was no way he'd be like: alright then, change up everything that happened before. That seems simple and not like a problem at all. He probably would have been able to feel that what I was trying to do was against the Skyfather's wishes.

Slowly, every evening took on the same form: Elken would come to me, wanting to sit and talk, like we'd been doing all that time before. He'd want to listen to my thoughts and kiss and fall asleep together, holding hands, with our heads leaning against each other.

"I'm tired."

"I'm not feeling well."

"I'm trying really hard to hear the voice, and I need quiet."

I told him whatever lie worked. And each time it hurt him because I think he could feel that they were lies; he knew that I just wanted him to leave me alone. He'd stand there for a second, watching me, looking sad and sweet and somehow still perfect, before wandering off, giving me space to ponder why time wouldn't obey me when I told it to be different.

"Make it so Preah never got sick."

"Make my mom sick the day she died so she wouldn't go to work."

"Make my dad not go in her place."

I was focused and cold, and every moment that I was pulled away from my trials, I was irritated. I didn't want to stop what I was thinking to eat or sleep or take a bath with Elken or listen to whatever it was that he'd learned on his daily walk. I was used to not eating. I could go back to not bathing. Being tired was nothing new to me, and in a strange way, I was more comfortable with the discomfort. It's what I was used to. I didn't want to waste any more time.

I wanted to take some spare lichens (real ones, not voice-made ones, just in case that changed anything) and order them to get younger or smaller. They didn't listen, and I'd spend hours wondering why, rephrasing my request.

"Become young again."

"Grow backwards."

"Go back to being a seed."

I was sure that if I found the right instructions, my past would listen. I tried closing my eyes and telling myself that when I opened them, I'd be back at Ilona's lodge before I'd eaten her food. That didn't work, either. But I knew—I knew that the Skyfather wouldn't have forbidden it if it wasn't something I could do. Was it my body that needed to be different? Was it the sun and the moon that needed to move another way? I asked the moon to get less full, but it didn't listen. Was there something in the air that I should be speaking to? Something like all the feelings that poked at Elken?

Child. This will not end as you think it will.

I ignored him.

Child, please. Rest.

I thought about saying: *I'm too busy fixing what you broke*, but I didn't. I said, "I'm not tired."

I wasn't Elken, so normally I didn't feel what the Skyfather was feeling, but that day I could. He pitied me, and I didn't care. Not at all. *I pity you too*, I thought before turning back to the moon-shaped lichen in my palm. It must have grown wonky around a rock or something, but this gave me an idea.

"Make it so you grew in a different direction."

That didn't work either.

So while all this was happening, while I was reaching out for something I couldn't see or even fully understand, things got bad with Elken. I think he knew even then—that first night I rejected his company—that I was trying to do something I wasn't supposed to. I think he could feel where I was going, and he wanted to stop me before it was too late, but I wouldn't let him. He'd try to distract me, suggesting that we go on a walk somewhere new, or that we watch the stars, or that I come and paint with him during the day. He'd bother me to ask the voice questions on his behalf, and usually, I felt like his questions were dull.

"Can she hear me even when I can't hear her?"

"Always."

"Does she know that I'm trying? Like... that I'm really trying to do what she wants?"

I sighed. "He does."

"Is there anything extra I should be knowing or doing or—"

My voice couldn't have been emptier as I translated. "Nothing. You're right where he wants you."

"What does she think is up with your spear?"

That question was actually kind of interesting, but only because the Skyfather didn't answer. I asked again, and he laughed at me.

You won't like it.

Elken said, "Because the spear doesn't listen to your voice, does she? And... I don't know... it seems like she loves you."

She does.

So I got this silly idea in my head that my mother's spear had somehow... that Niyi had gone into it in some way because, if you think about it, the spear didn't get all lively until after Niyi had flown off in the shape of a bird. Maybe when the spear nudged me towards the temple, it was Niyi trying to get me to find Elken and be happy. Only I was with Elken and too focused on getting everyone else back to enjoy any of it. That time—when things were good between us—was far too short. I mean, I didn't deserve for it to be longer, I didn't deserve it happening at all, but Elken did. He should have gotten a few more months of happiness out of the whole exchange.

I think when people speak about broken hearts, a lot of them are thinking about this kind of thing. A time when you have someone and a part of your life is figured out, but rather than revel in it and savour it and love every moment of having that person nearby, you destroy it. And if you don't think that's what I was doing, you're not really listening. Or you're too cheery and hopeful and this isn't the right kind of story for you.

So we were fighting—a lot—because I wanted him to leave me alone, and every time he asked me, "Is everything okay?" my skin crawled with irritation. Because I was frustrated with myself for not figuring out how to change something after it had happened. Because my mother's spear kept trying to stop me from doing what I was trying to do—whacking me in the temple whenever I had a new idea for how I could go back and start over—and that made me miserable because it seemed like Niyi didn't want to come back to me after all.

I had nowhere to direct my anger, so I took it out on Elken.

The slightest thing he said or did, turned my mouth into a dagger. And I regret it now—even then, I regretted it, each time something awful came out of my throat. It hurt me to hurt him, but I did it anyways. I shouted at him, telling him not to touch me because I didn't want him making me less angry.

I cursed him. I used my voice to throw things at him, and when I was especially angry, I'd make something appear right beneath his feet, so he'd trip. And he was Elken, so he was sweet about it and forgiving, and always he'd say something like: "You can just talk to me about it. I'll listen. What are you feeling? Right now, what do you need?" Or he'd laugh and call me mean, but in the nicest way. And then, on top of everything, I was feeling guilty because he'd been so kind to me.

So I'll leap ahead here because there's no point in describing the brutal details of each of our arguments. All the times Elken swore that he'd always forgive me no matter what. All the times he told me that I was just testing him, pushing against him to prove to myself that everyone leaves me.

"I don't want to leave you." He'd said that almost daily (because we were fighting pretty much every day, or I was fighting with him, and he was trying to soothe me). "I promise. I don't want to be apart from you. You can tell me anything. I can't promise I'll understand, but you know I'll try, right?"

He would say we were going to figure it out, and sometimes I'd cry because I felt so guilty. He would hold me, and it would be sweet once more, for a few days, or a few hours at least. But before long, my mind would turn back to the task I'd given myself.

Other times I'd be annoyed. "Stop saying what you think I want to hear."

I remember going into the kitchen to take a helping of stew back to the room I was working in. Elken was sitting alone at the table. He put his spoon down so gently it didn't even make a noise.

"I don't know what I've done, Katya, if you would tell me I could—"

"You haven't done anything. I just feel like being alone right now." I used the wooden ladle to fill my bowl from the pot over the oil lamp and turned to leave again.

"Do you..." he got an embarrassed look on his face as he stood, seeming like maybe he was going to follow me. "Do you maybe want to talk to the hag? You could probably make her big again with your voice so you could hear her—"

"What?" It was only a single word, but I said it with so much venom that he took a step back.

"I'm only thinking, maybe you want to talk to a woman? Or someone you're not—" he hesitated, "so close to."

"You think speaking to the mad woman who MURDERED MY SISTER, who was going to EAT ME, would make me feel better?" I threw a spoon at him with my voice.

He ducked.

"I just... Katya, I'm running out of ideas... you're not happy."

I sighed. "So what?"

"She told me to take care of you and I... I don't know what that means right now. You say you want to be left alone, but it feels like it hurts you when I listen, like you want me not to listen, but that's—"

"You're calling me a liar?"

"No... just confused maybe."

My shoulders relaxed a little. He looked so earnest, so desperate.

"I'm just trying to figure things out," I said quietly. "Things you can't help me with."

And he looked at me in a way that I'll never be able to forget, strong but also soft. Brave and afraid and loving. "Do you not... like me anymore?" he said.

"No," I said. "I like you."

And then, because he didn't look like he felt any better, I added. "You're the only person I like."

It wasn't a lie. And even if I had disliked him at that moment, I still would have been grateful for him anyways because he'd given me hope. He'd suggested something that I hadn't tried yet.

Ilona had been collecting blue ears and tongues, right? She knew something about blueness and maybe that something had to do with how it worked. I was certain my voice could make her big enough that I'd be able to hear her again. And I was certain it would help me deal with her if she started playing tricks on me.

Please, said the voice.

"Make it so I can't hear the Skyfather anymore," I said to my ears.

TWENTY-SEVEN

SO WHEN ELKEN LEFT for his usual morning painting, my mother's spear hopping after him, I went into his room. I figured this was where he kept Ilona because I'd seen him carry little portions of lichens into it, and we spent a lot of time in the other rooms and I hadn't seen her anywhere else.

Her little vessel was on a table Elken had lugged into the room, but she wasn't inside the vessel; he'd made a living area for her on the tabletop, sort of like a pen only nice with a nest made from rags. She looked even more terrible than I remembered, frumpy and grey and sagging worse than Equah and the other elders back home.

"You say one stupid thing and I'm squishing you. You hear?" I said.

Her thick neck bobbled up and down as she nodded.

Katya...

The Skyfather's voice was barely a whisper. I might not even have heard it if I hadn't been listening extra carefully in case Ilona said something with her teeny, little throat. And I was disappointed, I guess, that my ears hadn't listened to my order completely. But also, I wasn't surprised that he'd figured out a way to be heard because it seemed like the annoying kind of thing he'd do.

I ignored the voice, took a deep breath, and even though I'd been giving my body the instruction all night, I told any remnants of Ilona's food to leave through my skin like sweat. Nothing came out, because I'd given that order so many times already. And then I spoke to my ears, "Make it so I can hear what Ilona says."

Yes, it was a risk, but I'd already done everything else I could think of, and my whole family was dead, except for Kid, so give me a break, okay? I'd decided to ask my ears to change instead of making Ilona's voice loud again or making her big enough to be loud again, because that way, if something went wrong, at least she wouldn't be able to affect Elken.

"Do you know how to go back," I said. "Back in your life and make things different?"

"Te-he. You're about to get yourself in a whole lot of trouble Crab."

I sighed. "Do you know or not?" I lifted the vessel up to her tiny little body as a threat, making it clear I'd be happy to stuff her back in the bottle and give her a few shakes. Maybe I'd bury her in the snow, and she'd freeze before Elken could find her.

"I've never been able to do it myself, but I've heard of it."

I'd spent a lot of time bartering at the market in Kettin, so I knew when people were trying to mislead me, and it didn't seem like she was.

For a second, I thought Elken was behind me, that he'd come home early and walked in and seen me talking to Ilona. I turned and looked but he wasn't there, and even though he wasn't, my heart still raced like I'd been caught doing something I shouldn't.

Ilona cackled. "You've not been listening very well," she said. "I think that's part of it. What does your Sky-God have to say about all of this?"

I paused. I'd never spoken about the Skyfather near her... had I?

Even tiny as she was, I could see she was smirking. "Elken told me darling. He needed *someone* to talk to, and I'm a very good listener."

It stung—the idea that Elken hadn't come to me, that he'd gone to some stupid, evil witch who was so small he couldn't even hear her.

"He cries when he tells me about it. The things you do. What you say. He cries on his walks as well."

I decided to squish her, and she must have been able to tell I was about to do it because she started rambling FAST.

"You've been told not to leave, right? Maybe that's part of it. Maybe you have to be where you were. The day you want to go back to and change—where were you?"

It was an interesting idea. In a heartbeat, I tried something new. In every past attempt, I'd been trying to go back to another time *and* another place. I tried only going to another time, just a few minutes earlier, before I'd walked up to Ilona's little table.

It worked.

I saw myself. My younger self (of a few minutes at least), standing right in front of me, looking at the table that held the owl-hag.

I said, "I figured it out."

And she—me—turned in my direction. She was startled, but I don't think she saw me because she was scanning the whole room and when her eyes passed over me, they didn't stop or seem to recognize what was in front of them.

"Katya, it's me... or...you?"

The other me jumped again and dropped the empty vessel, the bottle ringing as it shattered like ice. I could hear Ilona laughing (because I hadn't yet told my ears not to listen to her anymore). Colour bled in from the sides and then it was over. There was only one of me, but the bottle was still broken, and Ilona was still laughing.

"That poor boy... he has no idea... does he? Does he know about the things you've done? Selling children like they're lard? Letting other children get sick and die?"

My jaw wound so tight it hurt.

"He doesn't know he's got himself tangled up with a poisonous Crab-girl. You're making him sick; did you know that? Just like you make everyone sick. Soon he won't be able to go on his walks anymore, that's how bad it is. Already it takes him twice the time to get where he needs to go. But you've not been paying attention, have you? Have you even noticed the limping? How his teeth clench each time he takes a step? And he knows you don't care. Oh, he knows."

I tried to remember Elken's face from the past few days, but Ilona was right, I'd not been looking at him. I couldn't remember if he'd been limping when he left.

"He doesn't realize it yet, but he wishes he'd never met you."

It cut into me—what she was saying—so much so that I made a noise, an in-pain sound sort of like I was saying *no* but also *stop* and grimacing at the same time. When I made the noise, Ilona cried out too.

I'd hurt her with my voice; my cry had made her cry.

And it felt good.

So I did it again.

The door behind me opened with such a force that it thwacked into the wall.

"What are you doing?"

I spun around to find Elken—he must have come because he could feel the pain. His sandy hair was a mess, twisted and stuck up all funny from being out in the wind for so long. He was standing wrong, with his jaw clenched tight. His shoulder was slumped against the wall behind him, one leg not holding his weight fairly. His fists were balled up...

I was crying because of what Ilona had said and not really thinking about how the pain I was causing her would affect Elken even though I knew he felt what other people felt. I was a terrible friend to him. We've been over that.

And for some reason seeing that Elken was hurt didn't calm me down at all, it made me so much angrier because it felt like the witch had tricked me into hurting him. I ground my teeth together and groaned and Ilona screamed, and Elken came to me on shaky legs, wincing.

"Stop!" he shouted, and that was sad too because he never raised his voice, not ever. It was my fault. I was making him go bad, just like everything else.

"KATYA STOP!"

But I couldn't. I was too sore and achy and stinging, and my voice needed to let the pain out of my body. So Elken did something else. Something I didn't know he could do.

Everything went black around me.

TWENTY-EIGHT

WHEN I WOKE UP, Elken was kneeling next to me on the floor in his room, wiping my face with a damp cloth, looking all kinds of worried.

"What happened?" I said.

It felt like clouds were behind my eyes, and when I tried to sit up, the clouds got thicker.

"I'm sorry... I just... I'm really sorry." Elken shook his head, clenching his teeth. "I didn't mean to, only it hurt too much. I won't do it again, I promise."

"Do what?"

"I put you to sleep."

It didn't bother me nearly as much as it did Elken. I actually thought it was a pretty smart solution. I didn't say this to Elken though, I was too busy feeling guilty for how I'd talked to him earlier and how things had been between us lately and how I'd ended up hurting Ilona with my voice, not thinking at all about how it would make him feel. I looked into his sad, concerned eyes and thought it would have been better if he'd never met me. But then I remembered more clearly what had happened before he'd come to find me.

"Can you forgive me?" he said. "I know trust is—"

"Do you talk to her about me?"

He sat back on his heels and furrowed his brows. "Who? Ilona? Sometimes."

I probably shouldn't have felt betrayed, but I did. I wouldn't have told him half the things I had knowing that. "Why would you do that?"

He shrugged. "I thought she needed someone to talk to, and I mean... I can't hear her, so it's not a proper conversation, but I can feel her and when you're talking to someone, you... I don't know, you share things. You mention what's on your mind."

I could feel my face twisting into a scowl, the sort of expression that made Bayflower tell me to fix my face. "What have you told her?"

"Uh, not much. That we're... um, that we've gotten close. That I think we're doing something really important here, only I have no idea what it is."

He laughed a little, but when I didn't smile or laugh along, he got serious again. "I told her that I was going to try to convince you to let her go. I think I can make her big again. And heal her up some, so she doesn't hurt any more children."

If my mouth wasn't hanging open, it should have been.

"You told her about the Skyfather?"

"Uh, kind of? I guess. I asked her if she'd had any sort of experiences with gods... like me and the green goddess or you and the blue god. I didn't say anything about how you felt or thought or anything—"

Elken was lovely, maybe a little too trusting, but he was a good guy, entirely. Having a little reminder of that caved my chest in, but still, I said what I needed to say. I sat up and looked him straight in the face and said, "Elken, I have to leave."

"Where? I'll come if you want."

"No," I said pulling my knees out from beneath the blanket he must have covered me with while I slept. "I have to go far, back to my village. Farther than the green goddess said you could go."

"But didn't the blue god tell you to stay here, too?"

"Yes, Elken," I stood. "But I'm not going to listen. I've figured out... I'm going back to Kettin and then back to my life before my mother died. I'm going to set it all right. I figured out how to do it. And then, when everyone's living, I'll come back. I'll find you again. I promise."

"That sounds..." He shook his head as he got up too, looking at me sternly, or at least, sternly for Elken. "Katya, that sounds like something you shouldn't do. Did you ask for advice?" I got a terrible feeling, just now when you said that. Like everything we can't see is screaming at us..."

I sighed, adoring him because he was sweet and beautiful, but also because I knew we were parting, and he didn't fully realize it yet. "The voice told me not to go. But I'm doing it anyway."

Elken was still shaking his head. "No. This is really... you shouldn't. Something bad is going to happen, or it's not going to work how you think. Katya, listen to me, that's—" He reached out for me, and I took his hands in mine.

"Elken, it's my family. I have to."

"My mother's dead too," he said. "And I know it's awful, but that's part of how it all is. The green goddess, she only banned me from a few things. She said I couldn't bring anyone back to life after they died. What you're thinking of is kind of the same—"

My heart stopped beating.

"You can bring people back from the dead?" I was an icicle moments away from shattering.

"I don't know for sure; I assume so because why else would she tell me—"

I let go of him and took a step back, my shoulders shaking, my lungs spasming. "All this time..." I almost couldn't get the words out, my throat felt so raw and dry that I was whispering. "I've been crying and missing them, and you could have fixed it?" My face burned as the ache of what he was telling me settled into my bones. My vision blurred with tears, but I blinked them away. Right then, I knew whatever we were doing together was over. There was no way I could ever forgive him for that.

"Katya, no... I trust her. If she said not to do it, there's a reason. It's not going to be right, or it won't be them, not really, something like that—"

"I hate you."

"No, you don't."

"Yes, I do!" I shouted so loudly that the stones beneath our boots shifted, grinding against each other, making little pebbles and dust that rattled like a herd of elk was rushing by. Dust began to fall from the ceiling, and my shout had hurt more than the building. It looked like it was taking all Elken's strength to keep himself standing, like the air was pushing down on his shoulders.

"Katya, you're hurting me."

I backed away, not understanding how I could love someone so much and hate them so much at the same time, how Elken—the nicest, most caring person in the world—just didn't bother to do the one, kind thing that could have saved me from all my suffering and aloneness. That he'd let me ache for days and days and days when he didn't have to. That he was going to let me ache forever. The whimper-sound coming out of my clenched teeth rattled the walls.

KATYA ENOUGH OF THIS. YOU'RE GRIEVING, YOU ARE NOT YOURSELF—

"NO!"

The coloured panes in the windows shattered into countless little blades when I screamed at the Skyfather. I could feel the weight of his voice on me, but I could also feel the relief that came when my own voice pushed back.

Elken fell to his knees, blood seeping through his trousers from the glass shards he was being pressed into.

I need you here—

"Why?"

To understand!

That wasn't the answer I was expecting. "To understand what?"

For a moment, since all the shouting had stopped, Elken was free from the weight of our voices. He tried standing twice before he succeeded, making his way to me dizzily, reaching out for me, trying to comfort me.

Yes. *He* was trying to make sure *I* was okay, after I'd nearly squished him flat with my voice. But he must have known—he must have figured out I was beyond comfort by then. Surely he could feel it.

That suffering... that cruelty... I'm trying to understand if there are things more powerful than that. If there's a place for humans in the world. When the witches sided with the animals... when the coyotes changed sides... I must leave room for the possibility that they are right.

I laughed and stopped listening. We weren't being called to do something special, like Elken thought. The Skyfather had given me his voice and Elken his heart and the others—whatever he gave them—so we could help him learn about suffering?

Fuck this, I thought.

I was out. Out of whatever colourful-God-scheme was going on. Out of whatever had been happening between me and Elken because he casually chose not to bring my loved ones back to life. I was out of that gorgeous temple with shattered windows that I'd cracked with my voice. Just out.

I ignored everything Elken said as he pulled at my sleeve and tried to hug me or love me or heal me or whatever. And my mother's spear was fighting me too for some stupid reason I still didn't understand.

"I don't need you then either," I said to the spear, watching it shred into splinters from the weight of my voice. And it did hurt me to see that—one of the last pieces I had of my mother ripped into shreds. The shout pushed Elken back and I stormed out of the room, down the hall, and out those gorgeous doors.

The frozen world was dark and quiet, and the stars were painting the sky a milky pink, and it was cold enough that my nose and ears stung instantly. I started toward the direction I'd come from all those weeks ago.

The hailstorm came again but I screamed, and it couldn't touch me. If I wasn't so upset, I might have thought that part was a little bit cool—spears of ice bouncing away from me just before they crashed into my face, like I was in a foamy sea bubble where nothing could touch me.

Elken wasn't so lucky. He followed me outside, where he was whipped by the hail, his voice full of that teary sound that comes when someone's about to cry. "You know I can't go far," he said. "I was told to stay here. Katya, please, just come back. Let's talk about this."

I got farther away, and his voice was swallowed by the roar of the storm. The last thing I heard from him was, "No matter what happens, you can come back."

I know. Perfect. Stupidly fucking perfect. Getting all beat up by the ice for me and it didn't even work. I left Elken behind, and I didn't even cry over it... Well, I did cry, only much later.

I took my arrowhead out of my hair and set it on the frosty ground. I told it to grow and then I stood on it and told it to lift and float toward where I wanted to go. I was too torn up inside to walk.

As I sped across the tundra, the air around me warm at my request, the Skyfather tried changing my mind a few times, but his voice was so quiet it was easy to ignore him.

Just stop and listen to the air. Really listen.

And: *There's so much more going on than you can understand.*

And finally: *You will suffer for this.*

It was nightfall by the time I made it back to Ilona's lodge.

TWENTY-NINE

I HOPPED OFF THE arrowhead just outside Ilona's lodge, landing on the hard snow with a crunch, and then I whistled to tell the arrowhead to follow me because it was slowly becoming clear that I didn't have to give a full set of instructions to be obeyed; I only had to make a sound and mean the instructions.

The arrowhead hovered around my boots as I stepped forward.

Winter had ravaged Ilona's home—the wind had blown away boards and shingles, the cold had warped the beams and the whole thing was leaning a little to one side, looking more pathetic than I remembered it being.

Part of me didn't want to go inside because of everything that had taken place there, but at the same time, I remembered clearly what Elken had said about hags using parts of people for enchantments back when I'd brought up the tooth he kept in his bag. I had no doubt Elken was going to release Ilona now that I was gone and maybe they were such good friends she'd stay and they could sit together and talk for hours, but if she decided to go back to her home, I didn't want her finding a vessel with my hair in it. I'm not entirely stupid all the time it would seem.

I pushed the half-open door all the way open, the creak making my spine tingle. Trails of sparkling frost dripped from the door and the holes in the walls, having been blown in by the wind, but it didn't make the place look pretty like frost usually did.

I went straight to her hair collection and pocketed the first red curl I found before growing a little frantic at the sight of a different red curl in a different vessel. And before I knew it, I was throwing them all into the fire hole in the wall and ordering them to burst into flame, even the ones that weren't red because I was worried that I would somehow miss *my* hair and after I'd sorted everything out with my family, Ilona would show up and ruin it all over again.

The little glass bottles made popping sounds when they burst inside the fire and the hairs curled up like they were living, moving things as they burnt into ash. My eyes wandered to Ilona's shiny rock collection. I loaded my pockets with them, because why not? It was the least she owed me after all the trouble she'd caused, and maybe they could be traded at the market or to the sailors who came to Kettin in the spring. They were pretty enough that they might be worth something.

And then, as I was leaving, I still felt paranoid, so I burnt the whole lodge down. If you think the light of stars reflecting on snow is pretty, you can't even begin to imagine how beautiful it looks to see the pink and orange streaks of an entire home on fire reflected in sparkling white.

Watching that nightmare burn felt better than maybe anything that had happened to me so far in this story and I guess I got a little excited at the idea of fixing one wrong thing. The arrowhead was still following me, and I felt like we should mark the moment somehow, so I told my mother's arrowhead to shrink back to a reasonable size and then called a branch down from a tree and told it to cling to my arrowhead. I didn't need the old, disobedient spear. I had a new one.

I used the weight of my voice to smooth the wooden edges down until they were soft and then I called the oil from within the branch to the surface, making it the shiniest piece of wood I'd ever seen. So in a way, it felt a bit better than my mother's spear.

Except it doesn't have any iron in the middle, I thought. But then I thought that was a pretty easy thing to fix too. I told the iron cauldron from Ilona's lodge to roll out of the flames and become a different shape. It listened. I told it to wrap around the arrowhead, and suddenly, I had the best spear I'd ever seen, maybe the best one in the whole world. And I knew exactly where I was going to take it.

Or rather, where it was going to take me.

I told the spear to lay flat, and it did, hovering above the frozen ground. I sat on it and told it to move, and it did. I wouldn't be balancing on a piece of stone on my way to the winter sprite's strange pyramid-lodge, I'd be flying.

My chest was starting to ache for Elken, and my mind was burning because missing him was stupid, because he wasn't actually my friend. If he were, he would have saved my family. Instead, I knew that I was about to save them myself.

Only first I was going to take care of the sprite—the one who'd taken Niyi—because that seemed like it needed addressing too.

THIRTY

WHEN YOU USE YOUR voice to move through the air, it doesn't take very long to get places. If I'd been in a better mood, I probably would have loved it—racing beneath the stars as waves of pink and blue and green splashed across the sky. It didn't even take the whole night to get from Ilona's not-there-anymore lodge to the ice pyramid where the blue man had taken Niyi. The structure looked exactly as I remembered—as if not a single snowflake had changed position since I was there last.

It was waiting for me, I thought.

And I know that's a pretty selfish thing to think, but that was what I thought. I felt like buildings were mostly good and this one knew that the winter sprite was evil, and it had been waiting for someone to come and set things right. Even my blood was still smeared on the tundra from when I'd broken my leg, only it wasn't red anymore; it was dried and brown and there were some marks around it, meaning wolves had probably followed the scent of it and sniffed around a bit.

I told my spear to let me down on top, which it did, and I spent a few moments wandering around as I didn't see the blue man up there. The ice crunched beneath my boots as the wind lapped at the few curls that had come loose on the flight over. I could have left just then, in the calm, silent night. The flight had settled a lot of the anger that was in me, at least for the moment, so I could have left, and things would have been the smallest bit better for me. But of course, I didn't. Because this isn't the kind of story with little gifts scattered throughout.

Carved into the ice was a big, round tunnel, sort of like a gaping mouth, and I figured the sprite was probably inside because it was cold and nighttime after all. I whistled into life a little ball of fire, urging it to follow me into the tunnel.

It wasn't as dark as I'd expected it to be inside, and I think that was probably because it was made of ice and ice is a little bit clear, so the moonlight and starlight filtered through the walls and everything inside was pale and blue-tinted and sparkling but somehow warm. There were a lot of things carved out of the ice, but what my eyes went to first was a massive ice seat with a beautiful skyline carved into it. The carved clouds were more swirly than real clouds, but still, I knew what they were.

I reached out a finger to touch one, right where the carved sun's rays pierced through the scene to the tundra below. *How does it not melt?* I thought. When the blue man sat on it… wouldn't the heat of his body ruin the carvings?

It's not for him. It's for me.

I wanted to tell the Skyfather to shut up and I also wanted to ask him what he meant because as far as I'd known he wasn't something that needed to sit down, but there wasn't the time to say any of my thoughts because I heard the sprite coming and was lucky enough to roll a little to the side as his massive, speckled fist came down on the spot I'd been standing a few moments before, leaving cracks snaking through the ice.

He pulled his arm back, looking like he was going to swipe for me again, but I wasn't worried. I didn't need to be. I looked at his giant, crooked teeth, for a second thinking about what it would have looked like if he'd crushed Niyi between them, because what else was he planning on doing with her besides eating her? He was the same one—the winter sprite that had stolen her—I was sure of it. His wispy beard dragged along the ice near his bare, blue feet. His thin lips and droopy eyes were the same.

I screamed, and it hurt him.

He clutched his hands to his head, and I screamed louder because I liked that I was hurting him. I guess because I'm a bad person or whatever.

As I screamed, he began to wail, and as he wailed, he shrunk. Down, down, down—until he was just the little blue man I'd first seen, the one who'd hidden in the darkness with us who was no taller than my knee. He flopped around like a fish, banging his head on the icy floor in a pathetic attempt at stopping the pain my voice was causing him.

He choked out a lispy, whimpering howl. "Owwwww. Pwease. No more. No more. The birdie took the baby!"

I hadn't known he could speak.

"I know," I said, crouching near him, a little pleased with the spatter of blood that caked the ice right where he'd banged his own head. "But you took her first."

No response from him would have made me feel better. Honestly, it didn't matter if he answered at all. I only wanted him to have a few more moments of suffering, wondering what was going to happen to him, before I tore his head apart with a hum.

I'd realized that the scariest part of everything had been when Ilona put me in the pot, and I'd known I was going to suffer but it hadn't happened yet. I thought something that stole babies should feel that way too. It was only fair.

He was still flinching even though I wasn't screaming, and it took maybe a full minute for his hands to slide down away from his ears and his breathing to settle. "The baby..." he said.

"Yes. You took the baby."

"She had a bwue tongue. The wittle people would have killed her. They no like bwue, the little people. No... no they don't."

My chest sank. "What?"

"But the birdie saw her alweady. The birdie-witch."

Do you think I had no plan?

"The birdie came and took the baby away. Confusing..." He scratched at the few hairs sticking out of his mottled head. "Confusing because the sky said... the sky said she was pwotected. Unless someone gave permission, me or her other famwy, no one could touch her. Poor wittle bwue baby. Eaten by a witch."

It had been me.

I'd given Ilona "permission."

I'd said she could take my coat and go get Niyi from the giant.

I didn't want to tell you this way—

Salt ground against the back of my eyes. "I didn't know."

I know.

It hurt in all the ways I wasn't hurt yet. Before that moment, I'd really thought that I'd done everything I could. That I tried every possible thing and worked my hardest and still Niyi had died. But knowing that things would have been better if I'd done literally nothing. If I'd just let things happen...

Go back to Elken. Tell him what has happened. He will help you. Learn from this and do nothing until you've made room for the anger you feel now. Elken has already forgiven you. I have already forgiven you.

"Forgiveness isn't enough," I said, backing away from the tiny, crouched man I'd been battering with my voice. Even if forgiveness was somehow helpful, theirs it didn't matter. *I* hadn't forgiven me. I never would.

Forgiveness is always enough.

I called my spear, and it came, and I was on my way home. Back to Kettin. To where everything started to go wrong. And I was crying a little by then because every part of my life was sick (Elken had been right, anything can get sick, even a whole life) and maybe knowing I was about to set it right... I don't know, somehow that made it okay to cry about it.

I remember thinking to myself, *soon it will all feel like a bad dream.*

No one would remember any of the bad things that happened. I'd go back to before my mother fell through the ice and I'd tell her not to go to work that day. She'd listen. And then my father wouldn't have been bludgeoned to death by the village folk for putting her body in the wrong place. And I wouldn't have had to sell Kid to keep my sisters alive, because my parents would be helping with the work and there would be enough to eat. And if Ilona did come again, I'd catch her and kill her, and we could eat her the way she'd been planning on eating me.

By the time I arrived in Kettin, the stars were fading, and the faintest blue light covered the snowy mounds where lodges used to be—everyone was still beneath the ground.

It was fitting in a way, that everything looked blue. The whole world seemed forbidden. I sat on the cold, frozen ground with my legs crossed. I closed my eyes and told myself—my whole being—to go back. To the day my mother died.

And I went.

THIRTY-ONE

WHEN I OPENED MY eyes, the light was the same: a faint blueish glow coating the flat, silent white. The moon was a different shape though—it was shaped like a fishhook and dangling all lopsided like one too. The lodges weren't collapsed for winter either; they stood, loose flaps of fur or leather snapping in the wind. I could hear people rustling about in the early morning: fishermen and fisherwomen getting up for their day's work. Children cooed and murmured as their parents begged them for a few more minutes of sleep.

I ran to my lodge—our lodge—and pushed through the flap of fur-lined leather with my breath all wrong inside my lungs.

They were there. All of them.

All of *us*. I was there too—lying between my parents with Kid and Preah and Niyi. My chest burned hot as coals and I cried because I was so happy to see them, because we all looked so comfortable—cozy—because everything was going to be alright.

I crouched across from them in awe, waves of disbelief and belief crashing into each other within me. I thought about reaching out and touching my mother, setting a finger on one of her red curls. But I stopped with my hand hovering just above the wash of red. I didn't want to wake her just yet. She was always tired because of Niyi waking up in the night to be fed and she deserved to rest.

So I watched her sleep and admired how beautiful she was until Niyi woke her up. At first, my mother kept her eyes closed as she pulled the baby close to her, over top of the old me, and opened the front of her furs. When Niyi was feeding, she sat up, but slowly, keeping her eyes closed, savouring the little bit of sleepiness she had left before the day began.

Kid stirred and made a moaning sort of noise, and my father who was still fully asleep, only moving around, pulled him in close. Kid settled—messy hair stuck to his forehead from how much he'd sweat in his sleep, his mouth open, one cheek pressed against my father's hairy chest.

My mother opened her eyes and inhaled sharply. "Katya! You scared me!" She laughed in a whispery sort of way. "What are you doing up so early?"

I couldn't answer right away. It had been a while since I'd heard her say my name and, I don't know, it really got to me. To hear her voice again. To hear her laugh.

"Mom…"

I didn't know how to begin, and instead of explaining myself, I pressed my face into her neck and wrapped my arms around her and sobbed.

"Shh, shh, what is it? What's happened?"

She couldn't hug me back fully because she was holding Niyi against her chest, but she nuzzled her face into the top of my head and whispered into my hair.

"It's okay. It's okay, baby."

My mother had still called me baby before she'd died, and I'd always hated it, but after I felt like I lost her forever, it didn't bother me at all. I loved it. She could call me that until I was all wrinkly and faded and I wouldn't be annoyed in the least.

She grew still in my arms.

"Katya, baby, what's happening?"

She pulled me a little away from her to look at my face. She was scared, I could see it in how her eyes flitted back and forth between the me from before, sleeping next to her, and the me from now, crying in front of her. She seemed to feel it out, at least a little bit, because she said, "Baby, you're not supposed to be here like this."

I was still crying. "I know mom, I know. But I have to tell you—"

"No, baby, don't tell me anything."

"No, mom, you don't understand," I said. "You can't go to the ice tod—"

"Katya!"

I don't know how she figured out that I was from a later time, or maybe she didn't know that, she just knew that I wasn't doing what I was supposed to be. But when she shouted my name, me from before woke up, startled.

She looked at my mother—or *I* looked at my mother? And she didn't see me at all. She *couldn't* see me—or... I couldn't see myself, I guess.

My mother said, "Go back to sleep, baby."

And I could remember her saying that the morning she'd died. I'd forgotten until that moment, but she'd woken me up early that day and then told me to go back to sleep.

This really hurt my head maybe because remembering something while you watch it happening is confusing and backwards.

"Mom," I said, trying to sound serious and grown-up. "This is really important. I *need* you to listen to me—"

"Am I meant to know it?"

It was a strange question. "Meant has nothing to do with—"

"I'll pray," she said. And then she said again, "You're not supposed to be here."

And I couldn't handle any of it, and I most definitely didn't want her talking to the Skyfather about me because maybe he'd say I was bad or something and that would hurt her feelings, so I said, "Mom, you're going to die today."

She grew quiet, her brows furrowed.

"Is it painful? No. Don't answer Katya. I don't want to know."

"No, mom, I came to warn you so that you don't... Mom, you don't *have* to die..."

"Baby, come here."

Niyi was done eating and was sleeping again, and my mother opened her arms for me. I could feel her—her warmth—and smell her hair as her hands slid along my back.

"Baby, some things... some things shouldn't be touched with human hands."

"You don't understand," I cried. "After you is dad and... Preah... M-m-oom—" I couldn't finish what I was saying, I was choking on my tears and hiccupping. The idea of saying *everyone's dead except for Kid who I sold,* was terrible, so I said, "I'm all alone now. It's just me. Just please, please don't go to the ice today and I won't be alone anymore."

"Baby." Her voice was cracking too; I could feel her chest waver against my cheek as she tried not to cry. "No one is ever alone." She pressed me tight against her and rocked me back and forth like I was little. And slowly, the others woke up, including the me-from-before, and none of them could see me—not even my father. They couldn't hear me any either.

But my father did notice my mother was acting strange. When the kids were outside, except for Niyi, of course, he took her in his arms and said, "What is it?"

She shook her head. "A strange dream."

I knew she was lying, and I think my father did too, because he smirked and said, "You don't have to tell me, if you don't want."

She smiled a little, though it was a sad one, and a tear escaped. "I love you."

And the way she said it... he knew something was serious and wrong. He frowned and said, "Is there anything you need?" But he said it in a strange voice, a quieter version of himself, a whispery one.

She shook her head.

"No! Mom! Don't act like you're leaving! Just don't go to the lakes—just don't go out on the ice today! That's it!"

She buried her face into my father's chest while I shouted at her, and he ran his hands along her back and into her hair.

"I can chop ice today if you need the rest," my father said.

"No!" she said, so forcefully that he frowned again in confusion. My mother smiled a little. "Just hold me. This is helping."

My father listened to her, because he always did. And after a long time of this, she looked up at him and said, "Alright."

You can probably guess where this was headed, but I couldn't. I couldn't understand her then. She went to work. And I followed her and cried and begged and screamed, but my voice didn't have the same power in the past. I couldn't tell her legs to stop walking. Yes, I tried that. Of course I did. My mother was crying too, but in a cleaner way than I was; the tears coming silently. She sniffled and wiped her cheeks.

She tied herself to the blasted owl pillar and took safe little steps out on the ice, and each time she lifted her pick, I could feel her hesitate. I could feel her take a breath and ready herself, and whisper to herself, "alright." Sometimes she said, "If this is how it is...

this is how it is." Sometimes she said, "Look away baby, please."

But I couldn't. I tried dragging her away and taking the pick. Of course, I tried that. I tried pulling on her rope, so she'd slide into shore... I tried ordering the ice to remain firm...

She fell through just after midday. And I cried and wailed over the hole and walked with her back home after her drenched mittens gripped the ice lip and hauled her trembling body out of the water. She was shivering, obviously, and each step she took was slow as her legs were too cold to move properly or bend. Her body was already shutting down, her lips blue, her skin too white and watery. She took my hand as we walked and said, "I'm sorry, baby. That you had to be here for this. But I couldn't let your father go in my place."

And I watched as she arrived home, and my father stripped her clothes off and got the rest of the kids to lay beside her too. Except for me, because as I told you, I refused.

I screamed at myself from before. "JUST DO IT! Please."

Please.

And the part where my mother said, "But it's you who needs it the most,"—that meant something very different this time around. Because she knew. She knew I was going to be alone. When she spoke to my father about her body, I again tried to change what she did. I told her the truth.

"No, they'll kill him for it."

Needless to say, it was the worst day, or one of the seven worst days I've ever had. And it was all the more terrible because I felt like I ruined my mother's last day of life. She knew for hours—each time she lifted the pick—she knew it could be the end, and she did it all anyways, and I couldn't understand.

This time around, I didn't look away from her with embarrassment as she fed everyone. I cried, but I watched. She was so beautiful. She was so... she was everything that I should have been, but I wasn't. When she was dead, I opened my eyes, and it was still the pretty blue morning in Kettin with everyone sleeping beneath the ground.

You see? This is why I forbid it. There is nothing to be gained by it.

I clenched my teeth. I would try again. I would figure it out.

THIRTY-TWO

AND SO I WENT back, and I watched my mother die again and again. And no matter what I did, she didn't listen to me.

She has always felt me... your mother. She was not afraid of death. Afraid of leaving her children, yes, but not afraid to come home.

"LEAVE ME ALONE!" I shouted at the sky.

When I was hungry, I made something to eat out of the air. When I was tired, I slept, ordering the space around me to stay warm. And the rest of the time, I thought about how to fix things. I tried going back and saying it differently. I told lies. I said I was sent by the Skyfather because she was about to do something he didn't want. I said I was dead and watching over her. I said anything I could think of.

And there was the day I gave up on my mother. On saving her. That was hard, but I had other people to worry about, you know? I decided to work on my father; all he had to do to stay alive was not put my mother's body with the wolf bones.

I'd already noticed some of the sled dogs acted strange around me, so I figured when I went back, I was there but only faintly—it might take some time to get my father to notice me.

I waved at him and shouted and tried to push things in the lodge around. But of course, that didn't work any. I couldn't push the furs around in the past and I couldn't make my father see me. Though sometimes it seemed like he felt me just the littlest bit because he'd tilt his head and say, "Lena? Is that you?" (Lena was my mother's name).

"No! It's Katya!" I wailed. "Please, Papa. Please just listen to me. You should leave; take the kids and leave. Work on a ship like Hemi..."

He sat up straighter making me think he was almost hearing me, his eyes narrowing as he peered through the darkness.

"I miss you," he said in a gravelly whisper to the air, his eyes growing watery and dull all at the same time.

It was maybe the third time after he'd sort of heard me that he told the older me he'd have to go soon. "I hear her calling me."

So yes, it was me calling him. Not my mother.

I did see who killed him, though. I watched them do it. They beat him with clubs until he stopped moving, and it was a mean trick too because someone had run to him on his way home from hacking ice and said that a "beast of a whale" had been spotted and they were going on a night hunt.

They got to the edge of the village and there was no skiff waiting for him. Only clubs. As much as I wanted to turn away, I didn't want him to be alone. He was still living a little bit when they left him on the ice gargling, and I came and set my head on his chest, and it seemed like—maybe I'm crazy—but it seemed like he put the mushy thing that used to be his hand on my cheek.

All of them. I watched Preah whisper to Ilona. I watched Kid—sometimes I'd even follow him on board the ship when I needed a break from the horror of it all. He was scared at first, but the captain who'd bought him was kind and a good teacher, and watching Kid learn what it was like to have a full stomach and feel free—watching him discover that the future could hold nice things—that was my only respite.

When I felt like I could get back to it, I tried to save them. And I couldn't. Preah maybe heard me, but she'd start wailing and cover her ears. When things got quiet, she'd press flower stems inside her ear holes, trying to itch her ear or stop the pain. Finally, I'd given up on everyone but the baby. I tried to stop myself from going after Niyi.

"DON'T!" I said as I ran after myself running after the winter sprite. "Just let him take her. At least then, she'll have a chance."

So basically, I spent the winter trying to change the past. And I failed. Though sometimes it felt like the me from before could hear me—just for a second—it didn't do any good. And all that Elken had taught me about healing—about how the pains we don't give space to eventually turn mean and take the space they need—I wasn't thinking about any of that, but obviously, I was making things worse for myself.

I saw the lakerunners come and told myself to be unseen and un-smelled by them. They were lanky grey creatures with long snouts and longer forearms. They ran on two legs and travelled in families of three or four with momma lakerunners teaching their little lakerunners to follow scents and dig. I watched them eat a puffin, tearing it into shreds for the smallest among them. Sharing with each other. Simply being creatures together. They weren't monsters in the way

I'd been told. They were just hungry animals. Dangerous to be sure. But just animals like the rest of us.

Some days I followed the older me, and I begged her, "At least be kind to Elken. Be nicer to him this time around."

Nothing I did mattered, and I cried a lot.

Of course, eventually, I opened my eyes, and it wasn't that same blue morning anymore; it was the beginning of spring.

I could hear the ice on the lakes shifting and creaking and squeaking as it was broken apart by the black waves, and the townsfolk of Kettin shuffling around at the collapsed entrances of their holes.

Once the first brave villager dug her way out of her underground tunnel and saw that the coast was clear, she shouted to the others.

"The ice is melting!"

The little tufts of snow that marked where doorways used to be spit forth white dust and people staggered around blind while their eyes adjusted to the light. It took them a long time—especially the older people—to look around and really see things. To see me, sitting cross-legged in the snow, watching them all.

THIRTY-THREE

"CRAB, MY DEAR..." EQUAH smirked when she saw me sitting in the snow in the centre of our village, my legs crossed. "How was your winter? Any sprites? Any tiny naked winter men?"

I couldn't answer her right away. There was too much anger in me. She was smiling. *She* was smiling *at me*.

"I know it was you," I said.

"What was me?" She thrust a weathered hand against her chest in fake shock. Equah always liked things to be dramatic and showy. When she spoke of her dreams, she'd drag things out, and pause in the most annoying way to build the tension.

"You told them to kill my father."

"Crab, dear angry little Crab. Your father was struck down by the Skyfather. It was His will that killed him. Your father broke a most sacred tradition."

"No. It was you. You told Kelm and Devn to do it. They got their friends together, and they beat him to death with clubs when they were all supposed to be whaling."

People were looking now. They'd heard their names, or sensed the intensity of the conversation or the drama of it—people were like that, always knowing when someone was about to be put in their place. The funny part of it all was they probably thought it was me who was about to be leaned on and they gathered around eagerly to watch the unlucky orphan get embarrassed again.

I could see Kelm out of the corner of my eye. It bothered him that I knew what had happened—I could tell by how he kept crossing and uncrossing his arms. I could see the guilt smeared behind his eyes. I stared at him to make it worse, and he didn't seem to be able to handle that because he looked away and kept his gaze on his boots.

And just to be sure the others were squirming a bit beneath their skin too, I said word for word what Equah had said to them when it had been done.

"Such things are best for the Skyfather to deal with."

And they seemed really spooked by that, which, I'll admit, was a teeny bit fun.

Then Brint spoke up. "Niyi?" he said.

He was feigning concern, or maybe he really was worried about her—I'll never know. He was there when my father died so I can't imagine his care for Niyi was real.

And I think Equah, to her credit, figured out that some things had gone wrong in my winter. "No Preah either?" She raised her sparse eyebrows. "Don't tell me you ate them to stay alive?"

Eating people was the worst crime you could commit in Kettin. For obvious reasons, it had to be banned. People stuck underground all winter without enough to get them by got a lot of crazy ideas. At least, that was what Equah said.

Equah looked to Devn, her nephew, and I'm not joking, he came at me. A full-grown man came toward a seventeen-year-old girl. I couldn't be sure exactly what he'd planned on doing, but I assumed it wasn't going to be fun. I wasn't even acting like I was going to run or anything. I was just sitting there with my legs crossed, as everyone gathered to collect their gossip.

I told his feet to stop, and they did.

I told his legs to break, and they listened, too.

"What is this evil?" Equah hissed, pointing a long yellow fingernail at me. "Look! Her throat!"

Everyone was murmuring and taking steps back. It was kind of funny, you know, because the ice was melting, they couldn't run anywhere. They couldn't hurt me, and they couldn't leave. They just had to wait and see what I did.

I'm not going to lie. It felt good having them look at me with as much hatred as I had for them. It doesn't feel good hating things—trust me, I know—so I was happy they got some of that back.

And maybe up until this point, you felt a little sorry for me. Maybe, like Elken, you took pity on me because of everything that happened. That might change here. And I don't care. Not one little bit.

I told Equah's insides to come out through her mouth. And they did. She twitched and croaked a little before she died, and it took longer than you'd think with all her twisty, mushy insides climbing up her throat and slapping onto the snow: pink, squishy, steaming things.

Kelm was next. Beat to death by his own club. The same club he'd used on my father. I pulled apart the people who'd killed my father—breaking, splitting, squishing—and I didn't feel bad. At all. Not even when I moved on to the folk who didn't actually murder Papa, but who knew about it and hadn't warned him. The ones who lived to the eastern side of the village who'd heard the splattering sounds and shouts and hadn't come to help him.

And then there was Hallen. He proved to me that day he was made of sturdier stuff than I'd thought, not a pathetic man-child at all. Just a man, more than most. While people's bones were breaking because I'd told them to, he came and knelt on the ground in front of me, sweaty and shaking and reeking like underground hole.

"It's me you're angry at," he said. "For the offer I made you. I shouldn't have, but I did, and I regret it, only it's done now, and I can't change it. You don't have to take it out on them as shitty as they are. It's my fault. And I'll take the blame for it."

I was kind of shocked, to be honest. I think the others were too, given how mean they'd been to him since he'd become an orphan even though he always did a little more than his share of the ice chopping.

I wanted to laugh. "You're the only one I'm not angry with."

But his performance—or whatever you want to call it—did pull my mind away from the worst of my anger. I could hear the families crying, the husbands or wives of the people I'd snapped in half with my voice. And maybe I did feel a little bit bad. I was out of breath as my rage settled, still sitting cross-legged on the snow. I told the wind to blow them all away, except for Hallen.

Please don't think I was being nice. Being flung through the air into the frigid lakes killed most of them almost instantly, and a few of them—the ones who landed on bigger chunks of ice—they were set to die really slowly in a kind of horror. They could end it quickly by jumping in the water and freezing in a few moments, or they could let death come for them at its own pace as they starved. Most of them chose slowly, freezing out on the lake.

Hallen stared at me. I think in a mix of terror and confusion and maybe he was the smallest bit impressed? I'm sure he wanted them all to suffer too.

I held my head high. "Fuck them? Isn't that what you said?"

He looked like he was struggling to speak. His face was straight; only his shoulders were moving with big heaving breaths. He was sweating, and I knew that meant he was afraid.

I sighed. "You can just... go."

"Go where?"

I sighed. "I don't know, Hallen. Take a whaling boat and find some other place to live."

And maybe there was still some sweetness in him for me because he said, "The kids didn't make it? Through the winter, I mean?"

I didn't have to shake my head or nod or whatever you do in that sort of situation. He understood by my expression; I could see it.

He stood and said, "I'm sorry then."

And then he left. He got all his stuff—everything that would fit in a little boat—and he left.

Kettin was all mine. Of course, it was a terrible mess because of the blood and broken bodies and caved in lodges, but it was mine. An entire island in the lakes just for me.

THIRTY-FOUR

THE WOLVES CIRCLED WHAT used to be Kettin pretty soon after the slaughter.

They hunched themselves low and crept toward the pink-red-brown smears to stiff the bodies. Hints of their snarls and yips spread around the mess, and maybe that meant they thought some of the humans were still alive, and they needed to break apart the herd somehow, like they did with muskoxen. My mother had explained to me how they did it once; wolves wouldn't attack a big group, they'd try to get it running and draw one person out. When I was little, she told me that again and again, in case I was ever mixed into the herd that they were chasing.

I had time before they realized everyone was dead and moved in, so I stood there, catching my breath in the silent white as wispy snowflakes fluttered to the ground around me. You might think I would wonder what I was going to do, but I didn't. I walked to where our lodge used to be and stared at Preah's body.

Oh yes. It was still there. Frozen and blue and mostly chewed up—more like a clump of ice that looked sort of like a little girl than the body of a child, but it was there. I took her to the wolf mound. And I didn't use my voice any for it either.

I wanted it to be "real" as Elken would say. Like I wanted it to mean something, I guess. I put her bones with my mother's and then watched from the height as the wolves closed in and feasted on the others, their snouts growing pink with blood stains. When they'd had their fill, I told them to hear wolf babies alone out on the tundra, crying and whining, and they quickly headed north to seek them out, their bloody-pink paw prints trailing away into nothingness.

I went to the people mound where my father's bones were. I did use my voice then because I didn't know which ones were his. I had wanted to put him with my mother right after he died, but I hadn't been strong enough to carry the body with all his frozen flesh still on it, so a few of the men from town helped me move it. They sure weren't going to carry him up to the wolf mound. They'd only just killed a man for that.

I'd thought about cutting a piece of him off—like his hand—and taking that over to where my mother was so at least part of them could be together. But that didn't seem right either. What if there were two places you could go after death, and he woke up in one without a hand, and my mother was somewhere else with a set of severed fingers? It wouldn't have worked.

But after I'd slaughtered everyone—make no mistake, that's what I did (some of them were still wailing on their stupid ice chunks floating farther away from shore)—I called my father's bones forward, and they came. I lay them down on the snow with my voice, and then I gathered them up with my hands and took them to my mother and Preah.

I called for Niyi's bones. They came too, only they took a while to arrive because they were coming from so far. I tucked the teeny frozen bird between my parents' bones on the wolf mound and felt one drop of relief. At least almost everyone was together now.

When all that was done, probably someone else would have left. I did think about it—I considered going back to Elken even though I still hated him—I guess I hated him less than when I'd first left. But by then, the sound of the people stuck out on the ice was beginning to haunt me. I knew I'd done something horrible. I mean, I knew when I was doing it what was happening, only I don't think I understood how it would feel afterward. Both easier and harder than you'd maybe expect. I told the ice chunks to carry them away to the other side. Maybe they'd die before they got there, maybe not. But I couldn't listen to their crying anymore, and I certainly couldn't bring them back to shore and just go on living with them.

And as bad as I felt, I realized Elken could possibly be feeling much worse. He could feel what other people were feeling, but he was pretty far away, so it seemed like there was a good chance that he could avoid most of what I'd done.

The Skyfather wouldn't let me have that peace. *He'll feel it. It's travelling to him now. It will take four days. Everything that everyone here went through. He'll go through it too.*

"And he'll know it was me that did it."

Yes.

I knew I'd never be able to face him knowing that he felt... and he knew... I threw up. I got dizzy, and my stomach burned like I'd swallowed fire. If you've never ripped up a whole bunch of people with your voice—even if they were evil people who murdered your father and would have cut your baby sister's tongue out—if you've never done that, then you can't understand the sickness I had. It wasn't a feeling. It was something physical in my bones and organs; it was like I'd poisoned myself. And the grossest part of it was that the sickness didn't change too much of my life.

So I didn't go back to Elken. I stayed in Kettin.

My thinking was that Kid might return one day so I should be there when he did, in case he still wanted a sister even though I'd sold him so didn't really deserve the role.

Since I'd hopped back to an earlier time and seen him at sea already, I knew it wasn't likely that he'd be coming back. I'd watched him, especially the day he'd tried dessert for the first time, his black eyes growing wide as the sailors laughed and pushed their pudding toward him so he could keep eating (he ate so much of it he got sick later). It was just as the sailor said, his work wasn't too hard, and the crew was kind to him. So I knew... I knew he probably wouldn't come back.

Still, I would wait. Just in case. Maybe he'd get curious and want to know how me and the girls made out. And while I was waiting, I needed to do something.

I pushed the remains of Kettin into the lakes with my voice—the lodges, the hearths, the chunky frozen limbs—all of it went into the cold black depths. I hummed the land flat, boulders and rocks tumbling to the beaches, leaving me nothing but a great white space.

I built.

I told the ice and snow and rocks how to move, twisting them into spires and pillars and steeped roofs. For months I did this, folding ice with my voice until my lodge was greater than the giant's pyramid or Elken's borrowed temple. Of course, I got a lot of ideas from the temple—the skylights especially. I took my time and made each room exactly as I wanted it—calling in wood from the forest near where Ilona's lodge had been, whistling to summon flowers I could press into the walls.

I had a room for everything. A room for eating that had one ice wall that was hollow in the middle and filled with lake water. I ordered the water to stay the right coldness and then told fish from the lake to live in it. I could watch them swish around and twist together into a flock and it turns out fish are a bit smarter than you'd think because never once did one ram into the ice wall.

I had a room for sleeping. It warm with a flickering fire trapped inside the wall just like back at Ilona's lodge; it was a bit of a trick to teach the wall not to melt. I had to tell it to be like iron. There was a second level and a room up top just for looking out the big skylight—especially on nights when the sky was only dancing colours.

I even had a room for the days that I wanted to go back in time and sit with my mother... just watching her sleep. Or days when I wanted to watch my father as he sang to Niyi. I'd listen to what Preah said to Ilona while I was hacking ice.

There was a room for the wolves who kept coming around after feasting on the town. I kept feeding them... for the company I suppose. I gave them names and called fish out of the lakes for them and slowly they learned to leave me be.

I knew when the pain I caused caught up with Elken. I could feel it. I could feel that he was suffering, and that was the day I really started to miss him. I cried over him and everything. I kept telling myself not to be so stupid. That I'd only fallen in love with the first person who was nice to me because I was sick. That he'd fallen in love with the first person he'd seen because he was lonely. That we weren't a good pair. And now that I'm older, I definitely believe that. Like, I was probably the worst person imaginable for him.

Don't get me wrong. I still kind of love him, but it was foolish. I just liked him because he didn't treat me like unlucky rotten fish. And he liked me because I was proof that the green goddess hadn't sent him on a fool's errand.

I spent a long time like that. Building and perfecting and tweaking my lodge when I was feeling not so bad, making it perfect in case Kid came home—he had a room all ready, with thick bear furs and a skylight edged with whale teeth so he could pluck one out and sell it to the next sailor if he was ever short on disks, because sailors are superstitious and like to have something on them at all times that could trick the water into thinking they belonged.

And then there were the times I couldn't think of what else to add to the lodge and I was left feeling like my chest was going to burst from the pain I felt, and the pain I'd caused.

❋ ❋ ❋

I think some of the people floating on the ice, or maybe it was Hallen... someone who'd seen what I'd done got somewhere with other people. And I think they told the story of me because once or twice a year, some young warrior would show up wanting to fight "the witch of Kettin," or sometimes they called me "the hag of Kettin."

Needless to say, none of them did too well. Sometimes I'd tell the body to fling back to where it came from, thinking that might get people to leave me alone. And for the most part, it did. Can you imagine your village's prized hunter flying through the sky and landing splat in the middle of your town? You'd hesitate before sending another, now, wouldn't you?

But sometimes bigger groups came, so I devised a bit of a game—a challenge for them. I ordered the snow to form walls—all haphazard, creating narrow passages, most of which went nowhere. Hallways circling back on themselves or ending with just a big white wall. There was only one route through the mess that would take them to my lodge, but no one ever found their way through except for the wolves.

So I lived alone in a really beautiful home, in complete misery. Years passed, and some of my wounds closed up. Of course, I spent a lot of time opening them again; I don't know why—because I'm stupid? Or maybe I thought I deserved it. But I also wanted it? I guess because it was all I had left of everyone. Whatever. I made a room in my lodge for each kind of feeling—a room for crying, a room for shouting, a room for feeling so empty it's kind of like being dead—and I killed lots of witch hunters.

So, if you've ever wondered how an evil hag gets to be the way she is, living alone in the wild, messing with travellers, now you know. And at least one of us got something good out of this whole thing.

THE END

EPILOGUE ONE

NINE YEARS LATER

WHEN YOU LIVE ALONE and don't have to work to eat or stay warm or accomplish anything, you come up with ways to entertain yourself.

At some point, my favourite way to let time pass became sitting on the roof of my lodge and stirring up the lakes with my voice, watching the waves froth and leap. If I was lucky, maybe some whales would join in. Only there came a day my plans were ruined because there was a guy sitting up there already with dark oily hair and a cruel smirk. All lanky and leaning with his legs swinging over the edge, almost like he was waiting for me to show up.

I nearly pushed him over the ledge with my voice, thinking he was another witch hunter come to slay me. But then I saw two things that made me pause. The first was that his eyes weren't right. They were a colour I'd seen only a few times during a rare sunset: a deep, potent violet that didn't stop where eye colour normally stops. It spread out, getting fainter across his eyelids and brows and on his forehead. So I noticed that, but I also noticed he was holding *my* spear—not the one I'd built from the remains of the forest near where Ilona's lodge had been, but the one I'd left behind with Elken, my mother's spear—the one I'd shredded with my voice. It was near perfectly healed, pale veins visible where the wood had been split.

The moment I looked at it, I knew in my heart that Elken had repaired it. I could picture him sitting still and carefully pressing each piece into its place, coating it with some sort of sticky herb juice to make it hold.

Years of being alone except for the occasional person who'd come to murder me hadn't made me any friendlier. "You have three minutes to explain yourself, or I'm sending you over the edge."

"Sheep's wire! He wasn't joking—even your teeth—ha! Blue teeth... who would've thought..." He bared his own teeth and licked his lips as he stared at my blueness. "The lips too? And the tongue... does it change how things taste?"

"Two minutes," I warned him.

He snickered. "Now, that's no way to treat a guest."

"You're not a guest. You've snuck in."

"Snuck in? You made that whole test of the mind thing there out of ice... basically inviting anyone who passes by—"

I opened my mouth to tell him to fly back to where he came from, but he seemed to sense how serious I was. He cleared his throat and sat up straight. "I've come to bring you back your spear." He flipped the thing around in his hands, twirling it in a flashy show. "This is yours, isn't it?"

I swiped for the spear, but he pulled it out of my reach.

"Ah." His smirk was probably the most annoying thing I'd ever seen. It was almost too big for his face. "I also bring news."

I crossed my arms, making sure he knew full well how irritated I was.

He seemed to love it. He laughed.

"Take the salt down a touch, eh? The one-man-gang is about to leave the temple. I thought you should know.... I'd want to know if I were you."

I sighed. I wasn't going to play these games with him. I could tell right away he had the same sort of need to perform that Equah had. The way he spoke... he was putting on a show for me, dragging out some of his words to build my anticipation, and shoving others forward really quickly to knock me off balance. Whoever he was and whatever he wanted, I needed no part in it, but also, he'd mentioned one man in a temple, and I needed to know who he meant because there was only one guy I'd ever met who lived in a temple.

"One-man-gang?"

"Yeah, the guy with the heart problem. No one showed up—or I did, but it was *so* boring... chopping lichens... being cold... I left pretty quickly. The being he meets with, she's sending him out to find us all, the ones that didn't make it."

And thinking of Elken waiting all this time and having almost no one arrive hurt in a sickening sort of way even though I maybe still hated him. I wanted to be alone, to maybe go sit in my being-confused-about-Elken room.

I said, "Leave, you can keep the spear."

"Don't you get it? I'm warning you. He's not coming for you first, but at some point—he needs both of us. There's something we're all supposed to do or be or whatever, but the thing is, I don't want to do it."

"And you're bringing it up to me because..."

"Because I have a feeling that you don't want to do it either. And I've seen... I've seen all the possibilities. The ones where you and I stick together, those work out best for both of us."

"You've seen?"

"Yeah. Like you've got the voice. I've got the eyes." He pointed to his own face. "I'm not supposed to look into the future, but, like—" He raised his eyebrows. "How can you not?"

"I don't want any part in it or trying not to do it... please leave. I won't ask again."

He chuckled. "But you will! I've already seen it. There's no point in arguing with me, doll. I know what you're going to say already. And I know that there's someone you don't want to see. Well, I mean, you do *want* to see him. But you'll wish you hadn't once you do."

I knew he was talking about Elken, or at least I felt like I knew. Even thinking of him hurt. It had been what? Five years? Six?

"Nine years," he said.

"You can read my mind too?"

"Ha, no... only I saw you were going to ask, so..."

Nine years. Nine. Kid would be what?

"Seventeen."

I hated him for saying that. He was kind of sneering about it, too. Like he knew he was rubbing salt in a wound.

"You want me to leave Kettin then? Is that it?"

He shrugged. "Nah, I mean, you could, but... I guess. I'll just tell you. I'm gonna fuck with the big guy." He pointed up to the sky. "And I think you'd also like to mess with him, right? I mean, he could have just not told you about moving through time or whatever, right? He can see everything that's going to happen. And he told you not to leap through the hours anyway. He's kind of a prick, right?"

I didn't want to admit that the snarky, purple-eyed guy was making sense, so I kept my mouth shut. Still, I think he knew he was getting somewhere because he hopped off the ledge with a lot of energy—a big bounce in his step—and said, "You and me together... we wouldn't have to worry about the others. Let's give the guy a little bit of what he's given us, eh? Let's, you know, hurt him a little... take him down some."

"What do you mean? He's a god. There's nothing either of us could do to him."

And I think he knew that I was interested because his eyes lit up.

"We could still mess with him some. Don't you think? He's got this whole... plan, I guess? Throwing pieces of himself down here, forcing us all... You know every single one of us has no family left? They're all dead. He wanted it that way, I think. He needed each of us to be alone."

"He said he made us like this so he could understand suffering or whatever. That's what he told me."

I wanted to be in. Of course, I did. I was bored out of my skull, and I'd gotten my vengeance on everyone else except for the Skyfather already. But I pretended I wasn't because I enjoyed the feeling of someone wanting me... even if it was only wanting me because of what I could do with my voice... it was a lot more than I'd felt in a long time. Nine years.

But then something he'd said struck me.

I shook my head. "My brother is still living. Not all our families are gone."

He raised his eyebrows and stared hard into me—his eyes such a deep violet that they looked as black as his hair. He didn't use words, but he didn't have to. Either Hemi was dead, or I'd never see him again.

It had been nine years, and he'd not come back. He was almost a man grown now, nearly old enough to be a husband. And he hadn't come back for me. I felt stupid for hoping...

I pushed the pain to one side because of how the purple-eyed guy was looking at me. He was having way too much fun, revelling in my suffering with a big grin on his face. But it was more than that. I think that when you see someone, and you've both been through the same sorts of things, you kind of just know that, like instinctively, you know that you have the same scars, and because of that, you're sort of the same shape.

"I'm Lyf," he said, setting the spear against the ledge and holding out his hand.

I took it and I thought about telling him my name was Katya, but that didn't seem right anymore. That hadn't really my name since my parents had died, I mean, briefly, that was what Elken called me, but it wasn't right to go by it anymore.

I thought about telling him I was called Crab, but that also felt wrong.

"I'm the hag of Kettin," I said.

He laughed at that, and I think it was because he understood it.

"Are you hungry?" I said, humming a feast for us into existence. Elk and smoked salmon and herb salads like Elken used to make.

"I could eat."

He was starving. I could feel the lie in his performance—how he pretended he wasn't, how he forced himself to eat slow even though he was dying for more, his eyes flicking to the big pots that held the leftovers. Between bites he said, "First, I want to hear everything that he's told you so far… You're the only one he can explain things to…"

And so Lyf and I spent a few hours talking and eating as the stars started to shine through the pink hue of the sky. I left out the more gruesome details of my story, and I'm sure Lyf left out the terror in his own tale—we both knew there was no point in picking at the wounds. It felt good to have someone to talk to. It felt good to think about the things I could do again, to have someone be thrilled when I made dessert appear out of thin air. I didn't know if it would even work, but I asked for the air to become what I'd eaten at Ilona's (calm down, I didn't make it so that if Lyf ate it, he couldn't leave). I mean, I *did* think about it, but as funny as it would be—trust me, Lyf would have found it funny—it also seemed a little mean, and I was kind of hoping that maybe I could have a friend if I was nice and kept most of myself and the things I'd done a secret.

The only time his performance cracked was when I asked whether he could see the Skyfather.

Lyf nodded.

"What does he look like?"

"Horrifying. Not like sky or like a father." Lyf picked at something stuck in his teeth. "Like the deepest, darkest void."

It was quiet for a moment. I'd more wanted to know if the Skyfather had a beard or something. But I could tell the sight had really scared Lyf. He ground his teeth together and I thought of what Elken had said once when I ground my teeth around him. *You can just cry.*

"Do you want me to see how you're going to die?" Lyf said, his excited, fidgety energy returning.

I shook my head. "I'd hate to ruin the disappointment."

He laughed. "It's just as well. It's pretty boring anyway, I mean... not as dull as mine, but... not interesting either."

And that's how Lyf ended up staying with me.

EPILOGUE TWO

AT FIRST IT WAS sweet—lovely really—to have someone hanging around. I even made Lyf a room of his own our first morning he was there. I put on shows for him, telling the clouds to be people acting out myths my mother had told me, and he'd tell me about the crazy things he could see: a woman whose entire face was pierced with teeny metal rings so you couldn't see her expression at all.

"I'm guessing she makes a lot of noise when she walks," he said.

Or a bear with grey fur and a little black mask covering his eyes.

"There's a whole bunch of them, really far away. They look sneaky..."

A man who'd lost nearly all his fingers but could still tie together a fishing net that was better than any Lyf had ever seen.

I asked who the man was and Lyf shrugged. "How should I know? I just look around for interesting things is all—he's going to die when his village is raided next. They'll take his eyes out first and put them in his mouth, then burn him."

I know. That's a dark end.

Lyf didn't seem bothered though. He laughed. "I've seen worse."

Pretty fast, something became a little off about it all. I mean, I shouldn't be surprised. That's how life is. Things are never fully, wholly good. There's always a rock in your boot. Or a Lyf in your snow lodge.

The first night things went awry was when he said, "Don't worry. He's just as miserable as the rest of us."

"Who?"

"The guy with the heart problem. The one who thinks he's running the show cause he got the cathedral ready or whatever."

I stayed calm, and I think I kept my face straight. "I don't want to hear about him—"

"But you *do* though. I've seen it. I saw it way back, the second he wouldn't let me into your room."

"I don't have a room—"

"*That's* what I told him. I said you'd gone, so the room couldn't be yours—"

"STOP!" I lost my calm a bit—well, I lost it a lot, so much so that the ground shook when I shouted. Thinking of Elken sad and not letting anyone into my room was like having a fist pushed through my chest, grabbing my heart and twisting it.

Lyf smirked. "What's the story? He wouldn't tell me, and I've been dying to—"

I hopped on my spear and went for a flight, certain Lyf could look and see whatever he wanted, only he was enjoying picking at my scabs and watching me flinch. I thought about asking him to leave, but at the time, I chose being picked at over being alone. Stupid, I know.

And then we got into a disagreement about Niyi and the winter sprite who'd come to take her away. I thought the man was trying to help her and protect her. Lyf thought this was a convenient lie the Skyfather told me to make himself not look so terrible.

I said, "I don't think he lies."

"Of course he does."

I mean, yes, Lyf was clearly trouble, but I kind of liked that about him, you know? He could see into the future, and all his family was dead, so he was all mangled up like I was... How could he not be trouble? But also it was fun, having someone around to talk to, someone who understood. Everything he said that was off I put to one side of my mind because I didn't want to give up the company.

And yes, I did think about kissing him or doing more than that with him. My chest ached for it because it had been so long since I was hugged or held or even looked at kindly. And sometimes it seemed like he knew that's what I was thinking because he'd smirk and stare at me without blinking, and the space between us would get thicker. And then he'd smile, really slowly, and say, "What's on your mind?"

I'd feel horrifically guilty because it wasn't Lyf I wanted, even though he was pretty handsome if I was being honest. He just happened to be the only one nearby.

"Nothing," I'd say.

Of course, there was more going on than I knew. Because there always is and there always was, and probably there always will be. It was maybe the second week that Lyf was staying with me, when he was telling me about all the things he could do, that I mentioned I had good hearing. Or at least, that I was supposed to have good hearing.

"I have his ears too."

Lyf laughed uncontrollably. "And what do you hear with them? People's prayers? Lichens growing? Storms in faraway places?"

I didn't really hear anything out of the ordinary.
Because you haven't tried.

Sometimes I forgot that the Skyfather was still watching and listening. He'd been so quiet for years.

"It's no use," I told Lyf. "He's listening right now. He knows what you're up to."

Lyf smirked. "Oh, I know. I want him to hear. I want him to know how much I FUCKING HATE HIM." He shouted that last bit up toward the sky and it frightened me a little to hear someone speak that way to a god. Just because my life was terrible didn't mean all the rest of existence wasn't worth something. The stars were pretty, and baby seals were cute even if they did get dragged off by bears every so often, and snow sometimes felt like magic no matter how many times you'd seen it before. The Skyfather made everything else too, right?

I did. The Skyfather's voice was different that time. It was the first time I realized... that he felt pain, I guess. But thinking about it now, I shouldn't have been surprised. Elken had the Skyfather's heart, and he felt everything.

What Lyf said had hurt him—I could feel it in the hollow slowness of his words—and that left me feeling sick. No one ever talks about that, but just like a guy can not bring a girl's family back to life, twisting her feelings inside, or a sister can cover her ears and it feels like a punch in the stomach because no one wants to listen to you... we—people like you and me—we can hurt the things beyond us.

It is not pain in the way you are thinking, the Skyfather said. *It is knowing there is an easier way. With your kind, there is usually an easier way.*

I think Lyf sensed I was bothered, but it seemed like he thought I was afraid because of how he'd spoken in the presence of a god, like I was worried about him being put in his place by the Skyfather. "Don't worry, he can't do anything to me. I'll see it coming, and I'll change where I'm standing or how I'm sitting or whatever. He can't do anything to you either. The others he can halt and change, but us? We're more free than any other people."

My unease grew, I think in part because my mother's spear was sitting in the corner and wasn't moving at all. It didn't feel alive like it used to, and I hadn't noticed that yet. It didn't feel like Niyi was inside it any longer. Maybe I'd killed what was inside when I shredded it?

I said, "The Skyfather doesn't change what people do." *Even if it would be better if he did.*

Lyf laughed and my mother's spear did move, it flinched a little, sort of like it didn't like the sound. When Lyf put his hand out to grab it again—the spear dodged him. It didn't want to be in his hands any longer.

I stared at the spear, frowning, *what do you want then?* I wanted to say to it.

It was quiet for a moment, like really quiet. The snow sucked away all the noise, and for the first time, I understood how it was doing that—the feeling of it—of sound being muffled by the cold fluffy white.

I listened as the whisper of the wind was stretched into silence by the shape of the land. But it wasn't only that. There were other sounds as well. Other whispers... Voices.

I picked out Elken's voice right away—it was far, but clear. *And, if Katya comes back while I'm gone...*

That... that was too much. I mostly couldn't remember what his face looked like anymore, but when I heard his voice, it all came rushing back to me. His beautiful, goofy, perfect, stupid face. The way he looked when he'd just woken up, trying to force his eyes open but only partly succeeding, squinting into the darkness. My heart felt raw.

From behind me there was another voice.

My voice.

"Katya. It's me. Listen."

My head shot around like a spear, but I couldn't see the me that had spoken. Still, I knew she was there. I knew it was my voice I could hear, and I was uneasy to say the least.

"You're not looney, are you?" Lyf said, tilting his head to the side with narrowed eyes.

I tried to tune out the whispers I was hearing but they were smothering me almost, too quiet to be understood fully, all piled on top of each other like a flock of squawking albatross. Out from the thick of everything, I heard my own voice behind me: *Just listen. He's not telling you the truth. Listen, and you'll hear it between his words.*

I turned back to Lyf, and he did look sinister then. I could hear something, the yearning beneath his grin—almost like I could hear his thoughts—he was riling me up in his mind. *Come on hag, you can do it... just agree to come with me. I'll even fuck you. Come on, sad, lonely hag.*

It hurt hearing what he was thinking, but once I started, it was hard to stop, and I couldn't really talk while I was listening. I said, "None of the others can move through the air without touching the ground, right?"

He laughed. "Not that I've seen."

"I'm going to break up the ice tonight," I said. "To make sure no one can cross the lakes. You'll have to leave before then."

He frowned. "Don't be boring."

"Really. I don't want a part in any of this. If the Skyfather wants a voice for his plans... he should choose someone else. You too."

Lyf's smile got really terrible then. Like kind of scary and too big for his face. "You'll regret saying that," he said. "I've seen it."

"This is your last chance to leave peacefully."

He knew it. He knew I was ten seconds away from ordering his stupid, all-seeing eyes to pop right out of his skull. He skipped over to where my mother's spear sat, where he'd left it.

"That will stay," I said. "Thank you for bringing it back."

It irritated him that I'd said that. I could hear the mean words he used in his head, and those hurt too. He called me ugly and stupid and naive. He thought I was pathetic and dreary.

On his way out, he took long, casual, meandering steps designed to drive me mad. I could hear his thoughts as he sauntered. *Any moment now, she's going to lose it... any moment now.*

When he was on the ground outside, and I was back on the roof of my lodge watching to make sure he was really leaving, he shouted up to me.

"You be careful! Or your face is going to stick like that!"

EPILOGUE THREE

IT'S FUNNY. BEFORE LYF had come, I'd thought maybe I'd found some sort of harmony with things—a way of being that didn't ache too much or itch too much. But having had a conversation with another person who had thoughts and feelings, who was warm beneath their skin—it broke down the well-constructed lie. Hearing the Skyfather again stung too. Had he been watching me all this time? Doing nothing but building in the snow, pretending I wasn't miserable?

I didn't want you to be alone.

I was swallowed up by a storm of loneliness and guilt and... unworthiness, I guess, unable to hide any longer from the truth of my life. All the pain I'd caused. All the stupid mistakes I'd made. I'd killed Niyi. I'd ruined my mother's last day of life, broke Elken's heart, mistreated Preah, sold Kid like he was a tub of lard. I'd slaughtered the townsfolk of Kettin. I don't think I did one thing right in all my years. And still, he didn't want me to be alone. No matter how much I deserved it.

Deserve is a human idea. It is not how I see things.

I couldn't handle the layers of that, so I shouted up at him, spitting out the first words that came to mind. "Is Kid really dead?"

You tell me.

I wanted to roll my eyes, but a small part of me was warmed that he'd answered at all. I'd ignored him for years; still, he'd stayed near and answered me right away. I wouldn't have answered me.

Listen for him.

I closed my eyes. Silence.

I could hear the wind and the lapping of lake water against the shore. I could hear the wolves scampering around the labyrinth, sniffing and scratching. I could hear the scurrying of smaller animals. The roots of lichens stretching—reaching out into the soil. And laughter, from far, far away—not a voice I recognized. A lot of other people, actually. I didn't know how near the closest village was, but I could hear them in their homes. Eating and drinking and chatting. Dogs barking. Fire crackling.

I was stretching—reaching with a part of myself I'd not used before—careening past the closer sounds to the ones farther away. The crashing of waves in a great sea storm. The shrieks of birds on a far away shore. The sound of drinking and washing and sweeping. Boots stomping. Disks clacking. Whistling. Chewing. Blinking.

There was a man's voice. He was laughing, telling a story... or maybe being told a story? He was drinking something that made his tongue lazy and clinked when he set the vessel down.

"You wouldn't know it," he said. "It's a nothing place. Probably doesn't exist anymore."

"Everyone's got a home, a place where their momma plunked them to the earth. Come on. You got nothing? No place you'd like to see again?"

He laughed again, a beautiful laugh—full and ringing and grumbling... like my father's almost. "What can I say?" he said, "I like new sights. Not old ones."

"Leave the kid alone." It was a woman's voice that said that.

My heart raced a little. I wished I could see him, so I'd know whether I was being foolish or not. Like how I'd thought that Howl was my father. Or when I thought the spear was my mother, or Niyi.

It was a man's voice, not a little boy's voice, so it was deeper.

Still, I thought. *It could be him.* Kid.

I had to clench my teeth to keep a bubbly cry deep within my throat. To be maybe hearing him—his grown-up laugh, the words he picked, the sound of his chair as he leaned back, all relaxed. The fire sucking up air nearby keeping him warm. *If it's even him*, I thought.

It is.

My heart raced, and I leapt to my feet. I would go to Kid. That's what I'd do. I reached for my mother's spear, but it leaped away from me—just out of my grasp.

The Skyfather laughed. *You are a slow learner.*

"Well, maybe if you explained things better—"

Maybe if you listened better.

I sighed and crossed my arms, hoping that I was making it clear just how much he was frustrating me. "Okay. I'm listening. Why does her spear move?"

It doesn't move... or at least, not on its own. It is you who moves it.

I laughed; I wasn't doing anything to the spear.

Not you as you are now. You many years in the future.

That made me pause. Me from the future didn't want me to go and find Kid? I thought about Niyi, and how going after her made everything worse. I did something I'd never done before: I asked the Skyfather what he wanted me to do.

"Should I go to him? To Kid?"

Now you care what I think?

He sounded smug, and my chest grew hot. "Will something bad happen to Kid if I go looking for him?"

Yes.

It broke my heart, but I knew then and there that I wouldn't be going anywhere. I'd learned at least one lesson in my waste of a life. I ordered the ice surrounding Kettin to break and told the clouds not to let anyone in—to grow thick and make it so anyone wandering by couldn't see the next step in front of them.

I didn't want to mess up Kid's life, at least not any more than I already had—so I'd be staying put, but I didn't want anyone else coming and finding me and tempting me to leave or asking questions like Lyf had. Kid sounded happy when I'd heard him; that was more joy than I deserved.

"That is enough," I said. And it was.

Still, I blinked back tears because it hurt so much to think of not seeing him ever again, especially after feeling close to him for a second. He was the sort of person who made the space around you warm just by being near you. The more my chest burned, the louder the air became until it wasn't just air; it was other people crying too—far off in the distance—bemoaning their situation or actions. The villages scattered across the lakes were filled with more people than I could picture in my mind at one time. Begging and pleading, wanting rescue, or forgiveness. Regretting, hating, wishing for death or help. The sheer amount of pain in the world gutted me; it nearly knocked me right to my knees.

There is more than that. Listen.

And there was more. There was laughter and thankfulness. More music than I'd ever be able to comprehend. Surprise and awe. The more I quieted myself, the more I could hear them. Every sound tangled together, and it doesn't really make sense, but it sort of made a song, like there was a rhythm and pattern to the combined noise. And a weight. It felt like every person was a pebble tossed on top of me. Alone they'd be nothing to listen to, but together? They crushed me, and I couldn't close my ears.

A man shouting because he'd forgotten something he needed for his day's work. A toddler laughing. A woman wailing from the strain of bringing a child into the world. A student lying to a teacher about having practised. A man bemoaning the death of his husband—he reminded me of my father.

"STOP!" I said to the sound, squeezing my eyes shut and covering my ears in hopes that some of the overwhelm could be blocked out.

That is not how it works, I am afraid.

Lovers who hadn't seen each other in months embracing and giggling. A girl pleading because her brother had fallen through the ice and was drowning before her, and there was nothing she could do—she couldn't find him in the hole that was left. Her voice was the worst. Louder than the others. A shrill, shrieking that bit into my ears.

"Please. Make it stop."

I cannot. This is how it is. As soon as I interfere directly, there is no purpose to this plane, and it dissolves. Things can only exist with a purpose. From the moment your kind was born... I have had no rest.

I pressed my face against the ice floor, hoping the cold would slow down the rush of sounds.

The Skyfather laughed. *You, however, you could make it stop if you wanted.*

I whined as the cold bit into my cheek and lips. "How?"

He didn't answer me, but I didn't need him to. I could feel him—the Skyfather and his wishes—for the first time ever, I could feel what he wanted. One small piece of the whole settled into place, like the central stone in Elken's borrowed temple, from which all the other stones kept their balance.

I told the water beneath the ice to push the crying girl's brother to the surface. And though the boy was far away and nearly dead, the salty waves listened. Her screaming stopped.

The sudden lightness I felt made no sense. The weight that was gone when one of the many pains in the world had ended, despite how much more suffering remained, was nonsensical. There was still so much agony, how could one less wail cause so much relief? But it did.

The sky felt more airy and fresh and it was stupid and pointless, but the release was so uplifting that I cried. I'd never done something that right before.

Good, said the Skyfather. *Now another.*

THANK YOU!

Dear Reader,

You've finished CRAB & THE BLUE GOD, the first release in the THESE SACRED CURSES series.

Your time and attention are a legitimate gift, and I thank you with my whole heart. I'm so excited about this series and where this story is going.

If you want to support the book further, you can add it to your Read shelf on Goodreads, include it on any curated lists you have there, or tell a friend about it!

And remember kids, every time you leave a book review, a villain gets their redemption arc.

Love,
Robyn

P.S. The follow up to this book is called LUCKY DOVE & THE RED GOD. Lucky is a teenage girl whose toes are turning red... her story is just as gritty as Katya's but set much farther south in a rough and tumble world of iron mining and whispering mountains. To get access to early scenes, art, and playlists, subscribe to my author newsletter SPECULATIVE MYSTICISM.

ACKNOWLEDGEMENTS

This book was one that poured out of me quick and painful. Teenagers see and feel so much, and I don't take writing about them lightly, especially not one who could be as easily misunderstood as Katya.

To home skillet. Thank you for picking up chocolate and firewood so frequently. To Gizmo, the fluffy guru who gave me all the necessary cuddles to get through the emotional storm that was editing this book. To Renee, my younger sister, who this book is dedicated to. Your energy is medicinal. It's magic. So much of my understanding of healing comes from time spent with you. To Megan, Sydney and Rachel, thank you for combing through this tale so carefully with me. To the loveliest proofreader of all time, Tenaya MKD. You help with words, but you help with everything else, too. To my early readers, Frances and Caitlin, your notes helped me get this book polished up for readers. Thank you for sharing your imagination with me.

ABOUT THE AUTHOR

Robyn Abbott is a Canadian author who writes stories about good people doing bad things. Depending on her mood, she's either a tarot reader or adamantly against tarot. If you've read *A SIN & A HALF,* you know why.

Instagram: @writinginnovember

Manufactured by Amazon.ca
Bolton, ON